DESTINED FIRE

NEPHILIM'S DESTINY: BOOK 3

TESSA COLE

Gryphon's Gate Publishing

Destined Fire

Gryphon's Gate Publishing

550 King St. N.

PO Box 42088 Conestoga

Waterloo, ON

N2L 6K5

ebook ISBN 978-1-988115-70-2

Print ISNB 978-1-988115-69-6

CHAPTER 1

INKY, MALICIOUS DARKNESS POURED DOWN MY THROAT, drowning me and burning into the core of my being. I fought to breathe, to resist, to do anything, but the nightmare froze my muscles and will, leaving only my helpless thoughts screaming. It was the archnephilim, suffocating me with his writhing essence— No, the hellfire prince Ibizual flooding me with his demonic magic, howling with laughter at the thought that I'd erupt into flames and burn up—

No, it was Gideon's mating brand etched into my body, somehow twisted and evil.

Yes, it was the brand, and my soul had warped it, tainted it, because I was a nephilim, I was lying to him, and I wasn't the woman he loved.

There had to be a toll, a price demanded by fate for what I was doing. I had denied my supernatural nature, and now I was neck-deep in the supernatural world. I couldn't escape and couldn't break free. Not from the power now pouring into me, or from my destiny binding me to an angel who hated nephilim. I needed to scream my frustration and fear, but the nightmare wouldn't let me.

For a moment, my thoughts cleared, and I fought to keep calm. It was just a dream. Nothing more. But no matter how hard I thought that, I couldn't push back the terror of being discovered, or of being truly evil. And I couldn't just make myself wake up.

In the last few weeks, I'd had nightmares that hadn't been nightmares, since I'd been fully awake for the horror, where both the archnephilim and Ibizual had invaded my mind. I couldn't shake the fear that they were at it again, determined to have me, determined to possess me. Were they still alive? Had I failed in stopping them? I'd barely managed to live through facing them the first time.

They'd tried to take over my body, tried to cajole me, convince me, threaten me. I was like them. No matter how hard I wanted to believe I wasn't, I couldn't deny it. Good people didn't lie. How could I even claim an ounce of goodness? I'd been lying to everyone my entire life, and dedicating my life to helping others didn't make up for it.

They won't understand you.

They'll kill you.

You're powerless.

Your mate despises you.

Yes, Gideon hated me.

My thoughts tripped over that. I might have Gideon's brand on my arm, but he wasn't my mate. Marcus was. I knew that in the core of my being—

Except a part of me felt that wasn't everything. Marcus wasn't my only mate. I was still bound to Gideon, and his rejection made my soul cry. I was also connected to Jacob, and here, in the drowning, burning horror of my nightmare, I could see his essence entwined with mine. Just like my soul sobbed over Gideon, it thrilled at Jacob, and in my heart I knew it had nothing to do with the power of his vampiric claim on me. I was bound to all three men. They were mine—

And me? What about me?

The voice was soft, sensual, and turned the inferno burning me into bone-melting desire.

Are we not also connected?

Strong hands captured my cheeks, and Kol brushed his lips against mine. A whisper of his seductive power slipped into my mouth, drawing a moan, and his face came into focus. Hellfire and need blazed in his eyes, fueling my own. I'd already had a glimpse of the ecstasy of his power, the breathtaking desire, and the promise of screaming, shattering climaxes when he'd saved my life, pouring the magic that sustained him into me.

You belong to Gideon, he said as his hands trailed down my neck.

More whispers of delicious power unfurled under my skin at his touch.

You belong to Marcus.

His palms skimmed the sides of my breasts, teasing me, making me ache with want.

You belong to Jacob.

He pressed his perfect, naked, lean-muscled body

against mine, and his magic rushed through me everywhere our skin touched.

Belong to me, too.

Yes, I breathed... thought... begged.

I ached for him as much as I ached for Marcus and Gideon and Jacob. I needed his hands on me, his power engulfing me, his body inside me.

His lips captured mine, the kiss this time hungry and demanding. His magic surged down my throat like the archnephilim's had, but instead of drowning me, it filled me with breath and life. It infused with my essence, not just entwining through it like Jacob's. We were one, one breath, one soul, one aching desire.

I crave you, Essie. I'm tired of waiting. I don't want to ride your climax with Marcus, I want your climax with me.

His tongue plunged into my mouth. One hand found my naked breast and kneaded it while his other slid down my stomach, ratcheting up my desire with anticipation of where it was going.

I was alight with heated, liquid bliss, his power already teasing me to the edge, then his hand on my stomach dipped lower, fingers inching closer, and—

I jerked awake, my breath fast, my body thrumming with the promise of a mind-blowing climax while my skin burned with my out-of-control buzz and my insides ached, still raw from channeling the magic to stop Ibizual.

It had only been a dream. A part of me sobbed at that, aching to fully know Kol's touch, while another part was relieved. The archnephilim was dead and Ibizual still imprisoned. I was safe. Or as safe as I could get, being a nephilim pretending to be a human.

I stared at the lounge's ceiling, my eyes sore and gritty from having slept with my magic contacts in, and struggled to think past my headache and buzz to get my thoughts straight. We'd just defeated Ibizual, Marcus and I had ridden the ecstasy of Jacob's bite, and Gideon had just told me I was officially on the Joined Parliament team. I hadn't been able to return to Marcus's room because I didn't have a key, so I'd gone down to the lounge and curled up on the over-stuffed leather couch.

I must have fallen asleep.

A shudder of desire swept through me. I wasn't sure what was worse, the nightmare of being consumed by the archnephilim and Ibizual, or hot sex with Kol. Not that the sex part was a nightmare, but the idea that I was fantasizing about Kol when I was sleeping with Marcus. That wasn't fair to him, or Marcus, or any of the guys, no matter what Marcus had said about sharing.

If I was going to be on the team, I was going to have to figure out how to not think about Kol in that way, which, given that the incubus was made for sex and I'd already had a glimpse of his heart-pounding power, was going to be a challenge.

But I had no doubt Marcus's good will was already stretched thin. Wolves were notorious for their possessiveness, and I already had emotional connections—whether I wanted them or not—to Gideon and Jacob. Of course, it was a new day and there was a good chance Marcus now regretted his decision to be with me, that his fear for my safety would make him push me away again.

I rubbed my face and drew in a ragged breath, trying to dispel the yearning from the dream and the ache at the idea that Marcus might go back to avoiding me.

Outside, through the patio door at the back of the lounge, the sun shone bright and clear. It was going to be a beautiful day for my first day as a JP agent.

Yep, working for the agency I'd spent my life hiding from and being afraid of.

Fear seeped through the dream-Kol's sensual magic, and I shoved it back. No matter how dangerous it was for me to be mostly powerless and fighting supernatural criminals—not to mention living with all the angels in Union City—this was where I belonged.

This was who I belonged with.

All of them.

I pushed that thought back to join my fear. Wanting all of them was the dream talking. Nothing more. I didn't want all of them. I just wanted Marcus... didn't I?

I refocused on the light outside. There was something I was supposed to remember... something I needed to do this morning—

Shit. The team debriefing at o'eight hundred in Gideon's office.

I sat up so fast that my head spun and my buzz flared, the painful burning bites under my skin turning into an inferno. It joined with the pain from my raw magical channels, setting all of me on fire for an agonizing second before it calmed down. My phone, a room keycard, and a note lay on the coffee table beside me.

Have a debriefing this morning. Will make Gideon put you

on the team and will meet you in your room after the meeting.
Marcus.

He hadn't changed his mind. He was still going to fight to save my job and embrace the attraction between us, even though everything was complicated. What he didn't know was that Gideon had already offered me the position, and he didn't have to fight for anything... well, depending on what time it was, he might be figuring all of that out right now. Of course, if that was the case, Gideon was going to be pissed at me for being late for my first meeting.

I woke up my phone. 7:45 a.m. Thank God. I wasn't late. If I hurried, I'd be able to freshen up first. I wouldn't be able to change out of Marcus's T-shirt and workout shorts because I didn't have any more changes of clean clothes at Operations, but I could at least look like I'd washed my face and combed my hair.

For a second, I contemplated running to the bathroom in the triage waiting area to freshen up. It was closer, but I really didn't want to run into Amiah while wearing Marcus's clothes. Without a doubt the angel would be upset that I was still around. She hadn't wanted me anywhere near the guys, and she'd be furious to see me in my current state of dress. Better to spend the extra time to go up to my room to freshen up and not remind the team's physician of why she hated me.

Yes, I was going to have to face her at some point, but with luck the next few days would be uneventful, and I'd be able to convince her I wasn't a liability. As for dealing with her possible feelings for Marcus...? I had no idea. She knew Marcus and I were a thing. I'd overheard her saying to Gideon that Marcus had to give me up for the sake of the angelic mating brand. Something—if he'd well and truly decided we were a thing—his wolf would never let him do.

I hurried to the elevator, took it up to the fifth floor, and rushed into my assigned room. It looked like a hotel room, consisting of a bedroom with a small seating area and an attached bathroom, and was just as empty as a hotel room. I didn't have anything there any more. The day before yesterday, Gideon had kicked me off the team, and I'd packed my bag to leave. Then I'd been shot—and only survived because Kol had given me some of his magic—we'd stopped Jacob's vampire brother from releasing the hellfire prince Ibizual from his prison, and Gideon had changed his mind about me being on the team. My bag had ended up in Marcus's suite, and since I'd gone straight to his suite after last night's fight, my clothes—too bloody and shredded to be worn again—and shoes had ended up there.

A shiver of desire whispered through me and this time it wasn't from the dream, but the memory of Jacob's bite inflaming my need and Marcus taking over and bringing me to climax... a couple of times before we'd fallen asleep in his bed.

A part of me feared that what we had wouldn't last in the face of all my other romantic complications, but God, sex with Marcus was everything I'd imagined and more.

So far the first attempt at our strange arrangement, with Jacob feeding from me because his claim was so strong he could no longer effectively feed from anyone else, and Marcus having sex with me because I couldn't release the sensual magic of Jacob's bite without an orgasm, had gone well. Although that could have been because we'd been exhausted from our fight.

A part of me also wondered if Jacob was really onboard with the arrangement. He knew Marcus and I were involved and that fate had bound me to Gideon. He'd told Marcus our connection wasn't emotional, that he didn't have romantic feelings for me, but when he'd bitten me last night, there'd been a pain in his eyes, and with my weird empathic magic that pain had manifested as a barely-there mist, revealing his sorrow.

He'd said his claim didn't affect him like it did me, that he didn't have to have sex with his feeding, but I'd sensed he wanted to. And a part of me, a part that I was pretty sure now wasn't his claim, wanted him, too.

I splashed water on my face in the hope it would help me focus. I couldn't think about my feelings right now. I had to get to my first meeting and show Gideon that he hadn't made a mistake by keeping me on the team.

At least my reflection looked almost normal. The last handful of times I'd stared at myself in the mirror, I'd looked shocked and desperate. Now I appeared a little low on sleep, but not by much. The gash in my cheek had become a thin silvery scar, and while the ragged one from the feral vampire was now a pale pink, it still looked ugly. It probably always would. There were also still a few hints of bruises on my face, arms, and legs, since Amiah hadn't healed me completely last night. But the bit of better-than-human healing I had because I was half angel and the added enhancement from Jacob's claim meant I looked like I'd been in a car crash a few days ago and not last night—which I had been.

My gaze, like it always did when I looked at myself in a big mirror, jumped to the delicate gold lines of Gideon's brand etched into my forearm. It glowed, ever so slightly, but with my buzz blazing at pre-nicotine-numbing levels, I couldn't feel the hint of Gideon's electric magic that I usually did.

Just the thought of Gideon made my chest ache. I really hoped accepting me on the team meant he wouldn't be acting as coldly toward me. Just the memory of overhearing his rejection of me to Amiah, of never wanting to even know me, broke my heart. And it didn't matter how many times I told myself that I didn't know him and couldn't possibly love him, it still hurt.

Maybe fighting to stay with the team had been a bad idea. Leaving would offer some emotional relief. Except I knew it wouldn't. I'd already tried to keep my distance. After defeating the archnephilim, Marcus had let me return to my normal human life, and I'd been miserable. I couldn't go back to that, no matter how much staying risked exposing my secret.

I combed my fingers through my long light brown hair, but since I didn't have a hair elastic, I couldn't pull it back into a ponytail. And I wasn't going to think about the reaction I'd get from the team with me looking unprofessional in Marcus's clothes, no shoes, and my hair loose and feminine. It was 7:55 a.m. and I had to get a move on if I didn't want to be noticeably late.

Phone and keycard in hand, I rushed into the hall, tripped on a carry-on sized rolling suitcase, and slammed into a hard muscular body. We both lost our balance and crashed to the floor with me landing on top of him, the air knocked out of me—perhaps I wasn't as healed as I'd thought I was.

I pressed my palms to his shoulders to heave myself off, but froze when I met his gaze. Summer-sky blue eyes radiating angelic light. Gideon. And there wasn't a hint of hardness or ice in his gaze. It stole my breath and broke my heart. This was how it was supposed to be between us all the time.

CHAPTER 2

I WANTED TO PRETEND THE WARMTH FROM HIS EYES MEANT I was wrong about his feelings for me, but he'd made himself perfectly clear when I'd overheard him talking with Amiah and then again with his cold-shoulder every time we interacted. He didn't want me.

Well, God damn it. I didn't want him!

And yet I was forever connected to him. We were going to have to work something out. I wouldn't be able to spend my entire life with even a small part of me constantly grieving.

Except the look in his eyes didn't hold any hardness. Maybe there was a chance, not for a romantic relationship or even a friendship, but in the very least a truce.

I sat back and my mind stuttered. His perfect blond hair had been buzzed close to his scalp.

"What did you do to your hair?" And as soon as the words leaped out, my brain caught up. This wasn't Gideon. This angel's eyes were the same, and he had the same chiseled jaw, but his cheeks and nose were narrower and his eyes slightly farther apart. "You're his brother?"

Those beautiful summer-sky eyes locked on Gideon's brand on my right forearm, narrowed, and turned icy.

Yep, definitely his brother.

"You're his human." His gaze raked over my body, his expression hardening into disgust, and the temperature in the hall rose. "I can see why Gideon was so upset. At least you've come to your senses and you're here and accepted your fate." He grabbed the handle of his suitcase and stood. "I told him a human wouldn't be able to resist the brand. Your wills just aren't strong enough."

He turned and strode down the hall, deeper into the building toward the suites where the team members lived.

Jeez, what an asshole. I wanted to tell him off, but if he lived here—like his suitcase and the direction he was walking implied—it would be best not to make him any more of an enemy. It was going to be bad enough when he figured out Gideon and I weren't a thing and I was sleeping with Marcus.

Maybe if I didn't draw too much attention to the situation for the next couple of days, Gideon would have a chance to talk with him and explain everything. Like how he didn't want me. Ever.

I hurried to the elevator, realizing as I travelled to the first floor that Gideon had said to meet in his office and I had no idea where that was. With the buzz driving me crazy and the inside of my head being raw and making it hard to concentrate, I still hadn't managed to figure out what to do about that when the doors opened at the first floor.

Kol stood in the hall before me, and my breath hitched at the sight of him. God, he was so beautiful. His black hair, a little too long, curled around his ears and horns and was always slightly disheveled, making me think of sinful sex, while his T-shirt stretched taut across sculpted muscles and his jeans hugged lean-muscled thighs, making me want to join that sinful sex in whatever way he wanted.

Heat rose to my face, and the memory of the dream flooded me. His hands and mouth on my body, his power unfurling within me.

Hellfire flared in his dark eyes, and a shiver of desire swept through me. I bit back a moan, and the muscles in his jaw tightened.

"Gideon was wondering where you were," he said, his voice husky, sensual, turning my insides to liquid desire. "Marcus showed up for the meeting and you didn't."

It was just a dream. It wasn't him. But I couldn't convince my body that nothing had happened between us.

The elevator door started to close, and he stepped forward and stopped it with his hand.

"I—" My thoughts stalled, caught between aching need and my agonizing buzz. Holy crap, this was going to be a challenge. I hadn't had this reaction to Kol since our first meeting. How the hell was I going to be able to work on the team if I couldn't think straight around him?

He drew in a sharp breath, and the hellfire vanished from his eyes. The panty-melting desire within me softened to just sensual craving, and my buzz quickly consumed it.

Jeez, I never thought I'd be grateful for my buzz.

Focus on the pain. That at least wouldn't be embarrassing, since I had no doubt Kol knew exactly how I'd just been feeling about him.

"So does everyone know I'm on the team now?" I asked, making myself step out of the elevator without brushing up against Kol like I wanted to.

"I don't know." He headed down the hall, and I fell into step beside him. "I was running late because I still haven't figured out how to properly shield myself from you and Marcus. You've got to stop with the sex magic. It's too dangerous for a human."

"Kol, I swear. There's no sex magic. Just Jacob's bite." He hadn't believed Marcus and me the first time we'd denied it, and from his narrowed eyes, it didn't look like he believed me now.

But before I could continue trying to convince him, he stopped at an open office door. Inside, Gideon sat behind a perfectly organized desk, his expression hard, closed off, and not even a hint of a temperature change to reveal his emotions. He wore a pale blue button-down that accentuated his summer-sky eyes, and for a moment it was strange seeing him in something other than the T-shirt and fatigues he wore when he knew we were headed into a combat situation.

Behind him, framing the narrow window, stood two floor-to-ceiling bookcases with everything in place. The whole office looked like it had just been cleaned by a professional organizer, except I was pretty sure this was how the office always looked.

Jacob, looking like the Wild West gunslinger that he'd been before he'd become a vampire—even though he wasn't wearing his usual calf-length duster—sat on a stiff beige couch. His claim within me gave a slight tug, but not enough to make me fear he could control me. He'd pulled his shoulder-length hair into a ponytail at the back of his neck, his tanned face unblemished even after last night's fight, but strain still tightened his massive body and pinched at the edges of his intense black eyes.

He hadn't gotten enough blood from me last night to fully recover, since he'd needed more than I could give in one feeding, which meant the three of us were going to have to test our arrangement again, and soon, to bring him up to full.

Marcus sat beside him, his piercing green eyes bright with pleasure and affection. An affection that filled my chest with honest-to-goodness real emotion. It was the morning after—of a major fight and of having mind-blowing sex with Marcus. I was on the team, and he still wanted me.

"Agent Shaw." Gideon pointed to a chair across from Marcus, and I sat.

My buzz did a strange flicker, easing off for a moment before flaring back to life, and I resisted the urge to pull my chair closer to Gideon. I really needed to get to my bag and replace my nicotine patches, and I could only hope this meeting wouldn't take long, because it was getting hard to concentrate.

"—newest member of the team," Gideon said. "Agent Shaw?"

And crap, I'd already missed part of the conversation and everyone was looking at me.

"Do I need to arrange for you to have a suite?" Gideon asked, the rest of the question clear in his eyes: or are you moving in with Marcus?

Marcus and I hadn't had a chance to talk about it, but my immediate instinct was for my own space. I'd been living on my own since I was seventeen and moving into Marcus's suite while also working with him made a part of me panic. I'd be with him all the time. I wouldn't have a moment or a space to myself. That and maybe Marcus didn't want to suddenly share his suite. I couldn't make this decision without talking with him first.

"I don't know. Can I keep my assigned room and think about it?"

Marcus didn't move and his expression didn't change, but a strange mix of emotions swept through me and vanished before I could figure out what they were or what they meant.

"You can," Gideon said, his expression and tone flat. "I'd love to give everyone the day off, but we're still in the middle of the operation to shut down the zip trafficker in town."

"Is there anything we can do about that?" Jacob asked. "We tried to raid the lab two days ago, but..."

But Gideon had taken a life-threatening gunshot wound, and they'd had to race back to Operations to save him without completing the raid.

Jacob rubbed his face, looking tired when he should

have been looking rested. "I'm sure they've already packed up and moved."

"Which means you're back to starting at the beginning again," a rich masculine voice said from behind me.

Gideon stiffened, and we all turned to look at the doorway to stare at his brother—and now that I could see them together, I was more certain than ever that they were related.

"You know why I'm here," he said, his gaze never leaving Gideon.

"Of course, Cassius," Gideon said. "The team is yours."

The room's temperature dropped, but I couldn't tell which of the guys were afraid. No one said a word as Gideon and Cassius stared at each other, their expressions hard. My buzz chewed under my skin, and I fought not to squirm.

"Taking down the zip trafficker and his operation is still the team's top priority." Cassius glanced at his phone. "Since you failed to shut down the lab, we need to go back to the initial intel. Jacob and Marcus, I need you to run down one of the low-level sellers and bring him or her in for questioning."

"That will alert anyone higher up that we're looking to make a move," Gideon said.

Cassius lifted his gaze back to Gideon. "They already know we're making a move. They're just lucky we're not coming after them for killing an angel."

So he knew about Gideon getting shot. I wondered if he also knew it was the mating brand that had saved him. I shuddered at the memory of that. I'd almost had my throat ripped out by a feral vampire because of the brand. But I also knew I wouldn't be alive, even with Kol's life-saving magical transfer, without it, and we certainly wouldn't have been able to destroy Ibizual's key. The advantages and disadvantages of the brand went both ways.

Cassius's gaze dropped back to his phone, and he frowned. "You're missing your new human officer. An E. Shaw. We should report his absence to the chief of police and have him replaced."

"Shaw is here," Marcus said, jerking his chin toward me.

"You're Shaw?" The angel glow in Cassius's eyes flared. "You need to be reassigned."

"Officer Shaw isn't being reassigned," Marcus growled.

"Agent," Gideon corrected. "It's now *Agent* Esther Shaw, assigned by the Union City Chief of Police himself and approved by JP Head Office."

"Because they didn't know about—" Cassius gestured at me. "There are rules."

"Actually, there aren't any rules about branded mates or even just mates working together," Gideon said, his tone unreadable, making it impossible to tell how he felt about that.

"You risk your team thinking you're giving her preferential treatment."

I snorted at that. Yeah, no risk of that happening.

"Agent Shaw has already proven herself to be a valuable asset to the team," Jacob said.

Kol shifted forward from his spot by the door. "I'd

rather work with Gideon's mate, too. We already know she can handle herself in a crisis. We don't know that about some other human UCPD might assign us."

Cassius turned his attention to Marcus, who was sitting too still, his body tense, a hint of his wolf darkening his eyes. "Agent Diaz?"

"Gideon knows where I stand with Essie," he said, his voice low as if daring Cassius to start a fight. "We'd be dead, twice now, if it wasn't for her."

"I see." Cassius's gaze shifted to me, and the pain from my buzz increased. He looked even less pleased than before that I was who I was. "All right. I suggest you change into something more appropriate and return here to fill out the paperwork to begin your reassignment from UCPD."

Marcus's phone chimed, and he pulled it from his pocket as Cassius stared him down.

"The Union City wolf pack alpha is requesting a meeting," Marcus said. "Right now. Says it's serious."

"You're the pack liaison," Gideon said. "Kol can take your spot with Jacob running down zip dealers."

"Actually, it's Kol's day off," Cassius said.

Kol shrugged. "I don't mind."

"I do. JP team members have assigned days off for a reason. You're always on call, and you'll burn yourself out if you don't take time off." Cassius shoved his phone into his pants pocket. "If things escalate, I'll call you back in. Until then, I won't expect your reports for the last two days on my desk until tomorrow afternoon. You're dismissed."

Kol glanced at Gideon, who gave a tight nod. The

incubus slid his gaze to me, a mix of emotions flashing across his expression, and he left. His emotions were just as confusing as Marcus's had been over me not moving in with him, and for a messed-up moment, I missed the clear-as-mud temperature fluctuations instead of whatever the hell I'd just seen.

Cassius turned his attention to me.

Another snap from my buzz, and I clenched my jaw against reacting and revealing a weakness in front of this angel.

"Officer Shaw—"

"Agent," Gideon corrected.

"Agent." Cassius looked like he was trying to not roll his eyes at that. "Looks like you're starting early. Jacob, show her the ropes until Marcus is done meeting with the pack alpha and can replace her." He turned his glare to Gideon. "We need to talk about how you've handled the last couple of weeks. Head office is unsatisfied with your latest performance."

The temperature in the room dropped a few more degrees, but I still couldn't tell who the fear came from. Gideon's expression remained hard, but both Marcus and Jacob looked concerned.

"You have your assignments, agents," Cassius said, his words a sharp dismissal.

We stood and hurried into the hall where Kol leaned against the wall radiating a sexual intensity that I doubted he was even aware of.

Cassius closed the door behind us.

"Your mate?" he said, his voice low, only audible

because Jacob's vampiric claim enhanced my hearing. "You've put your *human* mate on the team?"

"I didn't *put* her anywhere," Gideon said.

"And right on cue, big brother storms in to fuck things up," Marcus growled, drowning out the rest of the conversation behind the closed door.

"After the fight with the archnephilim at Essie's apartment and then the mess in the park and the cemetery, head office was going to send someone." Jacob rubbed his face again. Gideon and I might have gotten shot in the last two days, but Jacob had been slowly starving for the last two weeks. And while Amiah could heal the gunshot wounds, even if she'd known about Jacob's condition, she wouldn't have been able to do anything about it.

"You need to feed again," I said.

He captured me with his intense gaze, stealing my breath for a second. "You need more recovery time first."

"I agree with that," Kol said.

"Me, too." Marcus shifted possessively close to me, his arm brushing my shoulder, but didn't reach to hold my hand or embrace me. I wasn't sure what that meant, if he was being professional while we were at work—or as professional as his wolf would allow him—or if he was upset that I hadn't wanted to move in with him.

I took his hand and threaded my fingers between his, a silent attempt to reassure him I was still his just in case he was upset—as well as to satisfy my own need just to touch him. "Fine. How worried should I be about Cassius?"

"Depends on how much he thinks Gideon has fucked up," Marcus said, tightening his grip on my hand.

"It's protocol for a team evaluation." Jacob jerked his thumb to the end of the hall. "Come on, let's get back to your suite so Essie can get her gear and shoes before you head out," he said to Marcus.

"Just because head office needs to send someone doesn't mean I have to like it," Marcus said.

We headed down the hall to the elevator.

"It is what it is," Jacob said.

"He won't understand the team." Marcus's voice darkened into a low growl, and his canines sharpened, his wolf threatening to break free. "And he won't give us time to figure out our new situation."

"Haven't you already figured the situation out?" Kol asked.

"Essie is still Gideon's mate. He won't be able to avoid that forever." Marcus glanced at me. "You won't be able to avoid it, either."

Given how adamant Gideon had been about never wanting to get to know me, I was sure he was going to avoid our branded-mates situation for a long, long time.

"And your wolf?" Jacob hit the elevator call button. "What will your wolf do about that?"

"You mean am I going to lose my shit on Gideon?"

"That's the worry," Jacob said.

A whisper of mist curled around me, and somehow I knew the grief came from Jacob. Both Marcus and Gideon had a legitimate, permanent claim on me, while Jacob's would eventually fade.

"Everyone shares," I said. And I meant all of them. I *hoped* for all of them. Which had to be because of my dream this morning and not because that was the way I really wanted it. How could I feel affection for all of them in so short a time? Except I did. They were mine. I belonged with them. This, with them, was the home I'd never allowed myself to have. My soul had recognized it already and now my mind was starting to catch up.

"Those are Essie's terms," Marcus said. "My wolf fully accepts them."

"Sharing. With everyone? At the same time?" Kol asked, his tone thick with innuendo but his expression playful.

"I didn't say that," Marcus growled, not noticing he was being teased.

"The terms are pretty open-ended." The elevator door opened and Kol slipped in first, hiding his wicked smile from Marcus. "You have a threesome going already with Jacob?"

"It's not a threesome," Marcus snarled.

Jacob's mist deepened.

"I'm already riding that high," Kol said. "I think I should join in."

"You're not joining in." Marcus released my hand, shoved Kol against the back of the elevator, and pinned him there with his forearm.

"Stop teasing him," Jacob said, his voice a dangerous rumble, his mist thickening and obscuring my vision. "I'm sure his wolf is already struggling with sharing Essie with Gideon."

And now I was certain Jacob was struggling as well.

CHAPTER 3

WE ALL GOT INTO THE ELEVATOR, JACOB'S MIST GATHERING on my cheeks. It would soon look like I was crying if I didn't change his mood, but I wasn't sure how to deal with it, and I didn't want to bring it up in front of Marcus and Kol. When Marcus had first told me he'd share my affection, he'd included Jacob as part of the agreement because sex went hand in hand with a strong vampiric claim. But then Jacob had denied an emotional attraction to me and we'd come up with our arrangement. I knew if I broached the subject now, Jacob would continue to deny that there was anything more to our connection than a blood exchange, no matter how much his misty emotions said otherwise.

We headed to Marcus's suite, and he pressed his thumb to the fingerprint reader on the door, unlocking it for us. With a growl and a whisper of heated frustration sweeping over me, he marched back to the elevator to make his meeting with the alpha of Union City wolf pack.

"If you keep that up," Jacob said to Kol, "he's going to seriously hurt you."

"Yeah, but then he'll go to Essie to tame his savage beast, and I'll be back up to normal." Kol leaned against the doorframe, a pinprick of hellfire in his eyes. "Possessive shifter sex always comes with a little extra juice."

Jacob rolled his eyes at him.

Kol flashed a wicked grin that made my pulse skip and my body ache with need. Horror flashed over his expression, as if he'd just realized what he was doing to me, and all playfulness and hellfire vanished.

"Hand me your phone, Essie, and I'll give you my number." He held out his hand and my pulse skipped again, even though he wasn't radiating any sexual energy. All I could think about was the dream, and his dream-hands on my body. "So I can... ah..." The hellfire flickered back into his eyes. "You know... when..." He cleared his throat. "When Marcus takes over with Jacob and relieves you, I can help you get settled in, show you around... like I said I would."

If I wasn't so turned on, I would have burst out laughing. Twice in almost as many days, I'd managed to make Kol tongue-tied.

"Sure." I handed him my phone and grabbed my duffle bag from the bedroom. I desperately wanted to apply two nicotine patches right now, but I didn't want Jacob or Kol to see me doing it. I certainly didn't want to remind them that there was something not quite right about me. I was sure eventually I'd have to figure out an explanation—Marcus had seen me naked enough times now that he'd probably noticed the patches. But until I could come up with a reasonable explanation, I wasn't going to draw attention to it, so I decided to wait until I was back in my apartment and changing my clothes to reapply my patches.

Kol returned my phone and rushed down the hall to his suite a few doors down, leaving me alone with Jacob.

"Let's get you to your apartment so you can change," he said, his tone brusque and not leaving a good opportunity to broach the subject of our possible feelings for each other. And really, how could I bring it up? I couldn't say that I knew he felt bad about the arrangement with me and Marcus, because I couldn't explain how I knew that. While I *had* come up with an excuse to explain my empathy, it was another thing I wasn't going to voluntarily bring up. I might be stupid enough to believe this was where I belonged, but I was still keenly aware how dangerous it was to be here.

I shoved my feet into my runners, and we returned to the first floor, taking a detour to the cafeteria so I could pick up a breakfast burrito before heading to the garage. Instead of taking one of the JP's gray SUVs, we got into a silver four-door sedan. Given that there was a chance we might be sitting around in the car waiting to catch a low-level drug dealer, the nondescript vehicle was the better choice than the SUV.

The back windows were tinted, hiding the metal screen separating the back seats from the front like a cruiser—which thankfully meant if we did manage to pick up someone, they'd be contained for the ride back to Operations.

I climbed into the passenger seat and dropped my

duffle bag at my feet. "Any idea who we might be looking for?"

Jacob pulled out of Operations' secure garage and headed out of the Supers' Quarter.

My buzz grew stronger the farther we went, as if even being in the same building as Gideon had eased it.

"There are two on the list who probably don't know we know about them."

"Any idea where we might find them?" A painful nip sliced into my neck, and I pressed my palm against it, as if that would somehow help... which it never did.

"One might be at Rouge."

My stomach clenched at the name of the nightclub owned by Jacob's sire. I didn't want to run into Victoria again... ever, if I could help it. She scared the shit out of me, and it had everything to do with the enormous vampiric power radiating from her and her willingness to hurt someone to get what she wanted. Not to mention the fact that Jacob owed her a full twenty-four hours of time with her for her help with stopping Ibizual. Which I'd been told would involve blood loss. Because that was the way Victoria liked her sex. And I wasn't going to think about how much it bothered me that Jacob had freely agreed to the price. He wasn't mine, no matter how much a part of me said he was. He could have sex with anyone he liked, even if that meant he'd need my blood to recover afterward.

"What about the other one? I'd like to avoid running into Victoria any time soon."

Jacob shot me a dark glance. "She's seen how strong

my claim is on you. That should keep her happy for a good couple of decades."

"One can hope." Except I wasn't so sure about that. Victoria also knew I had Gideon's mating brand, and I had no doubt that complication amused her.

We drove through the park ringing the Quarter that separated the supers' part of the city from the rest of the city and headed to my very plain, very human neighborhood. Jacob's mist was gone and the temperature in the car didn't fluctuate, but there was a tension between us that made me want to squirm. I hadn't thought we'd gotten close in the last two and a bit weeks, especially with a week and a half with no contact, but the awkwardness now between us hurt.

Jacob parked on the street in front of my apartment building, a plain four-story walkup at the back of a three-building complex of four-story walkups. My landlord's wife knelt in the garden by my building's front door and started to wave as we walked toward her, but she stopped when she realized it was me.

Yeah, I was no longer in her good graces. I might have been a reliable tenant who kept quiet and paid the rent on time, but I'd also just hosted a fight with five powerful supers that had scared the crap out of my neighbors and required the Joined Parliament to repair the damages.

Her attention jumped to Jacob, and she grabbed her gardening caddy and moved to the flowerbed on the far side of the courtyard.

I glanced at Jacob. He was hiding his vampiric intensity, just like he had the first time I'd met him. If I hadn't known what he was, given that he was walking around in the daylight—thanks to a magical bracelet from the JP that protected him—I would never have known he was a vampire. Of course he was still huge, about six and half feet tall with a massive muscular body. That was still enough to scare anyone.

My apartment was on the top floor in the corner. I'd fallen in love with it the moment I'd seen it, with its vaulted ceiling, two walls of tall windows, the skylight above the living room, and access to the roof.

The memory of being in Gideon's arms while flying made me shiver, and my buzz blazed, stealing my breath for a moment. A part of me ached at the thought of flying. I might be half angel, but I didn't have wings, and I would never fly.

I hadn't thought that was a problem. Except now that I was back here, I couldn't help but wonder if I'd subconsciously picked this apartment two years ago because I could sit in my living room or stand on the roof and stare at the sky.

"You okay?" Jacob asked.

And I realized I'd gotten lost in thought with my key in the lock, thinking about not having wings and never being able to fly.

"Yeah." I opened the door. "Sure."

"It's been a difficult couple of days." He followed me inside, his attention sliding over the room. I wasn't sure if he was looking for danger or checking if the JP had actually fixed my apartment from the fight with the archnephilim. "I'm sure if you talk with Gideon and Cassius, they'll give you a couple of days to adjust to your new position."

"Cassius already thinks I'm getting special treatment from Gideon." I headed into my bedroom and pulled out a change of clothes.

Jacob leaned against the doorframe with his back to me.

"Cassius also knows you're human. Once Gideon tells him what we went through last night, he'll know you're not fully recovered."

"And that will just give him another excuse to kick me off the team." Jeez, I'd been worried it would be Gideon who'd send me packing and give the chief of police reason to fire me from the force, since none of the other officers wanted to work with me. And really, I couldn't blame them. Dangerous situations with supers kept finding me, and my partners kept getting hurt. If the JP team refused me, I was sure I would be unemployed. And I had no idea what I'd do with myself if I couldn't be a cop.

"Essie." Jacob's voice was sharp, jerking my attention to him. His back was still to me, but it felt like he was focused on me and only me. It probably had something to do with his claim. I might be able to resist the compulsion to obey him now, but it didn't mean our essences were any less entwined. "You were shot yesterday and then barely got through last night's battle alive. I doubt Amiah healed you to full. You're allowed to recover."

A hint of mist curled around me, and what he didn't say squeezed my chest. If I died, he died. Not to mention if I died, Gideon would go insane because of the mating brand. And, given that Marcus's wolf had claimed me as his mate, I didn't doubt Marcus would suffer as well.

And yet I couldn't hide myself away to protect them. I needed to stand with them as an equal.

"Your claim has helped me heal." I changed out of Marcus's clothes into jeans and a T-shirt. "I can handle a little surveillance until Marcus relieves me."

"Cassius still should have given you Kol's day off."

"I'm pretty sure Cassius did what he did to see what I would do about it." I shoved Marcus's clothes and three more changes of clothes into my duffle bag. "He wanted to see if I'd use my connection with Gideon to get special treatment. He hasn't figured out that Gideon wants nothing to do with me."

"Gideon—"

"Don't tell me that isn't true. I know Marcus threatened to quit if Gideon didn't keep me on the team. I know Gideon hates that I'm his mate."

"He doesn't hate that you're his mate."

I replaced my two used-up nicotine patches with new ones, sticking them on the back of my hip—I'd changed them so frequently in the last little while, I was running out of different places to stick them to avoid irritating my skin. "I'm not what he wanted or even expected. I get it. I'm okay with it."

Jacob snorted. "Doesn't sound like it."

"I'm okay with him not wanting me to be his mate." I was. Honestly. I didn't want to be permanently bound to an angel who hated what I was. "It's him acting like I can't do my job that bothers me. That he doesn't even want to try to work with me."

"And yet here you are on the team."

"Because Marcus gave him an ultimatum." I checked my sidearm and holstered it in my waistband holster. I hadn't reloaded since last night, so I was still down to half a magazine of enspelled ammunition.

"Actually, we all did."

I turned to him. He was looking at me now, his vampiric intensity darkening his eyes and stealing my breath.

"We don't want a different human on the team. We want you." He shifted, as if he wanted to move to me, but the muscles in his jaw tightened, and he stayed put.

My pulse stuttered, and my buzz blazed stronger, searing through the still enflamed magical channels in my body. I ached for Jacob, just like I ached for Marcus and Gideon and even Kol. We were stronger together. *I* was stronger with all of them.

Which was crazy. I didn't know them. How could I know with such certainty that we belonged together?

"You belong on the team," Jacob said, his voice a low, sensual rumble.

"I also complicate the team." I couldn't forget that. Jacob wasn't happy with our arrangement with Marcus and the jury was still out if Marcus's wolf would accept me having something with Gideon... or anyone else.

"Stop arguing against yourself. We both know you want to be on the team, and we both know you belong here." Jacob jerked away from the door, stepping into my living room. "Now, come on. You're clearly not going to take the day off, so let's go find a zip dealer."

"But not at Rouge." I hurried past him to my bathroom, loaded some toiletries into my bag, and tied my hair back into a ponytail.

"I know someone in Squatters' Row. She might know where to score some zip. We'll try her first." Jacob pulled up a picture on his phone and handed it to me as we headed back to the car. "This is who we're most likely to find. Floyd Webb."

The guy was handsome, not breathtaking like all my guys, but then very few men could be.

My heart thrummed at that. My guys. All of them.

I pushed that back as deep as it would go, concentrating on my blazing buzz to help distract me. Only Marcus was actually mine. It wasn't right to claim all of them.

I refocused on Jacob's phone. Floyd had a build similar to Marcus's with powerful compact muscles, and his sandy blond hair hung in waves to his shoulders that any woman would envy. His brown eyes though were hard, as if he wanted to kill whoever was taking his picture.

"He's a weretiger, was originally muscle for the Claws but sources say he's graduated to drug dealer. Zip for the humans and fentanyl for the supers. Apparently his good looks make him a good salesman."

"Yeah, and that death look probably means they always pay up front." I handed the phone back to Jacob.

"We'll see if we can get a line on his location, and keep eyes on him until Marcus can take over."

I opened my mouth to argue about that.

"Shot and almost died, remember?" Jacob said.

Right. Not at full. And my not at full was worse than

his not at full. If I didn't take it easy now, I'd pay for it later. As much as I wanted to prove myself and not be a burden, Jacob was right. I needed to be smart about this. The team was under scrutiny and me being reckless put all of us in danger.

CHAPTER 4

WE RETURNED TO THE CAR. I THREW MY BAG INTO THE trunk, and we headed back to the Quarter. Hopefully I'd packed enough clothes to get me through the next couple of days and wouldn't end up in Marcus's workout clothes again. I could just imagine Cassius's face the next time he saw Marcus wearing the shorts and T-shirt I'd been wearing this morning. Hopefully that wouldn't happen until after Gideon had explained the situation. But a part of me feared that even if Gideon did explain, Cassius wouldn't understand, not because angels believed only in monogamy—I had no idea if they did or not—but because their beautiful, sacred mating brand said Gideon and I were destined for each other and Marcus wasn't a part of that destiny.

Squatters' Row was a small neighborhood on the far side of the Quarter within the park ring. Only half of the area that had been expropriated by the Joined Parlia-ment to create the Supers' Quarter had been repaired or redeveloped. The supers' population wasn't particularly big, but no one really knew how long it would take—if ever—for the majority of humans and supers to feel comfortable living side by side, so the city planners had set aside space within the Quarter for population growth.

Most of the buildings in the Row were in decent shape. Michael's war hadn't spent much time in this part of the city—which was one of the reasons it had been picked to become the Quarter. But the buildings were owned by absentee developers, or by developers who'd gone bankrupt, and the city had other things to worry about than buildings it had no money to fix or fill with tenants. And just like many of the abandoned parts of the city, those who didn't care about—or had no other choice to —live without power or running water took shelter in the abandoned buildings.

These areas of town often bred violence and crime and every couple of months, my partner and I were part of a task force to clean up the abandoned neighborhoods in our precinct. It was pretty much an act of futility, since the residents just relocated to another abandoned neighborhood, but we usually picked up a few gang leaders and drug dealers in the sweep and criminal activity always settled down for a bit.

I'd only been to Squatters' Row once, and only recently. Because it was in the Quarter, it fell under the Quarter's policing jurisdiction, which was part JP team and part teams from the three supernatural heads of the community: vampire, shifter, and demon. That meant the Row was rarely cleaned out and housed many of the shadier supers—the threshold for criminal activities that required policing in the supernatural world was higher than in the human world.

The Row was where I'd found the witch who'd sold me the contacts that hid my glowing eyes... the glow that had manifested after my fight with the archnephilim and was supposed to have faded weeks ago.

I'd paid a lot of money for the witch's discretion, and she hadn't asked any questions as to why my essence said I was human but my eyes glowed with angelic light. In turn, I didn't ask her about her less-than-legal services. Better one shady witch suspecting I was a nephilim than everyone I worked with or met on the street.

Still, I'd taken a serious risk going to her. She could have easily gone to the authorities and told them she knew I was a nephilim. And while I hadn't outright told her I was one, just about everyone in the world could put two and two together. But I'd had no choice, and I'd hoped—which seemed to be the case—that me continuing to be a paying customer would trump reporting a possible nephilim.

Except I was going to need to deal with my glowing eyes a lot sooner than I'd expected. Yesterday, Sebastian Bane had said I had less than a week left before the spell on the contacts failed. They were supposed to have lasted months, and the fact that they were going to last less than three weeks worried me.

Scared the shit out of me, actually.

Things within me were changing. I really wanted to pretend it wasn't true, but I couldn't. It wasn't just my glowing eyes, but my buzz—

And speaking of buzz, we were back in the Quarter, at

least a fifteen-minute drive from my apartment. My
patches should have kicked in by now, easing the biting
agony under my skin to manageable levels, but it was still
just as powerful as before.

Jacob turned onto a narrow street lined with six-story
apartment buildings and stopped halfway down. All the
buildings looked rundown, but only half were completely
boarded up. Most of those that weren't boarded up—and
didn't look like they were going to collapse—had thugs
hanging on the front steps enjoying the early summer
heat. Only about a third of the thugs looked human—
and while they could have actually been human, the
better guess was that they were packless shifters or a type
of demon who could pass as human.

I got out of the car and every eye turned to me. Half
the gazes looked hungry, the other half slid to the Glock
holstered at my hip and recognized me for what I was—a
cop—and their looks turned angry. My buzz clawed
through my body, and I gritted my teeth. The patches
would kick in soon. They had to.

Jacob got out, and all but a few gazes looked away,
anywhere but at Jacob. They'd all become suddenly interested in the windows across the street or the crossroad
ahead of us. He released a hint of his vampiric intensity
and the remaining gazes vanished. His claim gave a
gentle tug in my chest, drawing a shiver, yearning for all
the intensity to be turned on me. Funny how everyone
else wanted to shrink away from it, knew it meant Jacob
was the most dangerous super on the block, and I
craved it.

We climbed the steep steps of the closest building,

making the three green-skinned demons perched there scurry inside. Jacob ignored them, and we headed up to the second floor, stopping at a scarred door in a garbage-strewn hall of scarred doors.

He raised his hand to knock, but slid his gaze to me instead. "We're here to talk to Fawn. Not save her."

I didn't like the sound of that. "What's that supposed to mean?"

"Things are different in the Quarter than the rest of Union City," he said, his voice a low rumble. "You're not going to like Fawn's situation. Most humans don't understand it."

"What do you mean by that?" A painful nip sliced through my shoulder, and I dug my nails into my skin, trying to grind the buzz away before that muscle started twitching.

"Just know that this is her choice." He knocked.

Footsteps shuffled to the door. The deadbolt clicked open, and Jacob tensed, but it didn't feel like he was tensing for danger, more like my reaction.

The door cracked open, still secured by the chain, revealing the face of a pretty demon with small delicate horns poking through long blond locks. If she'd been giving off any kind of sexual vibe, I would have thought she was a succubus, but she wasn't. In fact, she was barely giving off any demonic vibe at all. No hellfire in her eyes and no radiating heat from a raised body temperature. Save for the horns, I would have thought she was human.

My brain tripped on that, then realization kicked in. She was a half breed. Half human half demon. Something that, unlike me being half human and half angel, was entirely possible. The demonic half breed community was tiny, but there were enough of them worldwide for them to claim a community and have representation in parliament.

"Jacob," she said, her voice soft and dreamy. "Have you changed your mind about bagged blood?"

She shut the door, and the chain rattled.

"Your blood bunny?" I asked in a voice so quiet only Jacob could hear it and only because of his enhanced hearing. I had no idea how I felt about that. He was a vampire. I couldn't pretend he didn't use a blood bunny's service. Most did. And while most humans saw the job as prostitution with blood donation, bunnies had more protection and rights than a normal human because of the nature of their occupation. Not to mention they were paid very well.

"She used to be my bunny," Jacob replied, just as quietly, "but she started liking it rougher than I do, so I moved on. Victoria had to let her go a few years ago so she wouldn't lose her license to house bunnies."

"That rough?" That said a lot. There were only a few things bunnies weren't allowed to do and they were pretty extreme.

The door reopened in full this time, and I fought to keep a straight face. The half demon wore a pink slip that barely covered her, exposing a body covered in vampire bites. They were everywhere, some clean, some ragged, all in various stages of healing. Pink and silvery scars thickened her neck and wrists, and it didn't look like there was a single spot on her that hadn't been bitten. And because I could tell that, it meant the vampires feeding on her weren't properly healing her. Yes, their magic didn't completely heal the wound right away, but it continued to work over time, eliminating even the scar.

I tensed, and Jacob pressed his hand against my back, as if hoping the physical contact would remind me of his warning.

"I don't do couples any more. Too dangerous." She leaned toward Jacob, her voice breathy. The need of an addict filled her eyes, and the temperature around me skyrocketed with lust. "But I know you're safe. I'll make an exception for you."

"We need information," Jacob said. "I'll pay and you don't have to bleed."

"Make me bleed, and I'll say you've paid." She ran her finger over a ragged bite just below her collar bone. The temperature turned sweltering, and her pupils dilated, her desire growing stronger.

Jacob was right. I wanted to save Fawn. She was a perfect example of the greatest risk for a bunny. Most would think it would be blood loss, or serious injury at the hands of a vampire, but it was really becoming addicted to the magic of a vampire's bite. There were successful forms of treatment, and the terms of a bunny's contract with a blood house ensured a comfortable retire-ment if he or she did become addicted. But Fawn had been fired from Victoria's club and must have kept working as a bunny on her own. Which meant she didn't have a contract to protect her from her addiction.

Except Jacob had made a point to warn me that this was Fawn's choice. It was a terrible choice, but it was hers.

"I won't tell you anything unless you bite me," she said, shifting closer to Jacob.

"You won't be able to tell us anything after I bite you."

Fawn pressed her hands to Jacob's chest and looked up into his dark eyes, her body trembling with her desire. "Please, Jacob."

A hint of mist crept through Fawn's heat, but I couldn't tell if it was because Jacob was sad for Fawn or something else.

"A bite," he said. "Nothing more."

"Jacob," she begged.

Another snap in my shoulder and the muscle spasmed.

"Nothing more." His tone was gentle yet firm. I wasn't sure how he felt about this kind of payment, but I was beginning to learn that some supers negotiated with non-monetary currency. Victoria traded in sex. Looked like Fawn traded with being bitten. There was a lot I was going to need to learn if I was going to work on the JP team, a whole lifetime of catching up, because I'd made a point of avoiding all things supernatural.

"What do you want to know?" She ran her hands down his chest, as if that might change his mind about biting her right away.

I ground my thumb into my shoulder, trying to stop the spasm.

Jeez. Why weren't the nicotine patches working?

"Where are the best places in town to score zip?" He grabbed her wrists as they reached the waistband of his pants.

Her desire flared, and sweat slicked my skin. "That

shit will kill you. It's not worth the risk. Leave it to the humans and us half breeds. They say less than a quarter of supers who take it survive."

"It's not for me," Jacob said.

Fawn's attention slid to me. "No matter what powers the zip gives humans, you can't make your bunny into a super even just for a feeding. She won't be able to give you what you want," she said, her tone clear that she could.

More of Jacob's mist swept around me.

"Of course she can't," he said, his gaze darting to mine. "But she's new in town and still looking to score."

"So do you know where I can?" I asked, playing along.

"I've heard the guys a few doors down talk about scoring at the Third Street bridge as well as an apartment above the bodega on the corner of Morris and West, but I don't know if their dealers sells zip." Fawn pressed her body against Jacob's and tilted her head, exposing her neck.

"Do you know who their dealer is?" Jacob asked.

"You said you'd bite me." Her breath picked up with need and desperation.

"I want to make sure the guy is the real deal."

"Lloyd or something. Something about a spider for his last name maybe?" She clawed at a barely healed bite near her ear, breaking the scab and smearing the trickle of blood on her neck. "We made a deal."

Jacob didn't react to the blood. His pupils didn't dilate, and his fangs didn't extend, not like they did when I offered myself.

The air in the hall was sweltering, filled with mist, and my body stung.

"Should we step inside?" I asked, uncertain if Jacob wanted to bite her while standing in the hall.

"Yes," Fawn breathed, her eyes half closed in anticipation.

"Here's fine." With his expression tight, he pushed Fawn back a step, putting some distance between them.

Fawn's gaze shot up to his, filled with hurt and anger. "We had a deal."

"We did." He brought her wrist to his lips and sank his fangs into her scarred flesh.

She moaned and grabbed the doorframe to steady herself. Her need blazed in the air around me even though the first few seconds of a vampire's bite were painful, and I wondered if she preferred her bite without a vampire's intoxicating magic.

Then he sucked, a gentle pull on her vein that I knew flooded his magic into her body. She moaned again, the sound deeper, filled with euphoria.

A shiver swept through me, not at the sight of Jacob feeding from her, but at the memory of his magic rushing into me. Pure spiraling desire with a climax that exploded in every cell, and I couldn't help but wonder if this was my fate, addicted to the magic of his bite

He withdrew his fangs without taking a second sip, his magic sealing the wound shut, but Fawn didn't seem to notice. Just a few seconds, and she was riding the high of his magic. Gripping her shoulders, he walked her backwards to a bare, beat-up mattress on the floor a few feet inside the door, and left her with her hands roaming her body. He rejoined me in the hall, shutting the door behind him, radiating dark vampiric intensity and surrounding me with a thick mist.

"I suppose these are the ropes Cassius wanted me to show you." He didn't sound happy about that and it broke my heart, consuming my fear that I was walking a dangerous line with Jacob and reminding me that regardless of my fate, I would do anything to protect him.

Which was another thought that terrified me.

I pressed a hand to his biceps—the muscle so big I wouldn't have been able to encircle it with both hands—needing to reassure him, and myself, with physical contact. "Are *you* okay?"

"I only have a problem drinking bagged blood." Which was why we had our arrangement with Marcus.

But his mist wasn't clearing up. He was upset about something. "I wasn't talking about that."

He pressed his hand over mine. What remained of his claim thrilled at his touch, while another part of me warmed at the rightness of it.

"There are a lot of ugly things about the supernatural world that we keep from humans. It bothers me that you had to see me do that."

"I don't judge you for using alternative currency, like your bite for information."

He raised an eyebrow at that, his expression clear he didn't believe me.

"At some point, you're going to have to start taking me at my word. I might not know everything about you, but I know who you are."

Mine.

I shoved that thought back.

"The team wouldn't work together as well as it does if your moral codes didn't align, and I doubt destiny would have said Gideon and I were soul mates if we didn't share a similar moral center." I rose on my tiptoes and brushed my lips across his cheek with a need to show him that I wasn't afraid of him or found him disgusting.

The mist vanished, replaced with a sudden wild heat.

"Essie," he rumbled.

My breath caught, my heart pounding. "Yes, Jacob."

CHAPTER 5

Jacob's gaze captured my soul, and my pulse pounded faster. The wild heat of his emotions blazed through me, consuming my buzz. But a second later the muscles in his jaw clenched and his expression tightened. The heat vanished, leaving me cold and stinging.

"Let's see if we can find a zip dealer." He squeezed my hand then realized what he was doing, released me, and shifted away.

The distance—emotional and physical—hurt. Almost as much as the distance Gideon put between us. "Yeah. Sure."

A sharp snap from the buzz cut down my neck, making me flinch.

Jacob's eyes narrowed, and I fought the urge to rub the twitching muscle and draw more attention to it.

"It sounded like Fawn might have been talking about Floyd Webb. The Third Street bridge is closest. We should check there first." I headed toward the stairs and

Jacob joined me. We were definitely going to have a conversation, just not while we were working and after I'd gotten my buzz under control.

A masculine laugh echoed from the stairwell.

"The look on his face," a rich baritone said in response as footsteps clomped up the stairs.

I wasn't sure how many people there were, but definitely more than two, and most of the steps were heavy, suggesting they were all male.

I tensed, and my buzz sliced up my neck again.

"The look on *all* their faces," another guy chuckled.

I rolled my shoulders. This was just a bunch of guys —most likely supers, but still guys. Yes, I was a cop in their territory, but maybe they wouldn't see the aura of 'cop' radiating around me. Half the guys on the street hadn't.

The group reached the top of the stairs and were so caught up in laughing about whatever they'd been talking about that they made it almost ten feet down the hall before noticing us.

There were three of them. The guy in front, a bulky demon with onyx skin, milky white eyes, and almost as big as Jacob, stopped and met the vampire's gaze and held it. Whatever type of demon he was, he clearly thought he could challenge Jacob for dominance.

The guy beside him, a demon with red scales all over his body, a thin prehensile tail, and slitted pupils, glanced at my sidearm then sneered, revealing a mouth full of pointed teeth.

Crap. Smart enough to recognize me as a cop.

"You thought bringing a vampire to the Row would protect you, cop?" Scales said.

"Actually she brought a JP agent." Jacob released more of his hold on his vampiric intensity, and a whisper of cold swept across my cheeks—fear from the guys. I shivered with the chill, and my buzz sliced through my neck again. Jeez. This was getting bad.

"Still, two of you and three of us," Onyx guy said.

"We're not here for you." Perhaps I could deescalate the situation, although I had a bad feeling these guys were just looking for a fight.

The guy in the back shifted into the space between Scales and Onyx. He was average height, well-built, handsome, blond, and the zip dealer we were looking for, Floyd Webb.

Well, shit. I guess we were there for them.

So much for just doing surveillance until Marcus relieved me.

"I've got the demons," Jacob said, his voice low and dangerous.

Which left me with Floyd, the weretiger. How the hell was I supposed to apprehend a shifter by myself? The chief of police really hadn't thought things through when he'd demanded the JP include a human member on the team. Jeez, I hadn't, either. I'd wanted the job, fought to be where I was, and now I was faced with the truth. I wasn't strong enough to overpower a super and arrest him.

But Jacob wouldn't be able to deal with all three of them by himself.

"Shot, remember?" I said, reminding him of his own words that I wasn't perfectly fit.

"Archnephilim," he replied, pointing out I'd dealt with much worse than a shifter.

Well, fine. Maybe my light strike spell would be enough to stun Floyd long enough for Jacob to deal with the demons.

Of course, my ability to summon divine light had been on the fritz, and then I'd channeled Gideon's power twice in as many days and my inner magical channels were still raw. Casting a light strike spell now was just as likely to fail or incapacitate me as it was Floyd.

Which left shooting him as my only other way to slow the weretiger down. Good thing Operations had a magical healer on staff.

I drew my sidearm to shoot, but Scales leaped forward and slapped my Glock with his tail. Somehow I managed to keep hold of my weapon, but in that split second the hall erupted into chaos.

Jacob bolted past me and shouldered Scales into Onyx, while Floyd shoved past them to lunge at me, his nails extended into wickedly sharp claws.

He swiped at me. I jerked back, his claws narrowly missing my chest, and brought my Glock up to shoot him. But he swiped again, forcing me to wrench my weapon away or be disarmed.

Behind him, Jacob punched Onyx in the gut, but Scales wrapped his tail around Jacob's neck. For a split second, I feared Jacob wouldn't be able to handle them— which was ridiculous, given what we'd dealt with in the last couple of weeks. He rammed his elbow into Scales's face and ducked under a swing from Onyx.

Floyd snarled at me and swiped again, lunging closer than before. I twisted to the side instead of wrenching back. His claws skimmed my shoulder, tearing my T-shirt and slicing into my skin with fiery agony, but it was worth it. Now I was positioned right next to him. I rammed my heel into his knee and my fist into his head. I didn't really want to shoot him, and I wasn't stupid enough to try to hold him at gunpoint when we were so close, so I needed him down so I could put distance between us and gain control of the situation.

He dropped to his knees, and I hopped back and aimed my weapon at him. "Hands on your head."

His eyes were wide and a nauseating mix of hot and cold washed over me. Anger and fear at me. Yeah, somehow this puny human had gotten the upper hand on him.

"Hands on your head."

Scales hissed and darted past Jacob, who had Onyx in a headlock. The scaled demon dove for me. I fired at him, but he twisted and the shot skimmed his ribs. Jacob heaved Onyx toward us and seized Scales's tail, but Floyd took my second of distraction, leaped to his feet, and bolted for the stairs.

I raced after him, praying Jacob could deal with Scales and Onyx quickly then help me. If he could, all I needed to do was keep Floyd in the area.

Floyd reached the stairs. I fired and skimmed his shoulder, making him stagger. It wasn't enough to stop him, but it did slow him down. Except instead of continuing down the stairs, he lunged at me.

I tried to stop my forward momentum, but I was running all out to catch him. My buzz snapped, making my neck and shoulder muscles spasm, and he grabbed the front of my T-shirt, his claws slicing into my chest.

With a roar, he tossed me toward the stairs. I dropped my Glock and seized his wrists before I could fall, but he was off balance and my weight yanked him down with me.

He slammed onto me, stealing my breath, then tumbled off. I fell after him, crashing down the stairs and careening off the wall. Pain exploded through my chest, head, shoulders. The world spun and flickered into darkness.

I landed in a heap on top of him, dizzy and filled with agony.

"Get off me, bitch." He shoved me aside, heaved himself up, and staggered out the front door.

I lurched after him even though I had no idea where my sidearm was. I didn't know why he didn't stick around to finish me off, but I couldn't let him get away. He might not have figured out that the JP was specifically looking for him, but there was a chance he'd tell his boss about the incident and then it would become harder to bring down the zip operation.

He was already at the bottom of the stairs when I reached the doorway.

"Floyd Webb," I gasped.

He turned and snarled at me, baring his extended canines. "You really want to fight?"

"I want you to get on your knees and put your hands on your head." It was the stupidest thing I could have said. I had no weapon, I was a weak human—more or less—and the world was still spinning.

Please don't let him notice that I don't have a gun And please, Jacob, show up behind me and scare him into compliance.

But Floyd's sneer deepened. "I want to see you make me."

He rushed up the stairs, death in his eyes and his rage searing the air around me.

Oh, shit.

I jerked back and raised my hands in a useless defense. Agony exploded in my palms, and a massive blast of divine light, summoned without even thinking the words of the spell, slammed into Floyd's chest. It tossed him off the stairs and across the street. He crashed into the building across from us, the force of my light strike so powerful it cracked the bricks.

Holy shit!

I sagged to my knees, my body on fire from channeling too much magic power too soon after the fight to stop Ibizual. Gideon was going to kill me. There was no way I could have summoned that much divine light on my own. Even though it hadn't felt like I had taken his power, I must have to have made that shot.

Jacob barreled down the stairs, holding my sidearm. "Essie."

"He's over there." I pointed to Floyd, lying unconscious in the sidewalk. I really hoped I hadn't killed him. That would just suck. Yeah, it had clearly been my life or his, but I had no doubt this situation would bring out the JP's version of internal affairs to investigate. And I was pretty sure that was Cassius... who was already here and hated me.

Jacob returned my gun, called Gideon for support, and hauled an unconscious Onyx and a dazed Scales down the stairs and into the back of the car.

I sat in the doorway.

I knew if I stood, I'd throw up... if I could stand.

If I was smart, I'd really rethink the being part of a JP team thing. Except just the thought of leaving made my pulse race. This was where I belonged. With the guys. They were mine. And if I wasn't strong enough to deal with the situation, I'd just have to become stronger.

Gideon, Marcus, and Cassius arrived as Jacob shut the door on the demons. He headed across the street to the still-unconscious—please don't be dead—Floyd, and the guys piled out of the gray SUV.

"A little excessive even for you, Jacob," Cassius said, crossing the street to him and standing on the sidewalk in front of Floyd, while Gideon and Marcus hurried up the stairs to me.

Light blazed from Gideon's eyes. God, he was furious.

The air temperature didn't change, but that had to be because of the buzz burning me from the inside out. The pain was so powerful, I couldn't even feel a hint of Gideon's electric magic in his brand, and that had been an ever-present sensation since I'd returned to Operations two days ago.

"I didn't know I'd taken it until the blast came out," I said. Maybe if I apologized right away, Marcus would clue in and try to calm Gideon down before he reamed me out in public, not to mention in front of his brother.

"Taken what?" Gideon asked, standing over me as Marcus knelt and gingerly took my hands.

My palms were burned. Again. Although not as badly as they had been when I'd destroyed the key that could unlock Ibizual's prison.

"What did you—?" Marcus's gaze jumped across the street, where Jacob had hauled Floyd to his feet. The whole front of the weretiger's shirt had been scorched away, and an ugly red burn covered most of his chest.

"Why didn't you tell me your human could produce a powerful light strike?" Cassius asked as he marched across the street to us. His gaze jumped from Gideon to Marcus, who knelt too close to me, and he cocked an eyebrow.

"It's a new development," Gideon said, ignoring the eyebrow, "and dangerous." He gestured to my burned hands and glared at me. "You really shouldn't have summoned it. Not after last night."

Oh, yeah, he was pissed and didn't want Cassius to know. And for some reason that made me pissed in return. It might have been dumb to cast it today—not that I'd cast it on purpose—but it did mean I wasn't completely powerless and therefore not a liability for the team. I'd thought we'd gotten past that when Gideon had accepted me on the team. Maybe, with his brother in town, he was changing his mind.

"Well, the next time I fall down a flight of stairs, lose my sidearm, and am about to have my throat ripped out by a shifter, I'll take a minute and think about the last time I cast a light strike spell."

"And that's why she can't be on the team," Cassius said. "You're playing with fire, Gideon. If something happens to her..." He didn't say the rest because we already knew it.

"This isn't the time or place for this discussion," Gideon said.

"There shouldn't be a discussion." Cassius glared at me. "Lock her in your suite until she sees reason."

Gideon's expression turned icy, but the fire in my body wouldn't let me sense any temperature changes. He was definitely rethinking about me being on the team. He could use this incident to prove to the other guys that the job was just too dangerous for me. And a part of me couldn't disagree.

Marcus growled, the sounds low and dangerous, and his wolf darkened his eyes. "It was stupid to just pair her up. Given the situation, any human on the team would have ended up like this or worse. She should always be support for the full team. Any human agent should be."

"Agent Shaw isn't just any human," Cassius said. "She's mated with an angel. Her life is not her own any more."

Marcus's canines lengthened and his nails sharpened into claws. "Her life is always hers."

"Back off, wolf. This isn't your business." A flicker of real flames danced around Cassius's fists.

Marcus jerked to his feet, and Gideon shoved himself in front of him before he could attack Cassius.

"Agent Shaw needs medical attention, and we need to

get Floyd and his demons to Operations." Gideon held Marcus's gaze as if daring him to try something. Or was he trying to will him into seeing reason? Fighting Cassius in the middle of the street was a terrible idea.

"Fine," Marcus snarled.

He bent to pick me up, but Gideon grabbed his shoulder and ever so slightly jerked his chin toward Cassius.

"Fine. I'll help Jacob." Marcus shoved past Gideon and Cassius.

"You need to get your wolf under control," Cassius said over his shoulder to Gideon as he headed back to the SUV.

Gideon knelt beside me, his expression still frozen.

I was in so much shit.

"Can you walk?" he asked.

"I have no idea." I hadn't tried to stand since blasting Floyd and with my buzz biting and burning me up, I couldn't tell if I'd broken anything. With the fall I'd taken, it was a miracle I hadn't broken my neck.

I reached for the wall to pull myself to my feet, but Gideon swept his arms around me and picked me up before I could fully rise.

The buzz vanished, and I almost sobbed with relief. One moment it was there, the next Gideon touched me and it was gone. Agony now sliced through me from the beating I'd taken falling down the stairs, but the biting, burning, every-inch-of-flesh-on-fire was gone. And all I had to do was get the man who wanted nothing to do with me to hold me.

I leaned my cheek against his chest and let his soft

scent of springtime envelop me. It broke my heart and made me angry at the same time. I didn't want to feel the things I did for Gideon, but my soul seemed to think he was as much mine as the rest of the guys. And every time he looked at me with ice in his summer-sky eyes, the brand made my soul cry.

I couldn't work with him if we didn't come to some kind of a truce. Which meant he had to know that I hadn't taken his power on purpose.

"I really didn't mean to take your power this time."

He headed to the SUV, the movement making my head spin. "You didn't."

"I must have." I closed my eyes before I threw up. Add concussion to my list of injuries. "I blasted him across the street, and my hands are burned. If it was my power, it wouldn't burn me."

"I don't know. It shouldn't have. But you're a human with an angelic mating brand. Brands enhance an angel's power. It might be affecting yours." He opened the back door to the SUV and set me on the seat, then turned to close the door.

My buzz reignited the moment he let go, blazing through me with blinding agony. I bit back a whimper and, without thinking, seized his wrist to stop the pain.

"Agent." His summer-sky gaze met mine, filled with worry and questions and tight discomfort.

Yeah, I know. He didn't want any extra physical contact. But I just couldn't deal with my buzz right now. It was so strong. Stronger than it had ever been before, and with my magical channels burned raw and my gut-churning concussion, I just couldn't stand it.

Except I had no idea how to tell him that, no idea how to tell him I needed him and still understood that he didn't want a relationship with me.

Especially with Cassius sitting in the driver's seat watching us through the rear view mirror.

CHAPTER 6

I OPENED MY MOUTH TO SAY SOMETHING, ANYTHING, HELL, just beg Gideon to let me touch him. While I'd come up with an explanation for my buzz—like with all my unusual abilities—I'd only wanted to use it as a last resort. Maybe this was my last resort. Could it get worse? But it would be safer if I mentioned the buzz when Cassius wasn't around.

Gideon must have seen something in my expression —most likely my fear and desperation—because the ice in his eyes softened. His expression, however, grew pained, and he climbed in beside me, helping me shift over just enough to make room for him. He carefully wrapped an arm across my shoulders and let me lean against him.

I closed my eyes, fighting my nausea, my soul crying. Even just sitting beside me upset him. And while I was sure I was a big part of that pain, I couldn't forget the angel he'd loved had only been killed a few weeks ago. That was a pain that didn't heal quickly, or at all, and I wished with all my heart that even if we never accepted the mating bond, I could ease his grief. Not enough to take it away. That would be a different form of torture. But just enough to take the edge off.

The SUV stopped, and I cracked my eyes open. We were in Operations' secure garage, parked in front of the sliding glass door instead of a parking space.

Gideon carried me inside while Cassius parked the SUV. Still without a word, we entered Operations' small triage area, where Amiah waited beside one of the three gurneys, glaring at me as we approached.

"Why are you still here?"

"Because head office approved her reassignment to the team," Gideon said, setting me on the gurney and stepping back.

My buzz screamed back to life. I gasped, unable to hold it back.

"What idiot thought that was a good idea?" Amiah grabbed a pair of scissors and cut away the front of my ruined T-shirt.

"The Union City chief of police," Cassius said as he entered. His gaze jumped to the ragged pink scar above my heart where I'd been shot.

Amiah's face lit up with joy and all her attention turned to Cassius. "When did you get back in town?"

"The human." Cassius jerked his chin toward me and returned her smile. "And I got in this morning."

"You should have called." Amiah cut off the rest of my shirt, leaving me in my bra. And if I hadn't been in so much pain, I might have been embarrassed to be topless in front of Gideon and his brother. One day. That was all I wanted. One day where I wasn't hurt and my buzz was manageable. Was that too much to ask for?

"She took on a weretiger and fell down a flight of stairs," Gideon said.

Amiah rolled her eyes. "Of course she did." Her attention fell on my hands. "Looks like she took your power again, too."

Gideon stiffened. Oh, yeah, that was something he hadn't wanted Cassius to know.

"She can take your power?" I couldn't tell if Cassius was shocked or mad. Probably a combination of both. "That's how she can cast such a powerful light strike?"

"It's how we managed to stop Ibizual from breaking out of his prison." The muscles in Gideon's jaw tensed.

"You have to pull her from the team," Cassius said, his expression darkening. If he hadn't been mad before, he was now. "If your connection is that strong, her death will kill you. I'm not losing my little brother because of some human."

Amiah sent a blast of her healing magic into me. It wasn't her usual blazing lightning, but it set off my buzz, snapping and slicing under my skin. I clenched my jaw and squeezed my eyes shut, desperate not to cry. That would just prove to Cassius what a disaster I was.

"Amiah, be careful with her," Cassius snapped. "That's Gideon's life you're endangering."

"I'm not flooding her with enough magic to cause brain damage." Her magic vanished and the buzz eased back to a searing agony. "It shouldn't have been enough to hurt her."

"Her magical channels are burned," Gideon said.

"Well, I can't heal those, and I can't heal her without pushing my magic into those channels." Amiah doused a piece of gauze in saline and wiped the blood from the gashes on my chest. "Her concussion, cracked ribs, and fractured vertebra are healed. Do you want me to finish the gashes?"

"Will they need stitches?" I gasped before either of the guys could respond.

"Not with Jacob's claim on you." Amiah tossed the gauze into a stainless steel tray on a trolley beside her, doused another piece, and went to work on my shoulder.

"And you let Jacob claim her?" Cassius's hands clenched and unclenched as if he wanted to hit something.

"She was claimed before the brand appeared," Gideon said. "It'll work its way out of her system eventually."

Cassius glared at me. "How eventually?"

The buzz flared, and I bit back a gasp. I really needed to replace my patches. Even if they'd been working before —which I seriously doubted—Amiah's magic would have ruined their effects. *Please, just slap some bandages on my cuts and let me go.*

"It's under control," Gideon said.

Amiah snorted.

"It's under control," he said again, light flaring from his eyes. "My mate. My business."

"Not if it gets you killed," Cassius growled.

"Agent Shaw is a member of the team who's proven multiple times that she's a valuable asset. Like with any human who might be assigned to a JP team, we'll need to pay closer attention to her assignments."

The frosted glass door slid open and Marcus marched in. His gaze jumped to me sitting on the gurney in my jeans and bra, and his breath picked up.

"Marcus." Gideon shifted in front of him, blocking his view of me. Yeah, telling Cassius that I was Marcus's mate would only add more fuel to the bonfire that already involved taking Gideon's power and being claimed by Jacob. "Are the demons and Floyd locked up?"

"The demons are in holding, and Floyd is in interrogation."

"Good." Gideon gestured to the door. "Cassius, would you like the honor of digging into Floyd?"

"I think we should make him sweat," Cassius said.

"You said we need to get a jump on shutting down this operation. If you won't interrogate him, I will." Gideon strode out the door.

Cassius growled and rushed out after him.

"The brand won't let Gideon let her go," Amiah said as she taped a thick wad of gauze to my chest. "He has no choice, Marcus."

"And you think I do?" His wolf darkened his expression with a sudden feral intensity.

I shivered with the memory of all his ferocity focused on me, which made my buzz snap again.

Amiah held his gaze without any fear of his beast. "I think you don't want to."

"If you think that, you know nothing about wolves," he said, but a wave of uncertainty—real honest to goodness emotion—rushed through me.

"The brand will make her choose him."

The uncertainty bled into fear. He might be okay with sharing, but that didn't mean he wasn't afraid the brand wouldn't force us apart.

Amiah cut more tape and stuck another piece of gauze to my shoulder. "These'll scar."

"That's fine." What was a few more scars added to the ones I already had?

She peeled off her gloves, shot Marcus an angry, sad look, and left down the hall, heading deeper into Operations' mini hospital.

"Jeez, Essie," Marcus said as soon as Amiah was out of sight. He cupped my face with his hands and captured my mouth in a quick fierce kiss that stole my breath. "You were supposed to wait for me to take over."

"It wasn't like we were looking for a fight." I slid my fingers into his hair and pulled his mouth back to mine. I needed his passion to burn away my fear and heartache, reassure me that being on the team wasn't a horrible mistake. Not to mention reassure myself that he wasn't going to change his mind about us now that the crisis with Ibizual was over.

He kissed me like a starving man, his tongue plunging into my mouth and fueling my desire as if we hadn't had sex earlier that morning. I couldn't get enough of him. He, like Gideon and Jacob, was a part of my soul.

His hands skimmed my shoulders, brushed the gauze, and he froze. "You could have been killed," he murmured against my lips.

"We knew that when we decided I should be a part of

the team." *Please don't change your mind. Please don't push me away again.*

"I know. I just hadn't expected it to happen so soon." He eased back and sat on the edge of the gurney. "I should have known it would happen. You're a trouble magnet."

"I'm really not."

"What have the last two weeks been?" he asked with a wry smile.

"Terrifying." I leaned in and kissed him, slowly and sensually, showing him how I felt about him. "And amazing."

"I'm barely holding it together as it is, Essie. If you keep that up, I'll take you right here in triage," he said, his voice deliciously dark.

My pulse stuttered, and my focus shifted from my God-damn-annoying buzz to him and my need for him.

His pupils dilated with desire, but his fear seeped into me again. "My suite. Now," he growled.

He reached to pick me up as the frosted glass door opened and Cassius stormed back in. The angel froze mid-step, the light in his eyes flaring. Guess all the secrets were coming out right now.

"Agent Shaw," he said, his tone frigid.

Marcus snarled, and I squeezed his hand to stop him from doing something he'd regret. Cassius was his boss, and while I knew Marcus would do anything to protect me, I didn't want him to destroy his career.

"Cassius." I met his glare head on. *Yeah, you saw what you saw, and it's none of your God-damned business.* "Does Gideon need us?"

The room's temperature dropped. Not with fear but cold seething anger. His gaze darted to Marcus, and a flicker of fire danced over his hands then vanished. "If you're going to be a part of this team, Shaw, you should observe everything. That includes this interrogation."

"Do I get to put a shirt on first?" I asked.

The ice in his eyes deepened. Very soon he was going to get me alone and tell me what he really thought of me. He couldn't hurt me physically because of Gideon, but I couldn't help wondering if he'd hurt my other guys to get to me. How much did Cassius love his brother and how far was he willing to go to protect him?

"I have a bag in the trunk of the car."

"Jacob put it in your room. I'll let you in then show you to interrogation," Marcus said. He tugged my hand, urging me to hop off the gurney.

I wasn't sure why he'd lied to Cassius—Marcus had given me my keycard earlier—but I was grateful neither of us were going to end up alone with Cassius. I didn't know if he'd ever accept our weird situation or believe Gideon when he got around to telling his brother how much he didn't want a relationship with me, but Cassius had been hit with a lot of complicated information in the last ten minutes. He'd need time to process that, and I was more than happy to give it to him.

We hurried into the hall before Cassius could argue and rushed to the elevator.

"Do you have your phone on you?" I asked.

Marcus frowned. "Of course."

"I don't have Gideon's number yet, and we should give

him a heads-up that Cassius knows about us. I don't want him blindsided by all the rage we just saw."

"Yeah." He sent Gideon a text as another wave of his fear and uncertainty seeped past my buzz.

God, I wanted to confront this head on, tell him that just because I was being nice to Gideon didn't mean I was going to leave him. But then I'd have to explain how I knew what he was feeling. Besides, words were just words. I needed to show him that no matter what, I was still his. Even if we didn't have a brand tying us together, I would always be his.

We reached my room. I slid my keycard into the reader, tugged him inside, closed the door, and shoved him against it.

His eyes widened for a split second then darkened with desire. I captured his lips with mine and kissed him, willing him to feel all the desire and passion I felt for him. There'd always been something between us, and there always would be. I didn't know what was happening with me and the team, but I did know what was happening with me and Marcus. I'd known it the moment I'd seen him. I just hadn't wanted to accept it.

"You're mine," I growled against his lips.

He growled back, wrapped an arm around my back, and jerked me tight against his body. "And you're mine."

His other hand slid into my hair, capturing my head, and he took control of the kiss. Even before Marcus had become a werewolf, there'd been a ferociousness about him, a sense that something powerful and wild was curled deep within him. Now he released that ferocity with his passion. He jerked me around, pinning me to the door with his hips and grinding his erection against me.

I moaned, and he stole it with his kiss. The room spun, not from my fall down the stairs but from the whirling need spiraling tight within me. He was mine. Mine. I knew it with the certainty that I knew myself.

His hold in my hair tightened, forcing my head back. With a snarl, his canines pressed against my neck, not with enough pressure to break flesh but enough to tell me he was in charge.

I dug my nails into his scalp and snarled back.

He shuddered, his grip on me tightening, but he jerked his teeth from my neck and pressed his forehead to mine. "Essie, please," he gasped, his breath ragged. "Don't challenge my wolf. You know I have trouble controlling him when I'm with you."

"And I know he won't hurt me." He'd released his wolf the first time we'd had sex, and it didn't frighten me.

I shoved him with all my might—since I knew that was what I'd need if I had a hope of moving him—and caught him off guard. He stumbled back. His legs hit the bed, and he fell back on it.

"I could see him in your eyes last night. If you don't let him loose now, he'll take over later and you'll have no control." Then he might actually hurt me.

I stepped on my heels and pulled off my runners then reached for the button on my jeans.

"God, Essie," he groaned. "We can't. Cassius is waiting."

"He can wait." This was too important. Marcus and his wolf needed the reassurance that he was mine. The whole team needed Marcus and his wolf to be certain of that. If Marcus was worrying about us, he might miss something, and that could be dangerous for everyone. "We can make it quick."

"I don't want quick." He started to stand, and I pushed him back onto the mattress.

"Consider this your appetizer for later."

His expression grew hungry, his wolf turning it fierce. "Mine or my wolf's?"

I shimmied out of my jeans, leaving myself in my bra and undies. "This one is for your wolf."

"Then if you don't want to buy new underwear, you should take them off." His canines extended, and he dug his fingers into the comforter. "Now."

I unhooked my bra, but his wolf took over before I could step out of my undies. He grabbed me, yanked me to the bed, and leaned over me, taking the dominant position. His lips found mine and his hands roughly kneaded my breasts. I gasped at his ferocity and blazing passion.

The gasp made him growl low in his throat, and he plunged his hand down the front of my underwear and pushed two fingers into me without warning.

I bucked against him, my body reacting to his sudden invasion. My desire was as wild as his wolf's, and I was already wet and ready for him, already needing him inside me. I grabbed his T-shirt and dragged it over his head. He released me and pulled it off as I reached for the button on his jeans. He pushed my hands away, took off his boots and jeans, and stared down at me, gloriously naked.

He was stunning, a powerful specimen with ripped sleek muscles and a thick erection. He'd brought me to climax many times yesterday, knew how to work my body into a frenzy and send me crashing into bliss.

His gaze raked over me, heating my skin, and I bit my lip in anticipation of what was coming.

His attention landed on my undies. "Take those off," his wolf said.

I slid them off.

He squeezed his eyes shut. His chest rose and fell with rapid breaths, as if he was trying to regain control. Which I couldn't have. His wolf needed to be released. It needed to know I recognized it as my mate.

"Marcus," I breathed.

His eyes opened, and I skimmed my hand down my belly and dipped my fingers into my folds. The hunger in his eyes deepened, and I spread my legs so he could see better.

"This one is for your wolf." I locked gazes with him. "My mate."

His breath hitched, and for a second I had no idea how he felt about that.

Then he snarled, grabbed me, and flipped me onto my stomach. "Mine."

He jerked my hips back against his, and ground his hard length against me. My pulse thrummed faster with desire. A heat swelled in my chest, my need for him, my certainty that we belonged together.

"Mine," he said.

I shuddered with the possessive ferocity of that one word, and he drove into me with a fierce thrust. Another snarl, and he thrust again, pressing one hand against my back, holding me down. His other hand slid over my belly, and his thumb rubbed over my clit. I clung to the comforter, my head spinning with sensation, the promise of my climax twisting tighter.

He worked me into a frenzy, driving into me again and again, and when I was trembling on the edge, he grabbed my hips and picked up the pace. His nails dug into my skin, a glorious mix of pain and pleasure, until I fell over the edge, gasping with satisfaction.

With a roar, his climax seized him, and he tensed, his body tight against mine. His ferocious desire for me seared the air around me and flooded every cell with true emotion. He was a part of my soul. Now and forever.

"Mine," I gasped, and his desire within me turned to satisfied masculine pride.

CHAPTER 7

WE QUICKLY CLEANED UP AND I APPLIED FOUR NEW nicotine patches in the hope it would control my buzz, then we headed down to the secure section of Operations. I wished we'd had time to cuddle so I could cement the certainty with him and his wolf that we were well and truly mates, but keeping Cassius waiting longer than necessary was a bad idea.

I'd never understood this mate thing before. Especially with shifters. It had always seemed overly possessive and, being on the outside looking in, sometimes without reason. The attraction was often instant, the shifter's instinct recognizing his soul's mate before the human side of him did.

Now I understood. I'd fully accepted our bond and that knowledge thrummed within me. He was mine. Just like Gideon was mine. And Jacob. And Kol.

I pushed those thoughts back. Fate said Gideon was also my soul mate and something in the core of my being said Jacob was as well. But Kol? We didn't even have a whisper of a connection. Not like the connection I had with the others. My attraction to him had to be because he was an incubus and radiated sexual desire without even thinking about it.

And what I really needed to be thinking about instead was how to manage the situation with Cassius. My complicated relationships were still so new and fragile, and while I'd secured Marcus's certainty, I still needed to work out a truce with Gideon, and have a heart-to-heart with Jacob.

The secure section of Operations lay at the back of the converted 19th century warehouse. It sat on the first floor beyond two sets of heavy metal security doors that were locked on both sides with fingerprint scanners.

Cassius stood in the hall a few feet inside the second security door, holding a blue file folder and glaring at us as we approached. Gideon stood beside him, his expression hard and icy, while Jacob leaned against the wall opposite them. He appeared relaxed, but he radiated more vampiric intensity than he usually did, and a hint of heat in the air around me suggested someone was upset.

The heat could have been coming from Cassius, but I suspected if I was going to feel his emotions, they would be icy fury again. For now, he was emotionally locked down. Which meant the heat was most likely coming from Gideon. Just great.

My buzz softened the closer I got to Gideon. It wasn't enough to ease all of the biting agony, but enough to help me think straight, and now the gentle electric hum of his magic in our brand tingled over my forearm. Relief filled me. I hadn't realized how much I'd needed to feel that, how much not being able to feel it through the burn of my buzz had worried me.

"Agents," Cassius said, the word clipped and hard. He turned on his heel, unlocked a door with his thumbprint, and stormed inside.

"He can disband the team," Gideon said, his tone just as clipped as his brother's. "Play by the God damned rules." He unlocked the same door with his thumbprint and left the three of us in the hall.

"I take it Cassius knows about the whole mess of our situation." Jacob pushed away from the wall and entered the room beside the one with Cassius and Gideon, this one not locked by a fingerprint reader.

I followed him into an observation room with low lighting and a large one-way glass window looking into an interrogation room. Floyd sat facing us, handcuffed to a stainless steel table that was bolted into the floor, and Cassius sat across from him, the closed file folder on the table between them. Gideon stood by the door, his arms crossed, angelic light radiating from his eyes.

"Amiah spilled most of it," I said.

"Then Cassius caught me being an idiot." Marcus shut the door behind us and stepped possessively close to me. "I should have controlled my wolf better. But it's having issues, and Essie was hurt. I'd thought Cassius was with Gideon."

"Does Gideon know how serious my claim is and about our arrangement?" Jacob asked.

"No, but we should tell him about it sooner rather than later." I didn't want to complicate the situation between me and Gideon any more than it already was.

And if Cassius learned about the deal I had with Marcus and Jacob before Gideon did, there'd be no hope of a truce between us.

Jacob glanced at Marcus. Both had hesitation in their eyes, and I couldn't disagree. Telling Gideon needed to be handled carefully.

"I should do it." I didn't know when, but it had to be soon. Victoria could summon Jacob at any time to pay his debt to her for helping us with Ibizual, and twenty-four hours after that, I'd need to help Jacob recover. And then, because Jacob's claim on me was so strong and I was bite locked, I'd need Marcus to help me release Jacob's magic. There was just too much that needed to happen for Gideon or Cassius not to notice something was up.

In the interrogation room, Cassius drummed his fingers on the closed folder. "We have you on assault of a JP agent."

Floyd huffed. "I didn't touch the vamp, just the bitch cop he was with."

"That bitch cop is a JP agent." Cassius's tone remained even, but sharp icy fury flickered around me, telling me how he really felt.

Then Floyd's fear, colder than Cassius's rage but not as sharp, enveloped me. The weretiger leaned as far back in the chair as his handcuffed hands would allow in an obvious attempt to look unconcerned. "Everyone knows there ain't no humans on a JP team."

"There is now." Cassius opened the folder. "You've done time for assault before. This isn't a third strike, but I doubt the judge will care."

"Hey, I barely touched her." He pointed to his charred

shirt and the now half-healed burn covering his chest. "She almost killed me."

"You threw her down a set of stairs," Gideon said.

"Dude, she tripped."

Cassius's sharp cold blasted around me again, and his back and shoulders tensed. "Her life is valuable."

Yeah, valuable because I was permanently connected to his brother, not because I was me.

"I will personally tell the judge how valuable her life is."

Floyd's eyes flashed wide, and the temperature plummeted to a teeth-chattering freeze. He didn't know the extent of Cassius's threat, but the rage in the angel's voice said it all. Vengeance would be his. Funny how when I'd first met Gideon, I'd thought he was overly emotional for an angel. They were known to be emotionally frigid. But clearly Cassius was the hot-head of the family.

"I could also tell the judge how helpful you were." Cassius's tone remained dark and dangerous, as if daring Floyd to reject the offer.

"What kind of help do you want?" Floyd asked, his voice small, all sense of bravado gone.

Frost gathered on the backs of my hands, and I shoved them into my pockets to hide it. Jeez. I wished Cassius wasn't being so aggressive with Floyd. Except I suspected the angel needed to vent, and it was better Floyd than me.

"We know you deal zip." Cassius turned to another page in the folder.

I had no idea how long the team had known about Floyd, but it didn't surprise me that they hadn't picked him up until now. They'd probably spent a lot of time watching him, seeing who he met with in an attempt to identify those higher up the ranks of the organization.

Floyd's gaze darted to whatever was on the page then back to Cassius. "I'm not a snitch."

Marcus snaked a hand across my belly and drew me back against his body. A hint of mist joined Floyd's chill, and Jacob shifted beside us.

"There's only one deal on the table, and it's a limited time offer." Cassius closed the folder, stood, and turned to Gideon. "Looks like we should talk to the demons."

"They won't tell you anything," Floyd sneered.

"You sure about that?" Cassius asked. "They haven't been with you when you picked up a new supply or handed off your earnings?"

The frost swept up my forearms. I shivered, but I couldn't tell if Floyd's fear was because of Cassius or his employers.

Marcus wrapped his other arm around me, and I leaned into his warmth, hoping it would melt the frost before he noticed, since I couldn't just leave the room. Not without drawing suspicion.

Cassius raised an eyebrow at Floyd, who pinched his lips tight.

"Guess they haven't overheard you talking on the phone, either." Gideon pressed his thumb to the finger-print scanner and unlocked the door. "Pretty sure one of the demons will want to cooperate."

Cassius strode toward the door and Gideon opened it for him. "Doubt we'll even have to remind them of the penalty for trying to kill a JP agent."

"Pretty sure it'll be increased," Gideon said, following him out. "Everyone knows humans are fragile."

Floyd jerked forward, his fear blasting around me, and my breath misted.

Shit. My pulse stalled and panic—my panic—seized me. I couldn't stay here. I had to get away from Marcus and Jacob before they noticed something was weird with me—

No. I had to face this. That was the plan.

I'd known that if I stayed, they'd learn about my magic. I just never thought I'd be discovered on my very first day on the job. All I could do was stick to the lie, since there was no way out of this situation. There wasn't anywhere I could hide where Gideon wouldn't find me. And now that I'd completed the mating bond with Marcus, he'd turn over heaven and earth to find me as well. Running wouldn't work. *Please, God. Don't let this be the worst decision of my life.*

"Wait." Floyd jerked to his feet, rattling the cuffs against the metal bar.

Gideon glanced back at him, ice in his eyes. Floyd shivered. So did I.

"Why are you cold?" Marcus whispered, his breath hot against the side of my cheek.

A swell of warmth, his affection for me, bled into the cold. But my mother's words, words she'd told me again and again, rushed through me. *They can never know the truth. No one will understand. They'll think you're one of Michael's monsters, even though you aren't. You were born. Not made.*

Except I couldn't run forever, not with my soul saying this was where I belonged, working with these guys.

Marcus's grip on me tightened. "Essie, you're shivering."

"It's just a chill," I said, unable to force out the lie, years of fear screaming I had to keep my magic a secret.

"I know when they're getting their next shipment of stolen Divifend," Floyd said.

"It's more than a chill." More of Marcus's warmth seeped into me. I clung to it, trying to push out Cassius's anger and Floyd's fear. If I could get it to ease up, Marcus would relax and this conversation could happen another time. When I was ready.

But Jacob brushed the back of his hand across my cheek, his flesh hot against mine, and frowned. More ice whispered through Marcus's warmth.

Great. Now I was feeling Jacob's worry.

"We should call Kol," he said. "His increased body temperature might help."

"I'm okay." I was such a fool. I shouldn't have allowed myself to get close to Marcus. I shouldn't have given into the need for him or the need to belong. I knew joining the team was dangerous, and I'd still gone ahead with it.

But God, I wanted him. Wanted *them*. Wanted to belong, be missed by someone, thought of, cared for. And now I was terrified of losing the guys.

The plan. Remember the God damned plan. It will work. It has to work.

"You're not okay," Marcus growled. "Is it Gideon's brand? It's not our mating. Shifters and humans are supposed to be compatible."

"Could be a delayed reaction to her light strike," Jacob said.

"But she wasn't this cold last night."

"You know, I'm still in the room." I tried to push out of Marcus's arms to put some space between us on the slim chance I'd be able to think straight, but his grip tightened.

"We need to get you to Amiah." His fear joined the others' and the frost swept up to my elbows and my breath misted again. "What the hell is that?"

Stick to the plan.

"Is that your breath?" Jacob's vampiric intensity turned his eyes fully black.

Marcus's fear grew stronger and frost formed on my cheeks.

"Essie," he growled. "There's frost on your cheeks again. I thought that was from the magic of Ibizual's key manifesting."

"It's—" *Remember the lie. It's logical. You could have a super somewhere deep in your family tree. The mating brand could be affecting you.* "I'm not sure what it is. It started after the archnephilim. But it always goes away. Best guess is that it's your fear or worry."

Please believe me. Please work. I need this team. I need them.

"His fear?" Jacob asked.

"Yours, too. And Gideon's, Cassius's, and Floyd's." The frost slipped down my neck and my teeth chattered. "I think."

"How many times has this happened?" Marcus asked.

"Not many." My soul twisted at the lie. But it would be

worse if they knew the truth. Gideon's brand wouldn't be enough to protect me from the fury the world still held toward nephilim. Hell, it probably wouldn't be enough to protect me from Gideon. And Marcus— I didn't want to think about Marcus's reaction, how angry he'd be because I'd been so adamant to avoid the supernatural world.

Please. Believe me.

"It's got to have something to do with Gideon's brand," Jacob said.

"But she's human. Would the angelic mating brand really give her magic?" Marcus's fear shifted, and a strange hope whispered across my senses.

I tried not to hold my breath, waiting for them to come to the obvious conclusion. That I was a nephilim pretending to be human.

"Who knows." Jacob rubbed my forearms, melting some of the frost. "The archnephilim's magic could have affected you, as well. Not to mention blasting all that divine light into your body and channeling Gideon's magic. Who knows what could have changed in you."

My thoughts tripped at his words, and the fear churning in my gut eased. A bit. Did they actually believe me? I couldn't hear any suspicion in their voices. Not that they'd voice it in front of me if they thought I was a nephilim, but given how I was reacting to everyone's fear, the temperature would have changed if they were hiding such serious concerns.

"And who knows what's going to change," Jacob said.

Marcus's fear and hope flared with a nauseating snap from cold to hot. "She could have more magic?"

"Gideon's brand is only a few weeks old. It could take years before we know the full effects of it." Jacob's hands tightened on my arms, his body tensed, and his gaze grew unfocused. "Shit."

My pulse stuttered. "What is it?" I didn't think he'd realized I was a nephilim since his gaze wasn't focused on me, but something was wrong.

"Victoria's calling me." He pulled his phone from his pocket.

"She isn't even giving you a day to recover?" Marcus asked.

"Doesn't look like it." Jacob sent a text and took a jerky step toward the door.

"And she's compelling you to go to her?" Marcus growled.

Jacob staggered into the hall and pressed his hands to the wall across from the door, as if that would keep him from moving farther. "She's never been patient."

In the observation room, Gideon pulled out his phone, frowned, and glanced at the one-way window.

Cassius glanced at him, an eyebrow raised in question.

"I told you first," Floyd said, his voice sharp with panic. "The deal is mine. The courier is going to deliver the Divifend today."

Gideon jerked his chin to the door, and Cassius stood.

"We have a deal." Floyd's fear swept more frost over my cheeks.

"We have a deal if your intel checks out." Cassius strode to the door. "And not before then."

Gideon unlocked the door, and they stepped into the hall. Marcus and I hurried to join them.

"She's summoning you already?" Gideon asked.

"Can she wait until we've stopped the handoff of the Divifend?" Cassius asked. Guess he'd been brought up to speed on Jacob's deal with Victoria.

"You've met my sire." Jacob shot Cassius a dark look. "What do you think?"

"We've got this," Gideon said. "See you back here in twenty-four."

"Vampires still have to abide by consent laws with other vampires," Cassius said.

"Not my first rodeo with Victoria." Jacob shifted toward the doors leading out of Operations' secured section.

"Still," Cassius said.

"She plays harder than I like, but she's actually a very giving lover." Jacob's gaze jumped to me for a second, and a whisper of mist curled around me. "We couldn't have stopped Ibizual without her help, and given the stresses of the last few days— This isn't a hardship."

His claim—no, that thing within me that said our connection was deeper than just his claim—twisted in my chest. I wanted to be the one to release his stress, ease his misty sadness hanging in the air, not because I was jealous of Victoria—although I was, a little bit—but because my soul ached at his pain, at something I could mend just by embracing whatever it was that lay between us. Just like I'd done with Marcus and his wolf.

"Go," Gideon said. "We've got this."

Jacob hurried out the security doors, then rushed down the hall and out of sight with his vampiric speed.

"More Divifend means more zip on the streets, and that means more humans and supers will die," Cassius said. "We need to move on this handoff and track the Divifend back to the new lab."

"Agreed." Marcus shifted as if he wanted to step closer to me, but managed to stay at arm's length. "My meeting with the wolf pack alpha wasn't good. They have ten new zip deaths. Found a group of eight teens dead in the wolves' forest last night and two more in their apartment."

"Marcus—" Gideon said

"This isn't your op." Light flared from Cassius's eyes. "The mayor is breathing down the JP's neck about the human deaths and attacks from addicts suffering violent hallucinations. I won't let you turn this into another mess. Grab some lunch. We meet in Summer's lab in twenty to go over the op's details."

He marched away, taking the rest of the chill with him.

"I know he's your brother and all, but—" Marcus ran a hand through his dark locks. "How long is he supposed to be here?"

"Longer now because of you two." Gideon glared at me, the ice in his eyes breaking my heart.

"We should talk," I said. Now wasn't the best time to have a conversation about my arrangement with Marcus and Jacob, but I didn't think any time would be good.

"Is this about the upcoming operation, Agent Shaw?"

"You know it isn't."

"Jeez, Gideon." Marcus stepped possessively close to me. "Stop being a dick."

"If you want her here so badly, stop thinking with yours. Your wolf doesn't have to worry." Gideon's gaze captured mine. "The brand hasn't changed how I feel about you and it never will."

The truth in his words and accompanying emotion shook me to my core. He didn't want me, and he'd only let me stay on the team because the guys had threatened to leave if I did.

"Don't give Cassius a reason to disband the team." He stormed away, his desperation flickering in my heart, a mirror to my own need to be a part of this team. He needed this team so much that he was willing to let me stay even though just looking at me hurt. I reminded him of what he'd lost, what he'd wanted with Zella. Not talking to him was probably the best truce we were going to get, except I still needed to tell him about my arrangement with Marcus and Jacob.

Now, however, with his hurt and need still tightening my chest, wasn't the time. I had twenty-four hours. Maybe Cassius would be gone by then and the team could actually start figuring out our new normal.

CHAPTER 8

"Come on," Marcus said. "Cassius works like Gideon. We should grab food while we can."

I followed him out of the secured section and down the hall, heading toward the cafeteria and—if my growing buzz was any indication—away from Gideon. "If we're going to make this work, we should be more careful while he's here."

"I keep trying to tell my wolf that." Marcus's fingers closest to me twitched, as if he wanted to hold my hand but was resisting the urge. "I've fought him for four and half years over you and he doesn't give a shit about what Cassius thinks."

"Then tell him to care about what I think." Gideon needed this team, and so did I. "Let's not give Cassius more reason to stay."

"Yeah. He might have been sent here to review the team, but he won't leave until he believes Gideon is safe." Marcus glanced at me, his wolf, a feral energy radiating from his expression, threatening to break through. "That means ensuring your bond is safe, but, given that he already knows we're in a relationship, I'm not sure how we can convince him of that."

We rounded the corner and crossed from the old section to the new one, a five-story high rise added to the back of the 19th century warehouse. Ahead, I could hear the rumble of voices in the cafeteria.

"The best we can do with that is not constantly remind him of it." We could get more elaborate by staging a fight and pretending we'd broken up, but that might cause other problems, like Cassius thinking one of us needed to be transferred to another unit for the health of the team.

Marcus huffed a soft laugh. "Good thing you didn't decide to move into my suite."

The temperature didn't change. I couldn't tell how he felt about that. Of course, maybe the emotion was subtle, and I couldn't feel it past my buzz. "I thought we should talk about that first."

"You know you're welcome to move in. Even before we completed our bond, you were welcome."

We reached the top of the shallow steps leading down to the cafeteria, and my pulse stuttered with fear. It was close to lunchtime, more than half of the tables were occupied, and at least a dozen of those occupants were angels.

I forced myself to keep moving down the stairs and past the still-under-repair rock wall water-feature that had been damaged during the fight with the arch-nephilim. They didn't know I was a nephilim, and

Marcus and Jacob had believed my lie about my magic. They had no reason to suspect me. *Just stay calm.*

But there was a lull in the conversation and all eyes turned to me. My stomach churned and my buzz snapped through my chest. I gritted my teeth, trying not to react. I wanted this. I wanted to live and work in the one building where all the angels in Union City lived because I wanted to be with my guys.

"You do know you're welcome, right?" Marcus asked.

I dragged my attention back to him. "I know. I just—"

He headed toward the hot-food serving stations manned by a squat man who could have been human or any number of supernatural beings. Thankfully, his eyes didn't glow like an angel's, and I managed to grab a tray and keep it from shaking. So long as I didn't look at the angels behind me, I'd be fine. Really.

"This is just a big adjustment. I've been living on my own since I was seventeen."

"Yeah, and I have a lot of furniture and stuff," he said, referring to my nearly-empty apartment with my second-hand furniture—because what was the point in having a lot of stuff if you had to drop everything and flee on a moment's notice? "I'd embrace a minimalistic lifestyle for you."

"You know that's not why I kept my room."

"Essie." His voice softened and warmth fluttered around me for a second before my buzz consumed it. "Whatever you need. Always."

"The usual?" the man behind the counter asked Marcus with a smile, then his attention jumped to me and my right forearm where Gideon's brand glimmered as if it were real gold embedded in my skin and reflecting the sunlight. His eyes widened with surprise. "You're Gideon's human mate."

Those at the tables closest to us sat forward.

"The mated human."

"Have you seen a brand before?"

"—hundred years."

"Longer."

"No, I heard there was a pair during the war."

"—shouldn't be here. It's too dangerous for Gideon."

"Only here because of that brand."

The murmurs swept through the cafeteria, and I clenched my tray, desperate to keep my hands from shaking. This kind of attention— *any* kind of attention was bad.

And jeez, four patches and my buzz still wasn't under control!

Chris, a guy in his mid-twenties who'd helped with the cleanup at the cemetery last night, tipped his chair back and leaned closer. From the hint of feral intensity in his pale blue eyes, my best guess was that he was a shifter of some kind, but I didn't know for sure. He looked exhausted, as if he hadn't slept last night, and given the mess we'd left, that wouldn't have surprised me.

"I hear they've finally given in and put you on the team," he said.

"Un hunh." I didn't know what to say to that. From everyone's reaction, it seemed they all thought like Cassius, that I was a liability endangering Gideon's life.

"It's about time." He flashed me a warm smile. "Get the chicken. It's really good today."

"Ah... sure." My buzz snapped up my neck, making the muscles twitch.

He turned back to his lunch partner, a broad-shouldered angel in black fatigues. "Gideon lucked the hell out. The whole team did. That human can kick some serious ass."

The angel looked surprised, and Chris started recounting my *incidents* with the team as if they were major successes and not just a desperate fight to stay alive.

"She'll have the chicken to go," Marcus said, nudging my arm with his elbow.

I jerked my attention back to the server. "Yeah. The chicken."

"Make that two," Marcus said.

The guy filled two takeout boxes with a chicken, broccoli, and rice mixture, and handed it to us. It smelled amazing, and my stomach growled, reminding me I hadn't had much to eat lately. Most of my meals in the last little while had been eaten on the go or missed completely.

Marcus turned to head to an empty table deeper into the cafeteria when Chris shoved the empty chair beside him into Marcus's path.

"Come on, don't keep her all to yourself," Chris said. "Introduce the new hire."

Marcus glanced at me, his expression questioning. Did I want to join them?

"Sure." I sat in the offered chair. As much as I didn't want to sit with the angel—who was looking at me with awe—I needed to make an effort to fit in. I now worked and lived here. I needed to not look like an outsider any more than I already was.

"We don't have a lot of time." Marcus took the chair across from me and dug into his lunch.

Chris's expression turned grim. "I saw Cassius in the hall. He didn't look happy."

"Is Cassius ever happy?" Marcus asked.

"I think I saw him happy once," the angel said with a chuckle. He held his hand out to me. "Nathaniel. Did you really take on two feral vampires with just another human?" His warm brown gaze dipped to the ragged scar on my neck.

"Essie Shaw. I wasn't given much of a choice." I took a bite of the chicken and savored the rich juicy flavor. Wow. Chris hadn't lied. It really was good.

"And the ferals' nest? Did they really come back to life?"

"I hope I never run into that again," Marcus said between mouthfuls. He glanced at his phone. "Two more minutes. Then we need to run."

Nathaniel shook his head, his expression still awed. "We all thought it was trouble, a human mated to an angel. But if half of what Chris says is true— Wow, Gideon is lucky."

I glanced at Marcus, afraid the comment would rile his wolf, but instead he met my gaze with a satisfied, heated look. "Lucky indeed," he said. "Let's go."

I shoveled in two more mouthfuls and decided not to take the food up to Summer's lab. Chris said he'd return our trays, and we hurried to the second floor, my emotions a strange mix of fear and hope.

Nathaniel hadn't been angry or disgusted by me, and Chris seemed to think I could more than hold my own on the team. I could make this work. I could do this job, a job I knew in my heart I was supposed to be doing, and be with my guys.

My buzz was even easing off a bit, but that was because I was getting closer to Gideon, not because of the patches. If they were working, they'd have kicked in while Cassius and Gideon had been interrogating Floyd... which worried me, but not enough to dampen the joy of being exactly where I belonged.

Summer's lab was a large room filled with gleaming stainless steel tables and shelves, and a white spotless floor. Machines hummed at various stations, one of the many computers was running something with images and pictures flickering in rapid succession on the screen, and one whole wall was lined with locked cabinets.

The petite angel stood near a keyboard, looking at a satellite image on a large screen that hung on the wall beside her. Gideon and Cassius were staring at it as well. Both had their arms crossed, their hard expressions identical, which accentuated the family resemblance. Both could have been poster boys for angelkind with the same chiseled jaw, straight nose, and broad shoulders. Clean cut and handsome, radiating divine light from their summer-sky eyes. But only Gideon made my pulse pick up with a yearning and heartache I didn't fully understand and didn't want.

Kol stood a few feet behind them, leaning against an empty table, looking sexy as hell, his thick black hair hanging low, nearly veiling his eyes, adding to his bad boy aura. God, he was just standing there. He wasn't even looking at me.

The memory of my dream swept through me and drew a shiver of need.

His attention jumped to me, and liquid desire swelled in my chest and sank low. My breath stalled and I was captured for a long, sensual second, then he rolled his eyes at me, and the swell of desire—that had to have been his magic affecting me—eased.

"You were supposed to call me," Kol said as Marcus stepped past him to stand beside Gideon.

I hung back with Kol to keep a professional distance between me and Marcus. "Not until I got off work."

"Not what I was talking about," he whispered as he shot a glare at Marcus's back then gave me a knowing look.

Crap. Right. He needed a warning when Marcus and I were going to have sex to shield himself against our sexual energy. Even when we weren't releasing Jacob's magic, Kol had said our energy was too powerful and the last time that had happened, he'd ended up high.

"Are you okay?" I tried to read his expression. He didn't look high, but an hour had almost passed since I'd reassured Marcus's wolf. Kol might have found a way to release the excess magic.

He leaned toward me and hellfire danced in his eyes. "I felt it coming this time so I could prepare. But jeez, Essie—"

Gideon scowled at us, and Kol snapped his mouth shut and straightened, shifting away from me.

"We have less than an hour before the courier delivers

the Divifend." Cassius pointed to a squat rectangular building with a gravel parking lot along one side and the back. It sat on a tired block of mixed commercial and residential buildings with a tree-filled ravine running behind it. "Floyd says the courier will make the drop at this bar, Hacksaw."

Not a surprise. There were a lot of potential places where an exchange like this could happen, abandoned areas of town, parts of the Supers' Quarter, and other bars that attracted a seedy clientele, but Hacksaw was one of the seediest and sat right at the edge of the still-occupied parts of Union City. If you were coming or going anywhere east, like New York or Washington, you ended up on Hacksaw's road. No one would notice guys coming or going from the place and a courier could make a quick hand-off then get back on the expressway. Most of Hacksaw's clientele were human members of the Nephilim Purge, a biker gang that had formed after the war and had hunted the remaining nephilim, often killing them gruesomely and posting it on social media.

"Do we know who's making the pickup?" Kol asked.

"No," Gideon said. "All we know is one of the bodyguards is a pit fiend and the pickup man usually has two guys with him."

"Let me guess." Kol hopped up and sat on the table. "We don't know who's making the drop, either."

"Or how many guys he'll have with him," Cassius said.

Kol flashed a wicked grin. "This sounds like fun."

"Fun?" Marcus growled.

"Yeah, you know, like the jobs we used to do before we started fighting feral vampire zombies and archnephilim," Kol said. "Anything's got to be easier than that."

"True." Marcus turned back to Gideon and Cassius. "So what's the plan?"

"Since we don't know any of the players, we need to identify the bag of Divifend." Cassius's gaze met Kol's. "You're magically sensitive. Do you think you can sense a bag of Divifend?"

"Depends on how big the bag is," Kol said. "I'd still need to be within the room and concentrating. Divifend isn't powerful, so I won't be able to sense it from a distance."

Cassius gave a tight nod. "Then we send you in, you identify the pickup man, and we trail him back to the zip lab."

"If that's the plan, Essie should come in with me," Kol said.

Light flared from Cassius's eyes. "No. We—"

"Trust me. If I go in alone, I'll be noticed." Kol's expression turned apologetic. "Unless I'm walking into a demon bar, I get noticed. If I go in with Essie, everyone will jump to conclusions and won't think twice about me."

Which was true. I'd seen him walk into a hospital emergency department and every female eye, along with a few male ones, had turned toward him regardless of what they were doing. And as soon as he'd sat with me, the doctor had immediately assumed we were having sex, even after Kol had said he was a JP agent.

"Absolutely not," Cassius said. "I'm not putting Agent Shaw in the line of fire."

"Identifying a pickup man isn't being in the line of fire," Marcus said, his tone calm with no hint of his wolf in his voice, making his statement sound entirely reasonable... which it was. "Besides, Kol is useful for a lot of things, but being unnoticed in a public place isn't one of them. If he's the only one who can sense the Divifend, then sending him in there with Essie is the best plan."

The muscles in Gideon's jaw flexed. He looked like he wanted to say something, but he kept his mouth shut. I didn't know what Cassius had said to him while Marcus and I were having lunch, but it was clear words had been exchanged.

I kept my mouth shut as well. While I wanted to be useful to the team, speaking up would only draw Cassius's attention.

"If she's a member of the team, then we need to use her skills like the rest of us," Kol said.

Cassius's glare deepened, and the room's temperature dropped. "Being your arm candy isn't a skill."

"No, but being dismissed as harmless while also being excellent backup is." Kol cocked an eyebrow. "You'd be wasting an opportunity to ensure this op's success by keeping her on the sidelines."

"She did apprehend Floyd," Gideon said.

"And was tossed down a flight of stairs." Cassius's cold deepened.

Kol jerked his chin to the screen. "Then it's a good thing the bar is one story."

Ice filled Cassius's eyes. He opened his mouth then

snapped it shut. His cold shuddered but I couldn't tell what that meant.

"Fine," he growled. "But if she gets hurt, I'm pulling her from the team."

Marcus's wolf snapped across his expression, sharpening his cheeks and darkening his eyes. "You pull her from the team, you destroy her career."

"She doesn't need a career. She's Gideon's mate." Fire danced over Cassius's hands.

The guys glared at each other in an obvious attempt for dominance without actually fighting. Hot and cold snapped around me, Cassius's hate and Marcus's protective fury. This wasn't getting us anywhere, and it certainly didn't give Cassius reason to believe everything was fine and he could leave.

"We have an hour." No one looked at me. "Cassius," I snapped, using my command-the-perp voice and drawing his attention. "You're in command. What's the plan?"

He held my gaze, his cold forcing me to clench my teeth to prevent them from chattering.

"Go in with Kol," he said, his tone sounding more like a dare then a command, making me wonder what his threshold for "hurt" was. If I got something as small as a black eye, was I off the team? Probably.

CHAPTER 9

WITH NO TIME TO GO HOME AND FIND GANG-BAR appropriate clothing that covered Gideon's brand, I accept a loan from Summer. We agreed my jeans and runners would do—since I didn't want to wear a dress and be flashing the world if I got into a fight—and I changed from my T-shirt to a form-fitting top that revealed an obscene amount of cleavage. I used some of her makeup to look like I was actually Kol's arm candy, but kept my hair in a ponytail to keep it out of my face, then I hurried down to the garage to meet the guys.

Kol was the first one I saw. He stood on the other side of the glass door in the garage with his back to me, wearing a pair of tight leather pants that made his ass look amazing and holding a motorcycle helmet and a leather jacket. He turned to face me, and my thoughts stuttered. I thought he'd looked stunning before just hanging out in Summer's lab, but now he was breathtaking.

He exuded dangerous sexual need. His black T-shirt

clung to his perfectly sculpted chest and arms, and all I could think about was running my hands across all that hard muscle. Hellfire danced in his eyes, flaring as his gaze landed on me, and I staggered to a stop, too stunned to make it out the door.

"If I'd known leather pants were your thing, I would have bought a pair," Marcus whispered in my ear, making me jump as his hot breath filled me with more yearning. I hadn't even heard him approach.

"So I'm allowed to drool over the incubus now?" I asked, breathless.

"Drool over anyone you want." The temperature rose with his desire, and he brushed his knuckles across the small of my back, the whisper of contact making my breath hitch even with my burning buzz. "You know I said that because I was afraid."

"And now?"

"I know you won't dump me for Gideon, or Jacob, or even pretty boy over there."

"Even with pretty boy's sex magic?" I didn't know why I pressed the issue. Kol and I didn't have that kind of a relationship, no matter what my dreams yearned for.

"You still want me after the magic of Jacob's bite is released. You'll still want me after Kol's."

Kol's expression turned wicked, the hellfire fully consuming his eyes. I knew he couldn't hear us through the door, but he could sense the desire rising within me. And God help me, I wanted both of them.

Marcus stepped past me, brushing his arm against mine and drawing a shudder of need, and opened the door. "You look hot, by the way," he said over his shoulder.

"Yeah," Kol said, his gaze never leaving mine. Then realization flashed over his expression as if he'd just remembered who he was looking at and who he was agreeing with. The hellfire vanished, turning into a wicked teasing gleam. "My threesome offer still stands."

"You'd have to talk to Essie about that," Marcus said.

Kol's eyes widened in shock. "Seriously?"

Marcus burst out laughing. "You should see the look on your face." But I got the impression his offer wasn't just to surprise Kol. Which surprised me.

My buzz suddenly softened. Gideon was near.

"Are we ready?" Cassius asked from behind me as he and Gideon headed toward us. Both wore bulletproof vests but neither had a sidearm. Gideon didn't need one because he could summon a sword of divine light, and I could only assume Cassius's magic was just as powerful.

Cassius's gaze swept over me, pausing at my exposed cleavage and drawing a frown.

"Remember we're looking for a pit fiend." Gideon handed out the coms. "You're taking your bike?"

"Thought it would work best with our cover." Kol handed me the helmet and leather jacket.

"Marcus, take the sedan," Cassius said. "Gideon and I will follow in the SUV."

The guys piled into their various vehicles and left. My buzz flared with Gideon's departure, clawing under my skin and making my muscles twitch. I held up Kol's jacket to return it to him. "This is too big. It might be in my way in a fight."

"I know, but Gideon would kill me if I let you ride without it. I also figured you'd need someplace to put your sidearm." His gaze swept over me like Cassius's had a moment ago but there wasn't a hint of disapproval in his eyes. "I guessed right. You can take it off when you get into the bar."

I pulled on the jacket and slipped my hands into the pockets. My fingers brushed against the metal grip of a gun, and I drew out my Glock and checked the magazine —full, although the ammunition looked strange.

"Enspelled stun ammo specially made for Supers." He led me deeper into the garage and stopped at a motor-cycle that was black and sleek and sexy, just like Kol.

"This yours?"

"Oh, yeah." He grinned at me and straddled the bike. "Let me take you for a ride."

Heat swept through me, and all I could think about was a different kind of riding. Wow, have a few days of amazing sex and that was all I could think about.

He cleared his throat and yanked his attention away from me. "Not that kind of ride."

"Sorry. I've got—" I bit the inside of my cheek. I'd been about to lie and say I had Marcus on the mind, but remembered we had coms in and they were live. "I've got our roles for this op on the mind."

"See," Kol said with a laugh. "I told you guys, chicks like bikes."

"I'm beginning to hate this plan already," Cassius said over the coms.

I pulled on the helmet and settled in behind him, wrapping my arms around his waist and tucking myself tight against him. He hadn't put on a helmet or a jacket and his increased demonic body heat instantly enveloped me. I tried not to think about my hands against his sculpted muscles. But I couldn't stop thinking about my dream and *his* hands and lips on my body.

Jeez, if I didn't do something, I was going to be a quivering mess by the time we reached Hacksaw and then Cassius would have more reason to hate me.

We headed out, and I squeezed my eyes shut and concentrated on my buzz. It was easy enough. My patches weren't working and every inch of me stung. If I didn't get it under control soon, by the end of the day it would be all I could think about. And a week after that I wouldn't be able to control myself and I'd start clawing at my skin. Hell, who was I kidding. My buzz was stronger than it had been before. I wouldn't last a week.

God, I didn't want to go back to the time when I'd had no idea how to control it. I'd spent days sobbing. And that had been when the sensation had maxed out at the level of a low voltage electric fence. This was worse. The only thing that had worked to ease it had been nicotine. Now it was Gideon, and even if he wasn't trying to avoid me, I couldn't be near him night and day.

We arrived at Hacksaw and parked at the far end of the lot. Half a dozen vehicles—mostly trucks—and two dozen motorcycles filled the lot. On the one hand this was good. Kol and I could blend in with the crowd, but on the other hand so could the pickup man. Not to mention if things went sideways, there were a lot of bodies who could get caught in the crossfire or join the brawl.

The place didn't look welcoming with its two over-flowing garbage bins around the back, weeds growing from the foundation, and boarded-up windows. If it hadn't been for all the vehicles in the lot, I would have assumed the place was abandoned.

I pulled off the helmet and unzipped the jacket. It was too warm to be wearing leather, let alone wearing it while snuggled up to a natural furnace. I scanned the street, jamming a knuckle into my thigh to stop the muscle from twitching. The neighborhood looked like a lot of neighborhoods in Union City. Old and tired. About a quarter of the buildings were boarded up. The rest had murky windows, peeling paint, and broken signs. Pot holes made the asphalt uneven and weeds grew in every possible crack on the road and the sidewalk.

From the lack of destroyed buildings, it didn't look as if this part of the city had been hit by Michael's war, so the area hadn't been partially abandoned because of damage. Most likely the majority of residents had left because, with there being more places to live than people, the middle-class parts of town where the war hadn't touched had been dirt cheap in the first few years afterward.

I spotted Marcus's sedan, parked close enough to have a good view of the front door and the parking lot, but not close enough to be obvious to anyone coming or going from the bar that he was watching them. I didn't see the SUV and my buzz hadn't changed, so Gideon wasn't close, but I didn't doubt he and Cassius had eyes on us.

"The courier is supposed to arrive in less than thirty minutes," Cassius said in my ear.

Kol hung my helmet on the bike's handle and

wrapped an arm across my shoulders. He drew me close, hellfire whispering in eyes filled with wicked excitement, and released a panty-melting smile—something I'm sure he couldn't help. "Let's do this."

My buzz snapped in my chest, slicing through my desire. "Ready to be arm candy."

We sauntered across the gravel lot to the scarred metal front door and entered a dark smoky room that smelled of stale beer, sweat, and marijuana. Half the lights were out, mostly those at the edges, throwing those tables into a deep shadow that would have hidden the occupants if my vision hadn't been enhanced by Jacob's claim.

Blue and red neon lights illuminated the bar, catching in a mirrored back wall broken up by shelves of liquor bottles, while casting the bartender—a burly man with a craggy face—in a sickly light. None of the furniture matched, and the floor was sticky. I really hoped we weren't here long enough for me to see the bathrooms.

All eyes turned to us—close to thirty sets—and everyone, male and female, looked like they could handle themselves in a fight. Kol flashed a wicked grin at them, releasing a simmering flare of hellfire that thankfully felt focused away from me and didn't instantly turn me into a hot mess. He led me to a table halfway between the front door and the hall to the bathrooms, sank with a boneless grace into a chair, and pulled out a twenty.

"Why don't you get us some beers, babe."

"Sure." I reached for the bill, but he jerked his hand back, forcing me to lean forward to grab for it. As I did, his jacket fell open, flashing my ample cleavage and drawing a smirk, but the tease in his eyes was clear. This was the cover, the game, and he was finally getting to be himself.

Well, it was the plan. I might as well commit. Fighting my buzz to stay in the moment, I released my own smirk, slowly shrugged out of his jacket, making sure he and anyone able to see in the shadows got a good show, and set it on the table with the pocket holding my Glock facing up.

He cocked an eyebrow, not looking impressed. Yeah, not really a point for me. After a life of not letting myself get close to anyone, I didn't have a lot of experience flirting and pretty much sucked at it. But he didn't press it and handed over the bill.

Swishing my hips, I turned to head to the bar, but he jerked forward and slapped my ass with a loud hard crack.

Holy shit. I yelped in surprise. My butt stung, but a whisper of his magic swept through me, turning it into an exquisite need that shocked the hell out of me.

Someone at a nearby table snickered, and I managed to shoot Kol my sexiest smile instead of looking as shocked as I felt. An apology flickered in his gaze before the tease returned, and he jerked his chin to the bar, sending me on my way.

"What the hell was that?" Marcus asked.

"Just cementing our cover," Kol whispered. "We're fine."

"That didn't sound fine." Marcus's wolf turned his tone dark and edgy.

The bartender scowled at me as I ordered two bottles

of beer. No way in hell was I trusting anything in a glass in this place.

"We're fine," Kol insisted.

"Someone's just really getting into his role," I said, trying to subtly hide my lips by looking down, pulling on my shirt, and adjusting my breasts for maximum cleavage.

"Hey, I'm supposed to be an asshole incubus. Gotta play the part," Kol drawled. "We've got just under a dozen supers here who can see in the dark. Six shifters, three lesser demons, and a lethe demon."

"No pit fiend?" Marcus asked.

I leaned my back against the bar while I waited for the beers and scanned the room before returning my gaze to Kol's like a good enthralled woman.

"No," Kol said. "Did we just get sent on a wild goose chase?"

"There's still time." But Cassius's tone said he thought Floyd had lied, as well.

Movement in the hall to the bathrooms caught my eye. I turned back to the bartender as a burly demon, larger in height and bulk than Jacob, lumbered the few feet from the hall to a table in the corner. The guy had mottled black and white skin, a mouth that was too wide to be human, and leathery black wings tucked behind him. He sat backwards in his chair to avoid catching his wings, and laughed at something said by the other guy at his table, revealing a mouth full of shark-like teeth.

"Looks like the pit fiend was in the can," Kol said. "But there's only two of them at the table. Not three."

"What are the odds that two pit fiends would be here?" Marcus asked.

"There are less than twenty in Union City," Cassius said. "You do the math. Keep your eyes on that table."

Kol grunted his agreement as the bartender handed over our drinks. I paid, left the coins, and sashayed back to Kol. He took both of the beers and set them on the table, but before I could sit in the chair beside him, he grabbed my wrist and jerked me into his lap.

Heat surged through me, making my breath hitch and my nerves thrum with sudden aching need. I swallowed a gasp to avoid another comment from Marcus.

My gaze leaped to Kol's and stalled there. All hint of playfulness was gone, consumed by hellfire and surprise, as if he hadn't expected my instant desire— No, his body trembled beneath me and his shoulders were taut under my hands. Whatever this sensation was, it had struck both of us.

He drew in a shuddering breath and captured the back of my head with his hand. My pulse raced as he urged me close, brushing his cheek against mine. "Both of those guys can see in the dark."

Which meant we couldn't just stare at them. Not that we were going to.

"I've got the rest of the room." He nuzzled my neck, his body still tense beneath me.

I slid my fingers in his hair and concentrated on my buzz.

The pit fiend laughed again at something his friend said. The guy was small compared to the pit fiend and while he looked human, he had the same dark feralness Marcus had when his wolf was coming out.

"Do we know what kind of shifter he is?" I asked.

"Hyena." Kol's breath caressed my neck.

I clenched my teeth. *Focus on the buzz.*

Marcus growled, the sound rumbling through the coms. "What are the other shifters?"

"A wolf, three tigers, and a fox. And none of them are sitting together."

"Heads up," Cassius said. "You've got a group of three heading to the front door. Looks like the wolf is carrying a bag."

Daylight sliced into the bar, and I glanced over my shoulder to look at the new arrivals. All of the guys looked human... except not. The short one with the duffle bag had a shifter's feral intensity, but the others I couldn't figure out how they weren't human. Something about the way they walked? Or carried themselves? Or... hell, I had no idea, but I knew without a doubt that they were supers of some kind.

"Whoa." Kol let out a soft breath. "That's a whole lot of Divifend."

"Good," Cassius said. "Now let's follow it to the lab's new location."

The two non-humans sat at the table closest to the door, not bothering to order drinks, while the wolf with the bag walked past us.

"He's making the drop right away?" Kol asked, not turning to watch him.

The pit fiend and his friend didn't look up as the wolf

approached and walked right on by, heading into the hall with the bathrooms.

"He's gone into the back hall," I said. "Not even a glance at the guys at the table."

"Stay with the bag," Cassius said. "Both of you. I don't want Shaw left alone for a second."

Great. How were we going to make it look natural for both of us to go to the bathroom at the same time?

Well, they already thought we were here for sex—

I captured Kol's head before I could rethink the plan and kissed him. He tensed with surprise, then leaned into me, a whisper of his heated magic slipping between my lips. I concentrated on my buzz, on the biting stinging my skin and my twitching muscles. My right thigh was the worst right now. If I didn't do something about it soon, it would cramp.

His hands slid down my back and grasped my hips, and the air around me heated.

Focus on the buzz. On the buzz. Just make this look real.

I sucked in his bottom lip, catching it with my teeth, and slowly drew back. Hellfire consumed his eyes, but this close, almost nose to nose with him, I could also see the tension there.

"Come on," I said, not needing to work at making my tone sound like I wanted him. I slid from his lap, grabbed his leather coat and his hand, and pulled him toward the bathrooms. Hopefully everyone in the bar would think we were off to have sleazy sex in a bathroom stall.

"Damn it, Kol," Cassius said, his tone dark. "Stop seducing Gideon's mate. You're working."

"You wanted us to both follow the bag," I whispered

as we stepped into the back hall, lit by a naked bulb that barely gave off any illumination, in an unfinished light fixture between two unmarked doors—presumably the bathrooms. "We've barely arrived and there's only one logical reason for us to head to the back hall together."

The wolf with the bag, an average looking guy with stringy brown hair wearing a stained gray T-shirt and ripped jeans, stood at the far end beside a scarred metal security door. His eyes narrowed the moment we entered the hall.

Kol stopped a few feet in, tugged me close, and pinned me to the wall with his body. Glorious heat swept through me, along with the memory of his lips on mine two nights ago when he saved my life. Just the thought of his magic pouring powerful liquid bliss into my body stole my breath.

Focus on the buzz, not how close he is or the dream. I clenched my jaw against a shudder. My thigh cramped, and I embraced the pain.

"Trust me." Kol nuzzled my neck again, forcing me to turn my head toward the wolf. "This wasn't my plan."

"It fits your cover," Gideon said, his voice devoid of emotion, making my soul sob. "Just keep Shaw's head clear."

"Top priority." Kol glanced toward the bar. "The pit fiend and the hyena are here."

"Fucking incubus," the hyena said, as he and the pit fiend approached.

"Oh, man. You don't know what you're missing." The pit fiend's lips curled back, his expression hungry, sending a shiver of fear through me. "Hey," he said to Kol, "if you want a bigger meal, we'll fuck her, too."

"You honestly think I need your help?" Kol flashed the pit fiend a wicked grin and sent a surge of power through me that was a lot stronger than the whisper he'd used to ease my stinging ass.

I gasped at the sudden swell of power and a low throaty moan escaped my lips. Unable to stop myself, I arched against the wall, pressing my breasts against Kol's chest, and fisted my hands in the hem of his T-shirt. Too much clothing. Not enough kissing. Not enough—

Shit. Focus on the buzz.

I fought to catch my breath but couldn't stop panting. All I could think about was our kiss and my dream and how I wanted to ride his magic to its glorious, screaming end.

"What the hell, Kol?" Marcus growled in my ear.

"Told you they're all assholes," the hyena said.

"No shit." The pit fiend shouldered Kol into me—drawing another moan as our bodies pressed together—and headed to the wolf at the end of the hall.

Oh, my God. I was going to lose my mind and start ripping off our clothes. This was bad. Cassius was going to kick me off the team the moment this op was done. And really, it was only logical. How could I effectively work on the team when all I could think about was having sex with all the guys.

Except I'd managed to work just fine with Jacob that morning, and I knew, deep down, past all my aching desire, that I could work with the rest of the team as well. I just couldn't do it with Kol's magic flooding me.

Kol leaned close, the hellfire in his eyes gone, and I

fought the urge to rub against him again. "Just take a breath, Essie."

I drew in a ragged breath.

The guys at the end of the hall said something, but I couldn't concentrate past my consuming need to listen.

"Another one." The muscles in Kol's jaw flexed, and the heat of his magic rose to the surface of my skin then seeped out, evaporating in a swirl of red smoke.

My desire turned into an aching emptiness for an agonizing second before my buzz surged, setting off my cramping thigh. "How did you do that?"

"With a lot of concentration," he said, his expression pained. He glanced to the end of the hall.

The wolf handed the bag to the pit fiend and, with the hyena, headed back into the bar, while the pit fiend shoved open the back door and stepped out into the blinding afternoon sunlight.

"The pit fiend has the bag," Kol said. "He just went out the back door by himself."

I rubbed my thigh, trying to get the muscle to relax. "I thought he was supposed to be the bodyguard."

"I don't see him coming around into the parking lot," Marcus said.

My thigh clenched tighter. Jeez, that hurt—

Wait. "What if the real handoff is happening in the ravine?"

"Marcus," Cassius said, "get eyes on that bag now."

"I'm too far away to catch him before he gets out of sight in the ravine."

"We'll stall him." Kol grabbed my hand and urged me to the end of the hall.

I stumbled, my thigh screaming. God damn buzz. Kol's eyes flashed wide, but I managed to catch my balance, and opened the door.

The pit fiend stood a few feet away, his expression jumping from surprise to realization to anger. "You're JP agents."

Something roared, blocked from view because of the open door, then something crashed into the door. Kol shoved me out of the way as it slammed him into the metal doorframe and concrete wall, drawing a grunt of pain.

A massive demon with red scales, a prehensile tail, and slitted pupils, like the one Jacob and I had faced picking up Floyd but twice as big, snarled at us. Behind him stood a man with a ragged scar running down the side of his face and the feralness of a shifter in his eyes, and a tiger. An honest to goodness giant tiger.

The scaled snake-like demon wrenched the door open and swung it back toward Kol with a force that was sure to break his ribs, while the tiger pounced at me.

CHAPTER 10

KOL JERKED OUT OF THE WAY OF THE DOOR, CRASHING INTO me and making me stumble. But instead of catching my arm to steady me, he shoved me again. Hard. I lurched to the side and fell to my knees, narrowly missing a swipe of the tiger's claws.

"Follow the pit fiend," Kol said, grabbing the tiger's neck and wrenching it away from me.

I scrambled to my feet as Snake drove his fist into Kol's ribs. The pit fiend sneered and ran across the parking lot to a break in the trees, but the shifter, Scar Guy, sneered at me and slunk around Kol and the tiger, his expression clear. He was going to kill me, and he was going to enjoy it.

"Go. I've got them." Kol heaved the tiger into the bar's cinderblock wall and turned to punch Snake in the gut, but Snake's tail wrapped around his neck, shoved him out of reach, and choked him.

It didn't look like he had them at all. Except the mission was to follow the Divifend to the new zip lab, or, in the very least, reclaim the stolen Divifend so they couldn't immediately make more zip.

"On my way," Marcus said over the coms.

The tiger lunged again at Kol, and I pulled my Glock from the jacket pocket and shot it. It roared, its claws grazing Kol's back, tearing his T-shirt but not digging deep into his flesh. For a second I was sure I'd missed because it didn't look like it was bleeding or even in pain. But then red lightning exploded around it, and it tensed as if hit by a Taser.

With another roar, its fur melted into flesh and its body contracted into a man's. The guy panted on his hands and knees, completely naked—because a shifter's magic consumed whatever he was wearing when he transformed—and glared at me, feral fury in his eyes.

Oh, shit. One round wasn't enough to drop them.

Scar swiped at me, his fingers extended into claws. I heaved back, my buzz seizing muscles in both of my thighs, and hit the garbage bin. At the last second, I wrenched up Kol's jacket, catching Scar's claws. He tore the leather from my hand as Tiger leaped to tackle me. Kol, down on one knee and still being choked by Snake, snagged Tiger's ankle, crashing him to the ground. Then Kol grabbed a knife sheathed in his boot—I'd been wondering if he was armed, since I hadn't felt the sheathes he usually wore on his back—and sliced at Snake's tail, who released him before the blade cut too deep.

"Essie, the Divifend," he said. "I can handle them until Marcus comes."

"Not happening soon. I'm surrounded," Marcus

growled. I glanced around the garbage bin but couldn't see him. He must have been ambushed at the side of the building by guys coming out the front door.

"Shaw, go," Cassius said. "We're on our way."

I shot Scar before he could lunge at me again and bolted past him to the break in the trees where the pit fiend had gone without looking to see if the shot had even hit.

A rutted narrow path led down a steep incline and disappeared around a man-sized rock and a thick pine tree. Dappled sunlight shone among the branches, dancing with the breeze on the thick shrubs and weeds lining the path. Too many places to hide.

Someone screamed. It didn't sound like Kol, but I didn't look back to check.

I gritted my teeth against my buzz and listened for sounds of the pit fiend, to determine if he'd stayed on the path or plunged into the thick underbrush. But all I could hear were the guys yelling and grunting and breathing in my ear. Marcus was still stuck at the side of the bar. Something boomed over the coms and behind me. Kol slid down the side of the garbage bin then lunged at Tiger, who'd shifted back into his feline form. Gideon was almost to Marcus, and Cassius was off to help Kol.

There was no way I was going to be able to hear anything like this.

I shoved the ear piece into my pocket and squeezed my eyes shut. No footsteps, and no heavy breathing. Not that I expected the pit fiend to be close enough for me to hear his breathing.

A twig snapped in the direction of the path. *Thank you, Jacob, for enhancing my hearing.*

I skidded down the dirt incline and hurried, but didn't outright run. The point was to follow him. Which meant I needed to hang back, and he needed to think he'd lost me.

My buzz increased, turning from stinging bites to a full, constant electric shock. I didn't know if that was because I was getting farther from Gideon, or if it was reacting to my adrenaline.

The path curled around the rock, the ground a steep tumble to the bottom of the ravine on one side and a hard climb on the other, then disappeared around a cluster of trees and shrubs.

Another twig snapped. I was getting closer... but was that breathing?

It was hard to tell with my buzz. The twig's sound had been sharp, but it was blended with the yells of the fight in the parking lot, the rustle of leaves, and the rumble of cars on a nearby road.

I glanced around the cluster of trees.

No sign of the pit fiend.

I had to be wrong. It wasn't someone breathing.

The path carried on for about twenty feet then switched back, dipping out of sight, and I hurried toward it.

A branch snapped, right beside me, and the pit fiend crashed out of the underbrush, lunging for me. I jerked out of the way and aimed my Glock, but the demon flapped his wings, sending dust and debris into my face.

Grit stung my eyes, and he leaped the distance

between us and seized my gun. I fired before he wrenched it away, the bullet grazing his ribs, sending a crackle of red lightning lancing up his side, but not nearly as powerful as what had hit Tiger.

He tossed my Glock behind him, his gaze never leaving me, his expression hungry. My sidearm clattered against a stone on the side of the path and stopped half under a large tree root.

"I'm surprised the demon-whore didn't leave you to my guys." He sneered, flashing his shark-teeth. "Remind me to thank his corpse when I'm done with you."

With a snarl, he flapped his wings again. I turned my head and squinted to avoid the grit. He was going to jump at me. I had a second at best.

I hissed the spell to cast a divine light strike, and my buzz burst into wild lightning slicing under my skin. The pit fiend jerked close, and I released the spell.

Nothing.

Not a flicker of light or heat in my hands. Not a God damned fucking thing.

Are you shitting me?

Where the hell had the blast from this morning gone? Or did I only have one of those inside me per day?

The pit fiend grabbed my neck and squeezed. "I'm going to fuck you 'til you're torn in two then eat your heart."

My pulse stuttered. This was bad, and I had no way of getting out of it. I needed backup. Now.

He wrenched me close and licked my cheek with a long thin tongue. The temperature rose with his wild desire and the demonic heat radiating from his body. "You're going to be delicious."

I clawed at his hand and kicked him in the gut.

He grunted and squeezed, cutting off my air.

How could I have possibly thought I belonged on this team? Cassius was going to be so smug when he fired me. I shoved my hand into my pocket to grab my com and call for help, but the pit fiend grabbed my wrist and twisted, forcing me to drop the ear piece.

"I don't think so. Now be a good human and freeze." Red smoke, like the demonic magic that had flooded the cemetery during the fight to stop Ibizual, swept up my arm, immobilizing my muscles. My buzz burned, but the twitching was gone, along with all control of my body.

The magic swept across my chest and down my legs, immobilizing them as well. I couldn't let it cover me. I was dead if it did.

The light strike spell roared through my head and divine light shot from my hand, which was clawing at his around my throat. It didn't hit with nearly as much force as the blast that had sent Floyd flying, but it did make the pit fiend yelp in pain and release me.

My feet hit the ground, but only one of my legs held me. I staggered, but managed to regain enough muscle control of both legs to fall toward my gun. The pit fiend seized my ankle before I reached it and yanked me under him, pinning me to the ground with his hips, his huge palm crushing my chest.

"That fucking hurt," he snarled, and a blast of red smoke erupted from his hand and swept around my chest. My heart strained to beat, and I fought to draw breath. Every muscle within me went limp. With a growl, he ground his erection against me. "So I'll make you hurt."

Frozen panic stole my breath. I had to get free. Somehow. *Please, God.* I couldn't be helpless, not now, not when he was going to—

Another blast of smoke enveloped me, and my buzz roared into an inferno. My muscles went from limp to suddenly contracted, all of them in one agonizing instant. The pit fiend's eyes widened, and the temperature around me plummeted as the smoke billowed out from my body then rushed into me. Just like the demon magic when fighting Ibizual. My skin sucked it up, devoured it, and the fire within me blazed hotter.

"What the fuck." The pit fiend scrambled off me.

I crawled to my knees, my body back in my control. The demonic magic twisted tight in my chest then flooded into my palms like a light strike spell, except hotter, so much hotter.

The pit fiend lurched toward me and punched at my head, and I wrenched my hands up. A blast of red light, not the smoke I'd consumed, shot from my palms and slammed into his chest. He howled with pain and dropped, his entire body limp.

I seized my sidearm, aimed it at him, and scrambled to my feet to put some distance between us so he couldn't easily grab me. My hands stung, but they didn't look as if they were burned. Thank God for that.

"What the fuck are you?" he gasped before passing out.

I shuddered. That was a very good question. I'd

thought absorbing Ibizual's magic had been because of my connection to his key, but now I wasn't sure.

Someone crashed through the underbrush behind me. I jerked around as Cassius tackled a guy with the feral intensity of a shifter, but another guy was close behind them with a revolver. He stopped to aim at Cassius, who was wrestling to pin the shifter to the ground.

Instinct kicked in and I shot twice at the guy's chest before he could fire. Red lightning swept around him. His muscles seized, he dropped the gun, and he collapsed, unconscious. Looked like two shots did the trick.

Cassius glanced at the unconscious man behind him then turned a frozen glare at me.

And here it came, the dressing down and being fired —with the rest of the guys listening in on their coms. But the truth was, I'd made it through another fight by the skin of my teeth, and the next time I might not make it. I couldn't argue any more that being on the team was a good idea, especially if I couldn't count on my light strike spell.

"Thanks," Cassius said, his voice gruff.

My thoughts stuttered. Not what I'd been expecting him to say.

He jerked his thumb to the unconscious guy. "For dropping him."

I must have looked as confused as I felt.

Kol hurried down the path, his T-shirt shiny with blood, although most of it didn't look like his. His attention jumped to the pit fiend, and his face lit up in a smile.

"You took out a pit fiend all by yourself. How did you manage that?"

"Barely." I dropped my gaze to my hands. They were shaking and it was obvious, because I had my weapon aimed at the pit fiend again.

"Yeah, but you did it." Kol's gaze dipped to my neck, and his eyes narrowed. Yeah, I bet I had a hand-sized bruise forming there. But he waded into the underbrush beside me and pulled out the bag of Divifend.

Gideon stormed down the path, light flaring from his eyes, his hard gaze locked on me. "You went off coms."

Here was the dressing down I deserved.

And my God damned buzz wasn't easing off this time. I still felt like part of the demonic magic was vibrating inside me and amping up my regular agony.

"You're supposed to let the team know when you go off coms," he said. "Didn't you work with coms at all in the UCPD?"

"I'm a beat cop."

"Means radios only," Kol said.

"I know what that means," Gideon snapped.

"I'm sure she had a good reason." Kol jerked his thumb at the pit fiend. "Come on, enjoy the fact that Essie took out a pit fiend."

Gideon pointed to the com in his ear. "I heard. So much for following him back to the zip lab."

Cassius cuffed his guy and hauled him to his feet. I couldn't read his expression. It was weird, not quite angry but certainly not happy. And why the hell hadn't he kicked me off the team yet?

"He tried to ambush me. Thought I was Kol." My

buzz snapped a muscle in my neck, and I flinched with all of them looking at me.

Gideon frowned. But just like his brother, I had no idea what his expression meant.

"Let's get these guys back to Operations." Cassius pulled out his phone. "Maybe we'll get something out of them."

He sent a quick text, and we gathered the thugs and took them up to the parking lot. Tiger was nowhere to be found, but Snake and Scar were both unconscious, bleeding, and cuffed together. Beside them were three more shifters—one naked—along with an unconscious demon with green skin. They were all handcuffed together, and Marcus glowered at those who were awake, his Glock pointed in their direction.

My guys—and Cassius—put our three criminals with the rest of the pack while I hung back with the bag of Divifend. Kol beamed and said something to Marcus, who rolled his eyes and half laughed. Even Gideon shook his head in amusement at what had been said.

My heart filled with a mix of joy and sadness. These were my guys, in their element, kicking ass and, each in his own way, looking sexy as hell. And I didn't belong. This was the second time today I'd almost been killed. I had to accept the truth. This job was far too dangerous for any human.

Of course, my argument from before still hadn't changed. If I left, some other human would be assigned to the team, and he or she wouldn't have the magical advantages I had. Even if I couldn't always count on my light strike, casting it was still a possibility. Most humans couldn't cast the spell. Not to mention my new unnerving ability to absorb demonic magic and shoot it like a light strike.

The pit fiend had asked what the hell I was, and a part of me wondered that as well. I didn't think angels could manipulate demonic magic. Could a nephilim, because I wasn't fully angelic?

Cassius said something to Kol and they headed my way.

"A word, Agent Shaw." I still couldn't read Cassius's expression, and the temperature around me didn't change. "How badly are you hurt?"

I gingerly touched my neck, but couldn't tell how bad the bruise was with my buzz still blazing from absorbing the demon's magic.

"I'm sure all of us got a little hurt." Kol shifted closer to me, the temperature cooling. Fear. "This op didn't go as planned."

"They usually don't," Cassius said. "How badly are you hurt?"

"I'm a little banged up."

He didn't look as if he believed me, which made me wonder how bad my neck looked.

"Take Shaw to Amiah and have her checked out," he said to Kol. "Then both of you are on call for the rest of the day."

"On call? You've got a parking lot full of supers you need to move." Kol jerked his thumb to the group we'd arrested.

"Chris and Nathaniel are bringing the transport. If three angels and two shifters can't handle this group, we don't deserve to call ourselves JP agents." Cassius held out his hand. "Your sidearm, Agent Shaw. We'll discuss this op after we've got this group booked. Don't turn off your phones."

Well, that didn't sound good. I handed over my Glock, and he shot me another strange look. It wasn't icy, but it wasn't pleasant. God, what I wouldn't give for a little telepathy, or hell, even an empathic magic that actually let me sense emotions.

He strode back to the group, but the chilly air didn't change, which meant the cold had to be coming from Kol.

"We won't let him kick you off the team." Hellfire blazed in his eyes.

"I don't want any of you to jeopardize your career for me." Especially since it was getting harder to disagree with Cassius's argument. I hadn't even had one full day on the job, and I'd already risked my life twice.

But jeez, everything within me said this was where I was supposed to be. Could I *be* with the guys without being a JP agent? What the hell would I do? I couldn't just sit around, watching them work, waiting for them to come home. That would drive me crazy. But did I really have any other choice? Staying on the team was selfish. Gideon, Jacob, and Marcus all needed me. If I died, they went insane or worse, and I couldn't do that to them.

CHAPTER 11

I followed Kol to the bar's back door, where he grabbed his jacket from the ground and handed it to me. "Not being able to follow the Divifend back to the lab isn't your fault. Everyone but Cassius knows that."

I brushed the gravel dust off the jacket, cringing at the claw slices where I'd used it as a shield. "I barely got out of this fight alive. Again. I want to be on the team." God, I desperately wanted to be a part of the team. "But at this rate, I'd be surprised if I survived a week."

"That's because no one has really thought this through."

We headed around the building. Cassius watched us, his expression icy, while Gideon didn't even glance away from the thugs. Marcus and Kol shared a nod then Marcus's gaze slid to mine for a long second, filling me with heat, before he turned away.

The muscles in Kol's jaw clenched, but we kept heading toward his bike. "We're still treating you like you're a super."

"I won't be a useful member of the team if I can't risk being separated from one of you." I shrugged into his leather jacket and pulled on the helmet. "There will always be situations like today where we have to break up to deal with multiple perps."

"I'm not saying you have to be with one of us all the time. I'm saying you have no training for dealing with supers. I bet you have no idea what powers a pit fiend has." He straddled his bike and started it.

I climbed on and wrapped my arms around him. He tensed at the contact and didn't relax.

"I didn't even know a pit fiend existed or what it looked like until today."

"My point exactly."

We drove back to Operations. Amiah met us in triage, sent a slice of magic into me to find out just how hurt I was, then proclaimed I wasn't injured enough to waste her power. "Jacob's claim will fix that soon enough."

Which was fine with me.

Kol, from his perch on the arm of the couch in the waiting area, frowned at that, but thankfully didn't argue with her. My buzz still burned, the nicotine patches hadn't done a damned thing, and I didn't want another painful session with her.

"How about I show you around the Quarter and we get a bite to eat?" He flashed me his panty-melting smile, sending a shiver of desire strong enough to overcome my buzz sweeping through me. His eyes widened and the smile vanished. "Sorry. Forgot I hit you with a lot of magic at the bar."

"Do we need to talk about that?" I hadn't thought

there was something between us, but now, after that moment in his lap, I wasn't so sure. There'd been a connection, something deeper than me just being attracted to an incubus.

"I didn't have much choice. If I hadn't made my position clear, the pit fiend would have tried to take you."

A strange heat filled the air. Humid but not sultry, warm, not searing. It didn't feel like desire but it didn't feel like anger, either. It was complicated. Just like everything else at the moment.

"And before then?"

"You mean the ass slap?" A playful glimmer lit his eye and all sense of the strange heat vanished.

Perhaps I was only seeing what I wanted because my base human instinct was drawn to him. A part of me would always desire him, just like a part of every other straight woman and gay man.

"Yeah, the ass slap." I hopped off the gurney, and we headed down the hall to the elevator.

"Really wished I could have seen Marcus's face," he said.

"What about Cassius?"

We reached the elevator, and I hit the call button.

"Him, too, but Marcus always gives such a good reaction." His grin turned wicked, still sexually charged, but I got the sense that wasn't his intention. Guess I really had been mistaken about there being something between us. "We should take him up on that threesome offer, so I can watch him back out of it."

The elevator door opened. I got in and hit the button

for the fifth floor. "What makes you think he'll back out?" I asked Kol as he stepped in beside me.

"Come on, you don't honestly think he'd go through with it?" Kol frowned. "Okay, he might. But probably with Gideon, not me. He's your other mate. Marcus's wolf might see him as a part of you, which is why he hasn't lost his shit over this situation."

The elevator dinged, the door opened, and we headed down the hall.

"Oh, I'd love to see that." Kol chuckled. "You two propositioning Gideon."

"Yeah, that's never going to happen." Because Gideon didn't want me. Not that the idea didn't appeal—

Oh, wow! I just thought that, and... jeez... wow... had no idea how I felt or what I thought about that.

"Can you do it in front of Cassius?" The sinful gleam in Kol's eyes blazed, reminding me that he was still a demon, the chaos to the angels' order. "Pretty please?"

I bit back a laugh, imagining the look on Cassius's face.

Kol batted his eyelashes at me. "Pretty pretty please?"

"I'm going to get changed now." I unlocked my door.

"So that means you'll think about it?" Kol said as he headed down the hall to his suite.

"Depends on what you show me in the Quarter and where you take me for dinner."

He turned to face me, now walking backwards. "Oh, I'll show you such a good time, sweetheart, you'll do anything to make me happy." His eyes widened. "I didn't mean— You know what I—"

"Go get changed, Kol," I said with a laugh and stepped into my room.

I washed off my makeup, peeled off my four nicotine patches and didn't replace them. The level of my buzz didn't change, so it was clear the patches weren't doing anything. Not that I really had any doubts. I had red patches that I'd scratched on both thighs that weren't from my fight with the pit fiend, and another patch with fresh scabs along my ribs. I was already scratching and hadn't noticed. This wasn't good, and there wasn't anyone I could ask for help. I didn't know how much anyone at Operations knew about nephilim, but I couldn't confess that I was one in hopes that someone might know something that would help. And even if I didn't mention my half angelic nature, whoever I went to could still ask too many questions and stumble across the truth.

I changed into a fresh T-shirt. I only had one left from my hasty packing job that morning, but I didn't know if I should spend the afternoon packing so I could move in to Operations or not. Given Cassius's reaction to the op at Hacksaw, my money was on not.

Kol met me in the hall. He'd traded in his leather pants for jeans and his ripped and bloody T-shirt for another T-shirt. All hint of the hellfire in his eyes was banked, and his wicked playfulness was gone, replaced with the man who'd asked me three nights ago to stay on the team. He'd confessed that even though he was a demon, his heightened magical attunement meant he was repelled by and attracted to certain essences. Unfortunately he wasn't attracted to his own kind, but instead to essences on the light end of the spectrum. Angels, however, didn't usually like to hang out with demons, which made me the perfect find. I didn't look down on him like an angel, but my essence made him as comfortable as if I were one.

And I wasn't going to tell him that was because I was half angel.

We took a JP SUV and drove around the Supers' Quarter with the windows rolled down, enjoying the early summer warmth, while I tried not to claw at my body.

I'd already seen the vampire section of the Quarter with its UV-blocking glass canopy protecting a whole street and the park at the end, so we did a drive-by of the demon area, which looked a lot like the rest of the Quarter except that there were more demons on the streets and more businesses catering to demonic needs.

Next was Mercy Memorial, the JP hospital, a series of 19th century office buildings, converted and joined into a complex that catered to every supers' medical needs. It sat only a block off the main road near the ring park separating the Quarter from the rest of the city, so supers outside of the Quarter could reach it quickly, since supers couldn't go to just any hospital. Most human facilities—and all of those in Union City—weren't capable of handling a super in medical distress. And, depending on the super or the injury, it wasn't safe for humans to treat them.

This was where Marcus had suffered through his transformation into a werewolf after my horrible rookie mistake, and where he'd met Amiah. I still wasn't sure if there was anything between them. Marcus's wolf had clearly picked me, but that didn't mean there still weren't complicated feelings between them.

After the hospital was the shiny new UV-blocking glass and steel JP council chambers where the day-to-day running of the Quarter happened. The Quarter didn't have a mayor, but it still ran pretty much like a city inside the city. And while the community heads pretty much policed their own, there was an effort made to work together and uphold the laws they'd all helped make when supers had been given the right to representation in the world's governance. That, and supers paid taxes, got parking tickets, needed dog licenses, and everything else every other human citizen needed.

Kol shared entertaining bits of information as we drove, usually about this op or that, as if his whole life revolved around the team, and I couldn't help wondering if he had any family in the human realm or even in the Realm of Celestial Darkness. I didn't want to pry, so I didn't ask. I was sure it'd come up again at some point.

We ended up on the edge of the Quarter at the park entrance to one of the shifters' forests and stopped near a food truck.

"These are the best tacos in the city," he said, shutting off the engine and getting out.

I joined him, caught myself scratching my shoulder and digging in to get the muscle to relax, and forced my hand to my side.

We'd parked in a gravel lot beside a baseball diamond, a jungle gym, and a public bathroom. Three wolf cubs wrestled with each other in the grass a few feet away, while an adult wolf lounged on a blanket beside a shirtless man. At their feet sat an open picnic basket and a pile of dirty paper plates and cups.

"There are usually more trucks here on the weekend when the ball diamond is in use, but Tasty Tacos is here all the time."

The middle-aged woman in the truck waved at us as we approached. Silver streaked her black hair, and laugh lines crinkled around her eyes. She had the feral intensity of a shifter, but I didn't know which kind. Best guess was wolf and that this was the wolves' forest.

"I was beginning to think you'd forgotten about me," the woman said.

"You know I could never forget you, Bonnie." He flashed her a friendly-for-an-incubus smile that still made my pulse trip with desire.

She clicked her tongue at him and blushed. "You mean you could never forget my cooking."

"Only because I know you're taken."

"By the most handsome wolf in Union City," she said with a laugh. The air around me warmed, and I knew her affection for her guy was genuine. "Who's your friend?"

"Bonnie, this is Essie. Essie, Bonnie. She's new in the Quarter."

"And you just thought you'd show her around?" Bonnie winked at me.

"It's not like that," Kol said.

"Un hunh," she said, clearly not believing him. "What'll it be?"

Kol glanced at me. "Anything you want. On me."

"Anything?" I studied the menu. There were over a dozen options, all of which sounded delicious. "I should order one of everything to get back at you for slapping my ass."

Bonnie laughed. "Yeah, not like that at all."

"I can see introducing you two was a mistake," Kol said, but mirth filled his eyes. In fact, he looked more relaxed than I'd ever seen him. "We'll each have the brisket taco combo."

"Hey! I thought I got to choose."

"Too slow."

He paid for the food, and we sat at a nearby picnic table, side by side, facing out, to wait for our order.

I leaned back against the tabletop and stretched out my legs. My skin burned and my shoulder was driving me crazy. "You must come here a lot."

"I like Bonnie's food." He matched my posture and stared up at the cloudless sky, a perfect summer blue. The same color as Gideon's eyes. "And I like her essence. Sometimes the angels are hard to take."

"Because of their... attitude toward beings of celestial darkness?"

"Yeah." The word came out soft, weighted with so much more emotion than just frustration at how people at work looked at him, and the temperature dipped with a hint of mist. "And sometimes they remind me of things I'd rather forget."

"The war?"

"Just over twenty years and I still—"

The mist thickened, the droplets of water catching the afternoon sunlight like miniscule diamonds only I could see.

He ran his hands through his hair. "I can't make up for the things I did."

"You mean the things Michael *made* you do."

"It was still me enthralling those women." He squeezed his eyes shut, and I didn't need the mist or chill to tell me how much it still hurt. During the war, Michael had manifested him in the human realm to keep the women he'd imprisoned and used to conceive his nephilim army compliant. "I picked me over them. And the things he and his nephilim did to them... to us."

The mist swept around me, obscuring my vision and blocking out the sun. I didn't know what to say to him. There wasn't anything I could say that would heal this. All I could do was listen to whatever he wanted to reveal without judgment.

I shifted closer to him, brushing my shoulder against his, and took his hand. He laced his fingers between mine, his face still turned up to the sky, eyes still closed.

Mist gathered on my cheeks. Soon it would look like I was crying. Kol drew in a ragged breath, and his grip on my hand tightened.

"We need to figure out a plan for Cassius," he said, his voice raw.

"We need for him not to be right." My buzz snapped the muscles in my neck, making me twitch.

Kol glanced at me and frowned. "Are you all right?"

"I'm fine now, but if I wasn't, Gideon and Jacob would be in trouble. Marcus might be as well, but I don't know enough about shifter mating bonds to know for sure."

Bonnie stepped out of her food truck with our order and headed our way.

"How deep is a shifter's mating bond?" he asked her as she set the tray of food on the picnic table.

She propped her hands on her hips. "A true bond, not just being in love?"

Kol glanced at me, the look quick, but Bonnie's eyes narrowed. She'd seen it.

"I'd say true," he said.

"Throw yourself on your mate's funeral pyre deep." She heaved a heavy sigh. "If he catches you holding her hand, he's going to tear you a new one. Especially if he's a wolf."

"Doesn't she get a say in it?" Kol asked.

Bonnie met my gaze. "Your brain just hasn't caught up with your soul. If you're not in love with him now, you will be."

"Oh, I'm pretty sure I'm in love with him." God, I really was. I had been from the moment I saw him.

"Then leave my boy out of this." Feral intensity radiated from Bonnie's eyes, and her canines sharpened as her wolf came to the surface. Heat swept around me, and Kol's mist vanished.

"Whoa." Kol stood, grabbed Bonnie's hands, and met her gaze. "I'm fine. It's all good. Marcus isn't going to kill me."

Surprise flashed across her expression. "Marcus is mated? But he's hung up on a— Oh." She huffed and cuffed Kol on the head. "You still know better than to hold her hand."

He took the blow. It wasn't very hard, but I was sure he could have dodged it if he'd wanted to. "Yes, ma'am."

"Don't yes ma'am me." She rolled her eyes at him. "I'm too young to be a ma'am."

"Yes—"

She glared at him, cutting him off, but the edges of her lips curled into a smile for a second before she sobered and looked at me. "You hurt Marcus or Kol and I'll rip your heart out."

She headed back to her truck, and Kol dropped to the bench beside me with his usual boneless sexual grace.

"She really likes you," he said, nudging the tray closer to me.

"That's what that was."

He shrugged, his eyes gleaming, all hint of grief over the war hidden. "Wolves tend to be overprotective."

"Gee, I hadn't noticed." I picked up a taco and took a bite. Oh, wow. This really was the best taco in town. Just the right mix of hard and soft, salty and sweet. "We still need to figure out how to make this job safer for me or three quarters of your team is going to be in trouble."

"Three fifths. You're part of the team, too."

"I really want to be." I really did. "But I'm also not an idiot."

"The first thing we need to do is get you off active duty and get you proper training."

"Except the mayor and chief of police want me seen on the job with the team." I was pretty sure they were hoping I'd be kicked off the team and sent back to UCPD so they'd have cause to fire me.

"Then I guess we have to use your time off to bring you up to speed."

"You make it sound so easy." And it still wasn't a guarantee that any of it would increase my odds of survival or that it would be good enough soon enough to convince Cassius everything was fine.

"I'm all ears if you have a better idea."

But there wasn't one. I was staying, and I had to protect my guys, which meant I had to do everything in my power to make this job safer for me.

"Okay. Hit me with your knowledge, oh wise incubus."

He grinned at me. "I like the sound of that."

We ate and talked, mostly discussing the afternoon's op and the various demons and shifters we'd encountered. The breeze rustled the leaves and the sun warmed me as it slowly moved in the sky. The couple with the pups packed up and left, and about an hour later a beat-up hatchback pulled into the lot. Five teenaged boys piled out and stripped, tossing their clothes into the car. They raced toward the forest entrance, their bodies transforming as they ran with breathtaking ease, as if they'd turned to liquid, melting from one shape to the other. Even after seeing it twice now, I still always thought that kind of transformation would be painful—and if you weren't born a shifter, the first one always was, as the lycanthropic disease rewrote your DNA—but after that, I'd heard most transformations were mostly painless.

More cars arrived in the lot and kids in baseball uniforms and their parents gathered at the ball diamond. My head was full of information about pit fiends which, as far as I could tell, weren't supposed to be able to cast a paralyzing spell—and I didn't push for more information on that for fear of revealing that I could still absorb demonic magic—as well as the scaled demons, called nagas, and werehyenas.

"We should head back to Operations," Kol said, gathering our garbage and standing.

"Yeah." Except I didn't want to deal with Cassius or Gideon. Neither had called us, and I didn't know if that was a good thing or not.

Kol frowned. He must have heard my not-so-overwhelming excitement at his suggestion. "Okay, what would you like?"

"I want—" A moment, a breath, two seconds where things weren't a hundred percent crazy in a supernatural world. This afternoon with Kol had been good, but I'd still been neck deep in all of it. I'd spent my whole life avoiding all things supernatural, and while I was committed to Marcus, the last three days, let alone the last few weeks, had been overwhelming. "I want to go home. My home."

His expression softened. "Sure."

We drove across town to my apartment, settled on my beat-up second-hand couch with a bowl of popcorn, and found a light romantic comedy playing on the TV. It felt strange and yet comfortable. I'd never done anything like this before, never had anyone over to just hang out. And yet it felt as if I'd always been doing this with Kol. The weight of the last few days sank into me with bone-weary exhaustion. Except I was pretty sure it wasn't sinking in but being revealed now that I wasn't constantly on the go. Two nights ago I'd been shot. The night before that I'd almost had my throat ripped out by a feral vampire.

My buzz burned, and I didn't care if I was scratching

myself raw. I was just too exhausted to care. Amiah might have healed my injuries from the last few battles, but I'd been foolish to think everything was all right.

The rom com ended and turned into another one, and my living room started to darken with the setting sun. Kol's warmth seeped into me even though we were sitting side by side, and I couldn't keep my eyes open. Everything turned into a warm, soft hum, even my buzz —which, if I hadn't been so tired, would have shocked the hell out of me...

Sharp pounding jerked me awake. I must have fallen asleep for a good couple of hours since my eyes were gritty from my contacts. I lay against Kol, his legs on either side of me, my cheek pressed against his chest, and his arms wrapped around me. My living room was dark, even the TV was off, and through the skylight, stars sparkled in a cloudless night sky.

The pounding came again. From the door. Hard, insistent.

"We know you're in there," a guy with a raspy voice yelled from the hall. "Don't make me break the door down."

CHAPTER 12

I sat up and met Kol's gaze. Hellfire burned in his eyes, casting his face in a flickering light that made him look dangerous.

"Do you have a weapon?" he asked, drawing a knife from his boot and flipping the grip so the blade was hidden against his forearm.

"My off-duty Glock is in the gun safe in my bedroom."

"Get it." He stood and headed to the door.

"Victoria is summoning you, human." The guy pounded again. "Open up."

Kol glanced back at me. "Why the hell would Victoria summon—" Realization flashed across his expression at the same time it hit me.

"Jacob." I glanced at the clock on the microwave. It was a little after one, barely halfway through Jacob's agreed-upon twenty-four hours with her. "Something's wrong with Jacob."

And the moment I said it, I knew it was true. I couldn't tell what, and didn't know how—probably something to do with his claim on me—but without a doubt, something was wrong. The sensation sat hard and heavy in my chest, radiating dread.

I reached for the door, and Kol slapped his palm against it before I could open it.

"Or it's a trap," he said. "She's going to use you as leverage to get Jacob to go along with something else."

"Do you think she'd risk pissing off Gideon?" Last time I'd seen her, she'd been angry at Gideon and had tried to get him in her bed, but it didn't seem as if she'd been willing to make him furious to get what she wanted. And while Gideon didn't want a relationship with me, threatening my life threatened his, which Victoria knew, and that was sure to piss him off.

"You're right," Kol said, but he didn't sound happy about it.

He opened the door. Two vampires stood in the hall, both big and burly. The guy in front with his hand raised to pound again looked familiar. Best guess was that he was one of Victoria's lieutenants who'd helped with the fight at Rouge the other night.

His gaze landed on Kol, and his lips curled back in a sneer, revealing his fangs, before he turned to me. "You're coming with us."

"Lead the way," Kol said.

"Just the human."

The guy behind him fisted his hands and snarled.

The hellfire flared brighter in Kol's eyes. "Do you really want to make this a fight?"

The guy in front opened his mouth to say something, but his friend stiffened and his expression went blank.

"My offspring won't harm the human, but only if she comes alone," the guy in the back said, his voice flat. "Swear by it, Horatio."

The guy in front, Horatio, turned a wide-eyed stare at his friend. "Master, I—"

"Swear by it," his possessed friend said.

"Of course, Master." He turned to Kol. "As my master commands, we won't harm the human."

"I don't like this," Kol said, his voice low.

Neither did I. Especially since Victoria hadn't included herself in that promise.

I squeezed his arm, drawing his gaze to mine. "It'll be okay." At least I hoped it would. Not for myself, but for Jacob. The only reason he'd need me was if he hadn't been able to feed properly from a blood bunny or if Victoria, in her enthusiasm, had hurt him more than he could reasonably heal with a bunny's blood.

"Come on." Horatio grabbed my arm and tugged me into the hall.

"If I don't call you in an hour, tell Gideon."

We hurried down the stairs and out the door to a sedan parked on the street, the windows tinted and the engine running.

Horatio opened the door for me then got in beside me while his friend took the front passenger seat. My pulse picked up as we drove to the Quarter. If Victoria had been lying, I was dead. There was no way I could defend myself from three vampires. Even if I managed to get out of the car, I wouldn't be able to run fast enough to escape them.

I pulled out my phone. Horatio watched me with the

same unnerving intensity I saw in Jacob when he revealed the full power of his vampiric nature.

A shudder swept through me, and I tried to stay calm as I sent a text to Marcus letting him know something might be up with Jacob.

"My sire made me swear. You have nothing to fear, human," Horatio said.

"I want to know what's so hot about you?" the guy who'd been possessed by Victoria asked. He leaned around and swept his gaze over me, his attention stopping at my neck. I couldn't tell if he was looking at the bruise or the scar. "That's one heck of a scar. Is that why Jacob claimed you? You like it rough?"

"That's from one of the ferals, you idiot," the woman driving said. "Everyone knows that. Do you really think Mr. Humans Are Delicate Flowers would want a screamer?"

"You never know," the guy in the front said with a shrug.

My phone chimed with Marcus's reply. He was tied up in another emergency meeting with the wolf pack alpha that could last for hours, but he'd drop it all if I needed him.

I texted back that I'd let him know. Maybe, if I could get Jacob away from Victoria, the situation could wait.

We arrived at Rouge, my pulse thrumming. The closer I got to Jacob, the more my dread grew. Horatio took me up the backstairs to Victoria's suite, avoiding the nightclub part of the building entirely, while the other two stayed with the car.

Light from the crystal chandeliers in the hall glim-

mered in the polished marble floor and gilded frescoes on the ceiling. It had only been three nights since I was last here with Gideon and Jacob, and all hell had broken loose with feral vampires and Gideon nearly dying. That had been terrifying. A horrible second act to what had already started as a bad night.

Surely whatever awaited me now couldn't be as bad as that. Except the temperature kept dropping the closer we got to the end of the hall and Victoria's suite.

The lanky female vampire standing guard at the door watched us as we approached, statue still, radiating powerful vampiric intensity. It wasn't as strong as Victoria's, indicating she wasn't as old, but it was more powerful than Jacob. She gave Horatio a tight nod and opened one of the intricately carved wooden doors which depicted an enthusiastic threesome.

The cold turned frigid before I'd even stepped into the room, the fear so deep frost swept over my hands, making my pulse lurch. Someone inside was terrified.

Fury boiled inside me at the thought that it was Jacob's fear, but that flash froze into an arctic wasteland at the thought it was Victoria's. If it was bad enough to scare Victoria, it had to be terrifying.

I drew in a ragged breath and stepped inside. Horatio didn't join me, and the guard at the door closed it with a heavy thump, trapping me with all that frozen fear. I didn't even look to see if Victoria had completely cleaned her suite from the carnage of the other night. My gaze jumped instantly to the horrific frieze around her bed.

Victoria, Jacob's sire and Union City's master vampire, stood over him wearing a white gauzy negligee that did nothing to hide her voluptuous curves, her hair disheveled, her eyes big, and her complexion pale even for a vampire. Sebastian Bane, the only feakin I'd ever seen, with his pointed ears and his glowing translucent skin, sat on the edge of the bed beside a gasping, bleeding Jacob. He had one hand on Jacob's forehead, the other over his heart. A glyph between Sebastian's shoulders glowed through his white button-down, making the fabric as see-through as Victoria's, revealing a swirling, intricate black tattoo covering his entire back.

Only Jacob's hips and thighs had been covered by a red silk sheet, exposing the rest of his bulky muscular body and all the bleeding gashes covering him. He gasped as if he couldn't catch his breath and sweat slicked his skin, shimmering in the candlelight from the lit candelabras placed around the room.

He was dying. Every fiber of my being screamed that truth. I could feel it in his essence entwined with mine, and my soul wailed at that. That was the dread I'd felt.

And this was Victoria's idea of a good time? How much had all those gashes hurt? I didn't want to believe Jacob enjoyed that kind of violence, but I really didn't know him, just like I really didn't know Marcus or Gideon or Kol.

Except I was certain this hadn't been what he'd signed up for.

Jacob's eyes squeezed tight and every muscle in his body convulsed, arching his back off the bed and making the veins in his neck and arms bulge. He screamed, the agony wrenching at my soul, making my pulse stop completely in horror and fear, and I rushed to him.

"What did you do?"

Victoria seized my arm before I reached the bed, yanked me close, and grabbed my throat, squeezing. "What did *I* do?"

I gasped for breath, and her nails dug into my throat.

"What did *I* do, human?" she snarled. "What did *you* do? He won't take bagged blood, a bunny barely heals him, and my blood does that to him."

Jacob screamed and convulsed again. I heaved against Victoria's grip even though there was no way I could break free against her enhanced vampiric strength.

Sebastian slapped his own shoulder and another glyph burst to life with a blazing white light, joining the first one, revealing that Sebastian's tattoo also completely covered his arm as well. He pressed both hands over Jacob's heart, and with a groan, Jacob sagged back onto the bed, still unconscious, still gasping, and now twitching, as if even unconscious his body continued to convulse.

"I can't keep casting my sleep spell." He captured me with his icy gaze, pure frost, and not because he was upset with me—he barely knew me—but because his eyes were just that pale. "Whatever you're going to do, do it now."

Victoria shoved me onto the bed. I fell onto my hands and knees, one hand landing on Jacob's exposed calf. Even with the fear frosting my hands, his skin was freezing, proving just how close he was to death.

"Fix him," Victoria said, her voice low and dangerous.

Jeez. She hadn't even said *save* him. "He's not some toy. You can't do—" I pointed at his broad chest, my throat tight as I imagined how much all of that must have hurt. "You can't do that to him and expect it to be all right."

"I've been fucking your master for a lot longer than you've been alive. I'm more than familiar with what he can and cannot take." Victoria grabbed my chin and dug her nails into my cheeks, her dark eyes capturing my soul.

I shuddered at the enormity of her power as hard and icy fear churned in my gut.

"I don't know what you did to him or how you did it, but he's mine," she said. "My offspring, my *toy*, and mine to do with as I please. Now *fix* him. His debt isn't fully paid."

God, she was going to keep going? A fury sparked in my chest. "No."

"No?" She wrenched me close. My feet tangled in the sheets and I couldn't get them under me to support my weight, forcing me to clutch her forearm to ease the strain on my neck. Her nails bit deeper, and blood seeped down to my jaw. She laughed, a low, dangerous chuckle, and turned to Sebastian. "She said no."

"No," I gasped. "Not until you release him from his debt."

Her laugh deepened, and her enormous power swelled and gained physical mass, enveloping me and squeezing tight. "You're not in a position to make demands. You're his human and he's my offspring." She flashed her fangs with a wicked smile that made my fear churn stronger. "Didn't Jacob tell you I can use his claim to control you, just like he can? You're going to feed him and then you'll keep feeding him until his debt is paid."

"There are laws."

"You let yourself be claimed. You've given your consent."

Her power squeezed tighter, and pressure exploded inside my skull. It sliced through my buzz, making it twist into a sudden inferno coiled tight in my chest.

"The law doesn't work that way," I gasped.

"You will fix him, and you will like it," she said.

The compulsion contracted my muscles, straining to follow her command. I gritted my teeth against it. "Not until you release him from his debt."

"Fix. Him."

Her power crushed me, inside and out, and my buzz roared through every cell in my body into a whirling firestorm. It raced over my skin, crackling with the lightning I'd come to recognize as Gideon's magic, except it didn't feel like his. It felt different. It felt like mine.

It rushed into my palms, twisting tighter and tighter into a blazing supernova that threatened to explode.

Victoria jerked back, her eyes wide.

I met her gaze, fighting to not flinch away from the enormous power I still saw there. "His debt is paid."

A deadly fury darkened Victoria's expression and her fangs extended in full, revealing her monstrous supernatural nature. "You don't want to make an enemy of me."

"No, I don't."

Jacob screamed and convulsed again, fueling my rage. He wasn't her toy, and I wouldn't let her hurt him again.

"Fix what's mine," she snarled.

"He's not yours," I snarled back, matching her intensity. "He's mine." The certainty of my words rushed into my soul. He was mine. Just like Marcus and Gideon were mine.

My power flared in response, as if it had a mind of its own, turning Victoria's expression back to shock.

"His debt is paid," I said, my voice low, my rage barely contained. "Get out."

I didn't care if this was her suite or not. Jacob needed to feed now, and I wasn't going to wait even a minute for Marcus to get out of his meeting.

Victoria glanced at Sebastian as if looking to him for help. He was wide-eyed with surprise, but I got the sense half of that was an act and he was searching my soul for answers. I could only pray he didn't figure out the truth. But if he did... God, it would be worth it to save Jacob.

"Out." The power around my hands turned into a brilliant, crackling nimbus.

"She's mated with an angel." Sebastian jerked to his feet and grabbed Victoria's arm. "She's sacred. You don't want a fight with the entire angelic race."

Victoria hissed, wrenched her arm out of Sebastian's grip, and stormed to the door.

Watch yourself, Esther. You've made a dangerous enemy and burned through most of the spell on your contacts, Sebastian said in my head.

I glared back at him, unable to contain my rage at Victoria and this whole situation. If I'd made an enemy, so be it. I'd do whatever it took to save Jacob, and everything else could be damned.

CHAPTER 13

THE MOMENT THE DOOR SHUT, I DROPPED TO MY KNEES beside Jacob, the crackling power vanishing from my palms. I cupped his face, my pulse racing, fear consuming my rage. God, his skin was so cold, colder now because Victoria or Sebastian's icy fear had left the room, and his eyes were squeezed tight in agony. Blood wept from the gashes on his chest, and his body shook as he drew desperate ragged breaths that were too far apart.

"Jacob." *Come on. Wake up.* I didn't know how powerful Sebastian's sleep spell was, but I knew if Jacob didn't feed now, he was going to die. "Please, Jacob. Wake up."

I didn't want a repeat of the pain I'd experienced when I'd saved Jacob after the archnephilim had nearly killed him and he'd bitten me without his magic, but it didn't look as if I had much choice.

Jacob convulsed, his back arching off the bed, and screamed again, the agony tearing at my soul. The veins in his neck bulged and his face turned red. He gasped in a breath, then went limp, his chest still.

No. "Jacob."

He wasn't breathing.

No no no. He wasn't going to die. He couldn't. Everything within me howled at the idea of losing him. Just like when Gideon had been dying, my soul was shattering. I couldn't lose him. I couldn't.

"Just hold on. Please. Hold on."

I entwined my fingers to do CPR—which, if I'd actually thought about it, was ridiculous because he'd never had a heartbeat to begin with—but he sucked in a strangled breath before I could do the first compression or figure out what else I could do to save him.

I wrenched my gaze away from him to search the opulent room for something I could use to slit my wrist. There wasn't time to wait for him to fully wake up. I didn't know *if* he'd wake up.

Victoria didn't just happen to have knives sitting out —although it wouldn't have surprised me if she had some somewhere—which meant I was going to have to break one of the glasses on her sidebar.

I jerked to my feet, but Jacob seized my wrist and wrenched me back. I fell onto my butt beside him. His dark gaze locked with mine, filled with wild, powerful intensity. Its weight crushed inside me like Victoria's had, except his didn't scare me, his filled me with determination and yearning and heartache.

"You shouldn't be here," he gasped.

"Neither should you."

His attention jumped to my cheeks, where Victoria

had dug in her nails and blood still dampened my skin. The intensity turned hungry, the monstrous nature, akin to Victoria's, that he'd always kept hidden now fully revealed, and his lips curled back revealing his fangs.

"Essie." A convulsion seized him, and he dug his claws—not nearly as big as a shifter's but just as sharp—into my wrist. "Essie, please."

Agony and fear swept through me, and a cold mist enveloped me. He was in such pain, his heart broken, his body breaking.

I cupped his cheeks again and leaned close. "You have to feed."

"I'll have no control."

"If you take too much, Gideon's brand will keep me alive."

His heartache ripped into my soul and tears welled in my eyes.

"That's not all I won't be able to control," he gasped.

"I know."

"I told Marcus—" Another convulsion tore through him, turning whatever he'd been about to say into a scream and then desperate, ragged pants. "God, Essie. I lied. I said our connection wasn't emotional, that I'd keep my distance, but—"

"I know." His mist gathered on my cheeks and a tear broke free. "There's something more between us than just your claim."

"There can't be. Vampires don't have mates like shifters and angels." He wiped my tear away with his thumb. "It can't be anything other than my claim. We've just met. We don't know each other."

"And I don't know Gideon and we're supposed to be soul mates." I held his gaze, fighting back more tears. He couldn't die. Not when I'd just found him. "This is real. I feel this more deeply than I feel a connection to Gideon, and I know you feel it, too."

Another convulsion seized his body, and he let out a strangled scream.

Please. Please don't die.

He was losing strength, his breaths farther and father apart again. "You have to feed."

"Essie—"

"I won't let you die." I dipped in and kissed him, letting him feel my need and desperation and sorrow at his heartache. I wasn't crazy. There was something between us. It wasn't the instant sizzling attraction I'd had with Marcus. It was quiet, certain, intense, just like his vampiric power. It sang in my heart and soul, coursing through my veins with every beat of my heart. Our essences were more than just entwined. Whatever magic bound us together, it wouldn't fade like his claim on me. It was more powerful than that.

With a groan, he tangled his fingers in my hair and took command of the kiss with a desperate, hungry need. His sorrow deepened, as if he believed that when this moment was over we'd go back to the way things were.

But there was no going back. I couldn't go back. Not to my normal mostly human life, and not to a time without him, or Marcus, or any of them.

"Feed," I whispered against his lips and kissed my way across his cheek to give him access to my neck.

He groaned, his breath hot against my throat.

My pulse picked up in anticipation of his bite, of the moment of pain and then the glorious swell of his magic.

His grip in my hair tightened and slowly, with a slice of pain and a whisper of sultry need, he sank his teeth into my neck. But another convulsion seized him, and he clenched down, shooting agony into my neck and digging his fingers into my scalp. A terrifying mix of my pain and his grief sliced into me, and every nerve burned as if I— no, *he* had been lit on fire.

I screamed, crushed by Jacob's enormous power, unable to breathe or think. His back arched and his claws dug deeper. Darkness swarmed my vision for a second... for eternity. I had no idea how long his body and soul possessed me, only that my every cell was attuned to him with a connection a hundred times stronger than his claim.

The convulsion released him. He sagged back to the bed, his teeth still deep and painful in my neck, his breath ragged. His body trembled beneath mine, and the chill of his skin had deepened. I didn't know how much more of this he could take.

Then, with a groan, he took a weak pull on my vein, and relief flooded me. His bite was still painful, but he was feeding. *Please let this stop the convulsions, let this fix whatever Victoria did to him.*

A small spark of his magic curled around my throat, easing the pain, and he took a deeper, stronger pull. His hand on my head relaxed a bit, and he wrapped his other arm around me and pulled me tight to his massive chest.

Another, deeper pull, and heat and desire exploded within me with sudden, bone-melting need. The temper-

ature in the room jumped to sultry, and my breath caught
in my throat. My whole essence throbbed with my desire
and my certainty of us.

A moan of pleasure slipped out, and he moaned back,
the sound low and deep in his throat, vibrating against
my skin and into the center of my being. It was like the
first time he'd claimed me, except so much more. This
connection was deeper, consuming, blazing, and right.

With a growl, he rolled us over, pinning me to the bed
with his massive body. His erection pressed into my thigh,
oh so close and yet oh so far from where I needed him.
That, and I was wearing far too much clothing. I needed
to feel his body brushing against mine, sliding into me.

I clutched his back, savoring all that hard muscle
relaxing and contracting as he shifted and breathed and
moved against me.

His magic sank deep into my core, twisting my need
tighter, and he took another long pull on my neck. The
room spun and darkened. I didn't know how much blood
he was taking, and I didn't care, so long as he lived. He
had to live. He could drink me dry, and I'd die happy if he
lived. And that wasn't his claim talking, it was something
else, something deeper within me. The same something I
felt for Marcus. I knew I could live without them if I had
to, but I'd be broken, a shell of who I was supposed to be.
These men were a part of my soul, and I would do
anything to ensure they were safe.

My breath came fast, pressing my breasts against his
chest again and again, my nipples growing more sensitive
with every second his magic grew within me. He trailed
his hand down my side, not even coming close to the

edge of my breast and still making my breath hitch. His magic contracted, so much stronger than anything I'd felt before. All the other times he'd been holding back. Now, he had no control, and with his bite lock, it didn't dissipate, just kept growing, filling me, until I was wound painfully tight with need.

I squirmed underneath him, the slide of my T-shirt against my hypersensitive skin ratcheting up my desire.

Jacob rumbled his pleasure, and my essence jerked with a tremble of a climax at just the vibration from his body.

"Jacob—" I gasped.

His hand slipped under my T-shirt, his fingers blazing a trail of need to my breasts. I arched into him, crying when he pushed aside my bra and pinched my nipple.

He growled and sucked harder on my neck, sending more magic flooding into my aching core. I needed him now. Please, God. I was going to combust if his power wasn't released.

I grabbed his hair and pulled him away from my neck. The intensity in his gaze stalled my pulse and made me shudder, teasing the throbbing climax within me. I couldn't catch my breath. His breath was just as fast.

"I'm taking my clothes off," I gasped.

His pupils dilated. "Yes."

I grabbed the hem of my T-shirt, and he sat back, giving me a breathtaking view of his naked body, the gashes sealed shut, his skin smeared with blood and absolutely perfect. Perfect powerful muscles, bulky chest and arms, taut abs, and huge erection. My mouth went dry with anticipation, and I yanked off my shirt and bra.

He flicked open the button on my jeans and pulled them and my underwear down to my ankles where they caught on my runners. With a snarl, he yanked it all off, tossing it to the floor beside the bed, and stared at me with hunger and desire.

"You're so beautiful." His heartache swelled in my chest again, bringing tears to my eyes and swirling mist around me.

I met his gaze, letting my desire for him fill my expression. How I felt for him wasn't just the throbbing need of his bite, but a truth I recognized in my soul. We were mates.

I reached for him, and he met me halfway, sliding his cheek against my hand, savoring my touch, before dipping forward and capturing my lips with his.

The kiss was ferocious, intense, and stole my breath. The throb of his magic clenched in my core, teasing the promise of my climax, releasing, teasing, releasing, teasing, until I was dizzy and aching. I raked my fingers down his chest, through the dusting of pale hair along his abs, and wrapped my hand around him.

"Essie," he groaned.

I pumped my hand down his erection, drawing a shudder and a rumble of pleasure. His eyes rolled back, and I slid my hand up his shaft and rubbed my thumb over his tip.

"God, Essie." His lips curled back, revealing his fangs, his expression hungry for more than just blood.

I pumped again. His breath hitched. He pushed my thighs apart and, with trembling restraint, settled between my legs. His erection brushed my folds, sending a shock of desire exploding through me. I bucked and ground against him, urging his tip into me. I was already wet and ready for him. I needed him inside me, needed to release his throbbing magic and cement the truth of what we were.

He grabbed my hips and slowly, oh so slowly, pushed inside, stretching me. My muscles clamped in anticipation, teetering already on the edge. I tried to move, drive him deeper and faster, but he held me tight, and kept the slow slide until I was panting and desperate and he was buried to the hilt inside me.

With a groan, he drew out and just as torturously slowly pushed back in. I dug my nails into his forearms, the promise of a mind-blowing, screaming climax burning in my core. His magic twisted and spun. I didn't think it could build stronger and yet now my entire body blazed with its promise.

"Please, Jacob. I need you."

He squeezed his eyes shut and shuddered.

"Please. Release me."

"Not yet," he said, his voice strained. And he drew back out, twisting his power tighter. "If you're going to be bite locked, you might as well enjoy it."

The memory of the mind-blowing climaxes I'd had with Marcus made my muscles clench, making him moan. "Pretty sure I have been enjoying it."

He locked gazes with me, ran his hands up my belly to my breasts. Sensation snapped, stealing my breath, making my whole body clench in anticipation, starting my climax and yet not crashing me over the edge. "You haven't been getting the full effect."

He pushed back into me. My hips now free, I ground against him, my mind and senses on overload. His hands raked over me, tweaking my nipples, scraping against my too-sensitive skin, until I was one heightened, aching nerve. *Oh, yes. God, yes.*

Then he leaned forward, stretched me further, and sank his teeth into my neck. Ecstasy exploded through me. He sucked, the sensation blazing straight to my core and making the room spin. I was pure bliss and blazing magic. There wasn't anything else but the feel of him filling me completely and his power racing through every cell of my being.

Shuddering, his climax on the verge as well, he rolled us over. I ground into him, taking him deep, and he grabbed my hips to steady me, urging me to sit back and ride him. When I did, he slid a thumb to my clit and rubbed rough circles, spiking explosive ecstasy through me.

His hips rolled with mine, finding my rhythm, and with a moan, he tipped his head back, his expression filled with a need and joy that matched my own.

I closed my eyes and gave myself over to the feel of him, large and hard inside me, rubbing all the right spots. The climax, which had been teasing me from the moment we'd started, trembled, tightened, stole all breath and thought, and then exploded.

It roared through me, a blaze of light and sensation, and I screamed, the only way I could release all the pleasure. Jacob tensed beneath me, his fingers digging into my flesh as his own climax took him.

Heat and power erupted through every cell in my

body with the full force of his magic. I screamed again, a second wave taking me, and then I was on fire, my skin burning up. The inferno contracted around my heart, Gideon's brand, and then seared up my arm with blinding agony.

CHAPTER 14

THE PAIN TORE ANOTHER SCREAM FROM ME. EVERY MUSCLE in my body seized, ablaze for an agonizing moment, then I lost all control, my muscles giving way. I collapsed on top of Jacob, unable to catch my breath, the room spinning.

Jacob's chest, warm against my cheek, rose and fell with deep quick breaths, and all I could think past the agony was that he wasn't cold. *He's going to live, and I'm cold.* It was as if I had taken his chill, a teeth-chattering freeze that reached deep into my soul.

In contrast, Gideon's brand on my right forearm burned, radiating beyond the edges of the sigil all the way to my shoulder, and my buzz stung like a million bees.

"Essie." Jacob rolled me off him.

I slid to the mattress, twitching and shivering. Tears welled in my eyes. What the hell was wrong now? But I couldn't get my mind to work and figure anything out. I was so dizzy, so weak, and so cold. *He's going to live. Thank God.*

At the edge of my vision, the door flew open, and a blur of blue-white light rushed in. No, not light, Sebastian, with his semi-translucent glowing faekin skin.

Jacob jerked up, putting himself between me and the door, and snarled.

"You have to get out of here," Sebastian said, hurrying toward us as if he didn't care that a massive vampire was threatening him.

Jacob's snarl deepened, and this time Sebastian stopped, his hands raised. "You just severed your link with Victoria. She doesn't know it yet, but when she does, she's going to be pissed."

"How do you know?" Jacob's vampiric intensity radiated off him in palpable waves, adding to the cold and spinning room and making my stomach churn.

"I don't know how you did it—"

"How do you know it's broken, faekin?"

"I watched it break. Explode is more like it."

I struggled to sit up, to move, to do anything other than hug myself, shaking with the cold and on the verge of passing out.

"You have to go." Sebastian frowned. "Is that an angelic mating brand on your arm? Did you just get added to Esther and Gideon's bond?"

Jacob's attention dropped to his arm, but from my angle I couldn't see what he was looking at. "I don't—" He turned to me and I strained to read his expression. Had he really just been branded?

He grabbed my hand, slicing agony up my arm. Tears welled in my eyes, and the cold sank deeper into me.

Sebastian drew closer. "No wonder she made an enemy of Victoria over you. You're her soul mate... her other soul mate."

"Her other *other* soul mate," Jacob said.

"There's another one in the bond?"

"Not exactly." Jacob squeezed my hand. "We have to go."

I nodded. Or at least I thought I nodded.

Jacob's expression darkened, and his fear frosted over my cheeks and belly. "Essie?"

I opened my mouth to say something, but couldn't get the words past my chattering teeth. A tear leaked down my cheek and my buzz flared.

"Come on, Essie." Jacob helped me sit. The world lurched with the movement, and I sagged into his embrace. "What the hell is wrong with her?"

"She's in shock. Very few supers can channel the amount of magic needed to sever a link between a sire and her offspring. Add the formation of an angelic mating brand and the blood loss—" He grabbed my T-shirt from the floor, handed it to Jacob, then untangled my feet from the blanket. "You can't stay here."

Jacob pulled me close, his arms protectively tight, and snarled at Sebastian. "Don't touch her."

"I'm trying to help."

"Why?" I forced out.

He flashed me a wicked smile filled with sexual invitation, the look shockingly similar to Kol's, as if he were Kol's icy twin, but it felt more like an act than anything else. "Victoria will kill you for taking Jacob from her, and you're just too interesting to die."

"She can't kill me. Laws... Gideon..." My lips went numb and the room darkened. "Marcus."

"Ah, so the wolf is the other part of the mix. Would have thought it was the incubus."

"Bane," Jacob growled, the deep sound rumbling in his chest and making me tremble. He shifted me and tried to pull my T-shirt over my head. I struggled to help, but couldn't stop shaking.

I should have been embarrassed as hell that I was naked in front of Sebastian, but I couldn't make my mind work past the pain and the cold and the holy hell Jacob was a part of my bond with Gideon.

"No time." Sebastian ran a hand through his spiky white and silver hair. "Wrap her in the sheet."

Jacob bundled me up in Victoria's red silk sheet, then pulled on his pants—which had been on the other side of the massive bed—and picked me up. Sebastian piled my clothes on top of me, and Jacob carried me out the door, cradling me in his arms. I pressed my cheek against his chest and savored the warmth of his skin.

He's alive.

I couldn't think past that, couldn't get warm, couldn't get my teeth to stop chattering, and couldn't get the tears to stop leaking from my eyes. It didn't matter that an angelic mating brand was supposed to be a beautiful wondrous thing, that my soul knew this was exactly the way it was supposed to be. The shock was overwhelming, and I didn't have the strength to fight it.

Bane left us at the door to the back stairs. I wasn't sure

if he said anything to me in my head or not, but he had a strange expression. We hurried out of Rouge, Jacob's fear deepening as we went and fully frosting my cheeks by the time we reached the JP SUV Jacob had parked in a side lot near the bar.

"I'll be okay," I gasped as he set me in the front passenger seat and buckled me in.

He didn't look convinced, and the frost crept up to my elbows and down my neck.

"We need to get you to Operations."

"No. Not Cassius." I didn't want to deal with him. Especially since the first thing he'd see would be me naked, wrapped in a sheet, with Jacob's bite on my neck. Unless Gideon had already realized Jacob had joined our bond. Would Gideon know? I had no idea how it worked, and would the brand also make Gideon and Jacob fall in love like I was supposed to fall in love with Gideon? I couldn't deal with that now. I couldn't deal with any of it. More tears ran down my cheeks and I hugged myself, desperate to stop shaking.

"Essie—"

"Please. Not Cassius," I begged. "Take me home."

"You need medical attention."

"I was like this with Gideon's brand." I'd thought I'd been in shock over the attack from the archnephilim, and I might have been, but I guess I'd also been in shock by being branded with a true angelic mating brand. "Please, Jacob. I just—" More tears leaked down my cheeks. "I just need you." And Marcus and, God help me, Gideon, and—

Shit, Kol. I'd told him to tell Gideon about Jacob if I

didn't call back. I found my phone—which by some miracle had stayed in my pants pocket—and shoved it toward Jacob, my fingers shaking too much to make a call. "Call Kol."

"Good idea. He'll be able to warm you better than I can."

My buzz flared, stealing my breath and making the world spin and darken.

"It's about time," Kol said.

I blinked. I'd completely missed Jacob dialing... or the SUV starting... or driving down the street beyond the UV-blocking canopy of the vampires' part of the Quarter.

"Meet us at Essie's," Jacob said, pulling onto the Quarter's main street and heading toward the ring park.

"Jacob? What happened? Where's Essie?"

"Just meet us," Jacob growled.

"I'm already there."

"Good." He hung up as Kol started to ask another question, and gunned it.

The trees and buildings and streetlights whipped by, a twisting, nauseating blur. I must have passed out because the next thing I knew, Kol opened my apartment door and Jacob strode past him straight to my bedroom.

"What happened— Your arm!" Kol said, following us.

Jacob threw back the covers on my bed, set me on the mattress, and tossed my clothes and runners to the floor. I curled into a shivering, weeping ball. I just couldn't get warm, and Jacob's fear wasn't helping.

"What happened? She's so pale." Kol sat beside me, and I shifted closer to his warmth. "And cold."

"She severed my link with Victoria and—" Jacob ran a

hand over the complicated, delicate gold threads of his sigil. It wrapped from his elbow, where Gideon's brand ended on me, and up and around to his shoulder.

"Holy shit," Kol breathed. He brushed his fingers across my shoulder. God. They were so warm. So so warm. I grabbed his hand and pressed my cheek against it, clinging to his heat.

"It's okay, Essie," he said, but his attention was on Jacob. "I'll take care of you."

"Please," Jacob said, his voice soft and heartbreakingly desperate.

Kol climbed in under the covers, wrapped his arms around me, and tucked my back tight to his chest. A whisper of his magic seeped across my neck with each of his gentle breaths, and a warm darkness enveloped me.

The cold vanished. My buzz vanished. So too did the ache in my arm, Jacob's heartache, and his fear. There was only peace and warmth and love. Marcus's love and now Jacob's. It filled my soul, and yet it didn't reach the fragile fractured part where Gideon should have been. God, I didn't know how he'd take this new development.

The thought of his rejection or his anger was crushing. It didn't make sense. I didn't love him. But that was the terrifying inexorable power of our angelic mating brand. At least I had Marcus. Thank God for Marcus and being so clear in his agreement of the situation. I could deal with Gideon and Cassius and anyone else because I was certain of Marcus and Jacob. They were mine. And I was theirs.

My buzz returned first, biting and crackling under my skin at its new uncomfortable normal. With a groan, I cracked open gritty, sore eyes to brilliant morning sunlight streaming through my bedroom windows. Kol still held me close, his body warm and soothing, but Victoria's sheet had shifted and now his one arm lay, flesh on flesh, between my breasts, his hand pressed against my heart, while his other hand cupped my naked butt.

My pulse picked up. The fuzz rushed from my head and vision, but before I could panic that I was in bed and naked with Kol, my gaze locked with Jacob's. He lay on top of the covers, close—because with his bulk the queen bed was barely big enough for the three of us—but not touching me. He still only wore his jeans, giving me a stunning view of his muscular, gash-free chest. He also wasn't bloody any more, which meant he must have cleaned up while I slept.

"Hey," he said, his voice low, making me shiver with desire. Magical shock aside, last night had been amazing —terrifying because of what Victoria had done to Jacob and amazing—and now I was naked in bed with him and my smoking hot incubus—

Who, jeez, wasn't mine.

"Are you warmer?" he asked.

"Yeah."

"Thank God." He brushed a lock of hair out of my eyes, his cool fingers lingering on my skin and yet heating my heart. "I've been dying to touch you all night, but you needed warmth and even after I feed I don't reach human body temperature."

"You've been watching me sleep?"

Kol murmured something unintelligible and his lips

brushed the back of my neck, sending another shiver of desire through me.

"And Kol," Jacob said with a soft smile. "I don't think I've ever seen him this peaceful. He hides it well, you'd have to really know him to see it, but he still carries a whole lot of pain from what those animals did to him."

And by animals, he meant nephilim.

"How often do you watch me sleep?" Kol asked, his voice thick and drowsy. He nuzzled my neck, heating my desire even more, and sighed with contentment. "Is there something you want to tell me, Jacob?"

Jacob's lips quirked. "Sorry, man. Don't mean to break your heart, but I'm taken." His gaze, filled with absolute joy, held mine, warming me with a different heat. The ache of uncertainty and regret from yesterday was gone. We'd fully awakened that thing between us, and he had nothing but love for me. I felt it in the slightly raised room temperature and as an honest to goodness emotion in my chest.

Kol shifted behind me and lifted his head above mine. His hand left my ass to prop up his head, and he groaned. "There's something really wrong with a vampire making googly eyes."

"I could make vampire eyes at you instead," Jacob said, letting the full intensity of his power bleed into his gaze.

Kol snorted and brushed his lips over my shoulder, a whisper of his power leaking into my skin and thrumming through me. "I'm glad you're awake and warm." He slid out of the bed, still fully dressed. "I'll leave you two to it," he said as he left, closing the bedroom door behind him.

The intensity in Jacob's gaze vanished, or rather changed back to awe and joy, and it settled back on me.

My buzz crackled, and I clenched my jaw to keep from twitching. Just one moment. That was all I wanted. One moment of peace. But that wasn't going to happen until I figured out how to deal with the damned buzz.

Jacob frowned. "How are you feeling?"

"I'm okay. Just—" What could I say? On fire and wanting to scratch off my skin? Shocked and amazed at us, at last night? Terrified of it, too? "Overwhelmed."

"Yeah. Me, too." He traced his fingers over my shoulder, drawing my attention to the new delicate gold lines etched in my skin. They curled from the top of my shoulder, around my biceps to my elbow, and joined Gideon's brand on my forearm with no indication where one complicated sigil started and the other began. "I'd been wondering if our brands were identical, but didn't want to uncover you and look."

"Are they?" I was pretty sure my brand and Gideon's were identical.

Jacob sat up and turned his right shoulder to me. Delicate gold lines traced from his shoulder to his elbow in an identical pattern to mine.

"You don't have Gideon's half," I said. "Does this mean he doesn't have your half?"

"I don't know."

I tried to recall if I'd read anything about that in the many texts I'd pored through when trying to find a way to remove the archnephilim's false brand. There might have been something about an angel with two mates who were only connected to that angel and not each other, but I'd only skimmed that story because that hadn't been what I was looking for at the time.

"If he doesn't have your half, do you think he knows about us?" A new horrible thought struck me. If Gideon wasn't part of my bond with Jacob, how did I explain a human and vampire sharing an angelic mating brand?

My buzz snapped through my back, and I gritted my teeth.

Worry clouded Jacob's expression. "It'll be all right," he said, probably taking my clenched jaw as fear over Gideon's reaction. "We'll all work this out. Even if I have to beat it into Gideon."

"You can't make him love or even like someone he doesn't want to. I'm not Zella." Even if he did eventually accept our bond and love me, it was going to take time. You didn't just get over someone in a couple of weeks. Certainly not someone you loved with the kind of love I'd seen when he'd been sitting at her bedside.

And just thinking about that made my soul ache. I didn't expect him to stop loving or mourning Zella, but I needed him to not hate me.

I pushed back the grief that always welled within me when I thought of Gideon and sat up, pulling Victoria's silk sheet up with me. Not that Jacob hadn't already seen my breasts... a couple times, but... I didn't know. I suddenly felt awkward and exposed. The room tilted ever so slightly, and I drew in a quick breath to steady myself.

"Hey, take it slow." Jacob grabbed my shoulders to

steady me. "You're still really pale. I took a lot from you last night."

"Because Victoria almost killed you," I said, unable to keep my anger from my voice.

"She didn't know the extent of our situation." Jacob ran a hand through his shoulder-length hair. It wasn't in its usual ponytail and hung loose around his face, making him more deliciously rugged. "*I* didn't know the extent of it. The bunny's blood was almost ineffective, and Victoria's blood should have healed me, not send me into convulsions."

"Why did that happen?" I wasn't going to talk about how they'd gotten to that point. His relationship with Victoria was over a hundred and fifty years old, complicated, and something that was going to take a long time for us to work out. "Her blood helped stabilize Gideon when he was shot. Why didn't it help you?"

"I don't know."

"Did I really sever your link to her?"

"Yes. I looked for it last night and can't sense it." Jacob's expression turned grim. "I don't know what she's going to do about that."

My buzz snapped in my lower back again, and I dug my knuckle into the muscle to get it to stop spasming.

"We'll figure it out." He captured my cheeks between his large hands and pressed his lips to mine in a tender kiss.

A warmth seeped low within me, my desire for him flaring. I shifted to deepen the kiss and embrace another hot sensual round of sex with Jacob but caught sight of my bedside clock. 7:32.

"What time is the morning meeting?" I asked against his lips.

Jacob cut off our kiss and pressed his forehead to mine. "You're not going to work today."

"Given how yesterday's op went, Cassius is going to fire me today. I want to get that done and grab my stuff in one fell swoop."

"He's not—"

I pressed a finger to Jacob's lips. "And if he's not, I should at least try to show up on time for my second day on the job."

Jacob held my gaze, all that intensity making my heart flutter and my desire burn hotter.

"Unless you need more," I said, suddenly breathless.

"Yes, but you're too weak. I'll visit a bunny. Hopefully it'll be enough to tide me over."

Disappointment swept through me, and I tried to hide it. The decision was practical, not emotional. He'd been on death's door, and I only had so much blood. I didn't have enough to give what he needed right now, not without dying. Besides, it wasn't as if he had to have sex with the bunny.

"I'm yours, Essie." He captured my lips with a fierce kiss, stealing my breath with his passion. "I have been from the moment I entwined my essence with yours."

"I know. Just still trying to wrap my head around all of this."

"Me, too," he said. "And if you really want to go to work, you should get dressed."

"Yeah. Might as well face my firing head on."

CHAPTER 15

Jacob left to give me privacy to change, and I quickly pulled on jeans, a T-shirt, and my second—and last remaining—stretchy jacket. Even though it was early summer and we were in the middle of an unusual heat wave, last night's chill hadn't fully left me. I could only hope moving around and thinking about something else would shake off the rest of my shock—a shock that had been stronger with the formation of Jacob's brand than with Gideon's. I didn't know if that meant my bond with Jacob was stronger or if my bond had needed extra juice to sever his link with Victoria.

"We don't have time for breakfast," I said, hurrying into the living room.

"We have time for whatever you need," Marcus said, folding a blanket and setting it on my couch.

My thoughts stuttered over him being there quickly followed by a sense of immense relief and joy. "Did you sleep on my couch?"

"Your bed isn't big enough for the four of us."

Kol, who was looking in my fridge, snickered.

Marcus glared at him. "Don't you have something better to do?"

"Just waiting on Essie."

"I called Marcus," Jacob said, "figured he'd want to be here."

"But Jacob needed you more than I did and you needed Kol, so I got the couch." Marcus pulled me into a firm embrace, clutching me to his hard muscular chest and pressed his lips to my forehead. "You looked so pale."

"I'm okay." I clutched him back, savoring the feel of his body against mine and his ferocious love for me. It filled my chest with emotion and heated the room.

"You still look pale."

"Victoria almost killed Jacob." My throat tightened. I'd almost lost him before I'd even realized what he meant to me.

Marcus raised his head. "You didn't tell me that."

"Pretty sure Victoria didn't mean to," Jacob said, his voice a low rumble. "Now I need to see a bunny to see if I can get a little stronger, and you need to get Essie to work."

Marcus stiffened. "You're not seeing a bunny. You said the angelic brand severed your link with Victoria. Until we know how she's going to react to that, no one goes anywhere alone."

"I can't feed from Essie. She's too weak. I'll kill her."

"You'll also kill her if Victoria kills you." Marcus released me and turned to Jacob. "You can feed from me."

"We're *so* going to be late for work," Kol said with a gleeful smile.

Marcus rolled his eyes at him. "I'm not bite locked like Essie."

"But your mate is standing right there and you'll be hopped up on Jacob's magic. Twenty bucks says your wolf won't be able to resist her."

"I have more control than that," Marcus growled. "Besides, Essie gets a say in it, too."

"Hey." Kol raised his hands in defense. "I'm not saying it's a bad thing. Just that your bonds are all very new and you're all barely holding back your urges." Hellfire flared in his eyes and his smile turned wicked. "I'm getting high on your sexual energy just standing in the room with you."

Marcus raked his hand through his wild dark locks. "Fine. Bite but no magic."

"It'll hurt," Jacob said.

"Then make it fast." Marcus turned his pale green gaze to mine, his wolf turning his expression ferocious. "Why don't you freshen up while we take care of this?"

Meaning what? Get out of the room so I didn't have to watch?

The memory of Jacob's bite swept through me, drawing a shiver of desire for both of my guys.

Kol hummed low in the back of his throat before jerking his attention back to my fridge.

Right. Giving them some privacy was probably a good idea. Especially if I wanted to get to work on time.

I retreated to the bathroom, retied my ponytail, and splashed water on my face. I really wished I had time for a shower but it was at least a fifteen-minute drive from my apartment to Operations, and I just didn't have the time. Not that I supposed being late really mattered. Without a doubt, Cassius was going to fire me.

I yanked my attention from those thoughts to the mirror. Once again, the woman staring back at me was too pale, her eyes still a little too wide and—

I frowned and leaned closer to the mirror. A whisper of angel glow flickered in my eyes.

Oh, shit. The spell on my contacts was failing.

Sebastian had warned me. I'd just thought—

Hell, I hadn't been thinking at all. So much had happened last night that I hadn't given any thought to my contacts. All I'd been able to think about was saving Jacob.

But if I didn't deal with the contacts right away, Cassius would do more than just fire me. Everyone knew a being with a human's essence and glowing eyes was a nephilim, and while the team had seen my new glowy eyes, they'd thought it was an aftereffect of fighting the archnephilim and it was supposed to have disappeared over a week ago.

I could explain it away like I had with my weird empathy, but too many revelations too soon would certainly draw suspicion. Especially since Cassius was looking for reasons to lock me away to ensure Gideon's safety.

And what would the other guys think? Was my bond with Marcus and Jacob strong enough to survive that kind of revelation? *Hey, guys, I'm that monstrous, mindless animal you hate. No, Michael didn't create me, but—*

God, they'd think I'd falsely branded them like the archnephilim had branded me. A naturally born nephilim was supposed to be impossible, and I'd been lying to them from the start. They wouldn't believe anything I told them, not this early in the relationship.

A small voice inside me said they'd stand by me, that our bond was true.

But the voice of fear that I'd lived with my entire life was stronger. No one would believe the truth. No one would want to take the risk of letting one of Michael's nephilim roam free.

Someone knocked on the bathroom door, making me jump.

"You ready?" Kol asked.

No, I wasn't. Without a doubt, the truth would come out. There wasn't any way I could hide it forever from my guys.

My throat tightened.

I wasn't ready to say goodbye, and certainly wasn't ready to see the looks on their faces when the truth came out.

I squared my shoulders. If I could just buy myself a couple more weeks, Cassius would be gone, and I'd have more time to show Marcus and Jacob how much I cared for them, as well as what kind of person I really was. Gideon might even agree to a truce.

"Essie?" Kol asked.

"I'm coming."

The glow wasn't obvious—if it had been, Jacob would have seen it while we were staring at each other in bed— so I could deal with the morning's meeting, but then I had to find a way to slip out to Squatters' Row and get my contacts re-spelled.

I rinsed my mouth with mouthwash and opened the door, my gaze instantly jumping to Marcus and Jacob by the front door. Jacob, still without a shirt since his had been left at Victoria's, looked a little less pale. I was surprised at how fast he'd healed, since Marcus was essentially a bunny and his blood shouldn't have had an immediate effect. Marcus looked good, too. He was tying up his combat boots, and I couldn't see a bite on his neck or either of his wrists, which meant he must have shifted and healed the wound, hiding the evidence. It also meant I'd spent longer in the bathroom staring at myself than I should have if he'd had time to donate and shift.

We piled into our vehicles, Marcus in the sedan, Kol in the SUV we'd taken yesterday afternoon, and Jacob and I in the SUV he'd driven to Rouge. I'd expected an argument from Marcus about who I rode with, but he just brushed my cheek with a quick kiss and told me to go with Jacob.

"You're looking better," I said as we drove to the Quarter.

"I can put to rest any doubt you might have about your connection with Marcus." He squeezed my knee, sending warmth fluttering through me. "His blood doesn't heal me as quickly as yours, but my essence recognizes your essence bonded to his. He's more effective than a bunny."

"That means Gideon's blood probably would be, as well."

"I'm not asking Gideon for a donation," Jacob said. "I'm not asking Marcus again, either. Not unless he lets me use my magic."

"If we had the time, I'm sure he would have."

The temperature in the SUV rose and Jacob glanced at me. "We'll figure this out, but things are... well, complicated."

"Now that I'm mated to three of you?"

"That, and keeping ourselves controlled while on the job. Certainly while Cassius is reviewing the team." He stopped at a red light. "Kol was right about our bonds being too new. All I want to do is take you back to bed. It wouldn't surprise me if Marcus wants that, too."

And all I wanted was to go back to bed with all of them.

"We're just going to have to be adults about this. We have a lifetime to figure this out." If they didn't learn the truth about me. "We don't have to rush."

Jacob's expression darkened, and I realized I had a lifetime, but Jacob and Gideon would outlive me.

Except I had no idea how long I'd live. The nephilim during the war hadn't allowed themselves to be captured. The only way to stop them was to kill them, and if by chance the Angelic Defense did get ahold of one, it was said they always turned their magic on themselves and committed suicide. Which meant I had no idea what the life expectancy of a nephilim was. For all I knew, I could be as long-lived as an angel—

And then I'd be alive and well with Jacob and Gideon, mourning Marcus when old age took him.

Jeez, I hadn't realized how complicated this whole situation really was.

"We'll figure it out," Jacob said. Again.

"Is that your new mantra? You've said it three times

this morning and we've been awake for less than an hour."

"Because you keep looking like you're about to panic. I'm not saying it'll be easy, but the brand on my arm says we're soul mates. The bond between you and Marcus says the same. We *will* make it work," he said, with such conviction my soul sang.

The light turned green and we continued to the Quarter, my buzz easing the closer we got to Operations. It was still painfully distracting, but clearly better. Which made me nervous. If Cassius did fire me and Gideon didn't want me around, was I going to spend the rest of my life feeling like I was hanging onto an electric fence?

Jacob followed Kol and Marcus into the garage and as their vehicles ahead of us turned and parked in their usual spots, my gaze locked on Gideon, standing straight ahead, without his shirt on. My thoughts stalled. He wore shorts and runners and held his shirt wadded in his hand. Sweat slicked his gorgeous muscular body and his breath came just a little too fast, as if he'd just finished running and had really pushed himself.

His brand hadn't changed, confirming I was the link between the three of us, and I was going to have to figure out how to answer the obvious question when it arose about a human and a vampire sharing an angelic mating brand.

Jacob parked, and I got out of the SUV. Gideon's gaze instantly landed on me, icy and hard, making my chest ache for even the possibility of a friendship.

He turned his back on me and glared at Marcus and Kol as they got out of their vehicles. "You all show up with Agent Shaw. Are you trying to get Cassius to disband —" Light flared from his eyes as Jacob came around the back of the SUV. "What. Is. That?"

"Guess what?" Kol said brightly. "Essie and Jacob are soul mates, too."

Gideon's expression jumped from shock to horror, and the temperature fluctuated so fast it made my stomach lurch. My buzz sliced through my neck, making me twitch, and still, even though it was clear the situation appalled him, I yearned for him.

"We'll deal with this later," he said, his tone sharp and cold. "Cover that up before Cassius sees it."

"Yeah," Jacob said, heading toward the door. "I'll be in your office in five for the morning meeting."

"Don't bother. It got postponed to eleven because you were supposed to be with Victoria. Didn't any of you look at your phones?" Gideon's eyes narrowed. The temperature lurched again, then he squared his shoulders and I was surrounded by a mild chill—probably the actual temperature of the garage. He'd locked his emotions down and become the emotionless angel he was supposed to be. But I didn't need to feel anything more from him. I already knew how he felt about me.

"Your text didn't indicate it was urgent and last night got—" Jacob glanced at me, and I could see the question in his eyes: did we tell Gideon everything?

He was going to find out eventually, if he hadn't already figured it out. Might as well tell him now.

"The short version is," I said, "Jacob's debt is paid but Victoria is one pissed master vampire." My buzz snapped through my neck again, and Jacob shifted toward me.

The muscles in Gideon's jaw clenched. "My office in three hours," he said and stormed to the door. "And eat something, Agent Shaw, before you pass out."

"Well, that went as well as expected," Kol said.

My throat tightened as Gideon left. Why the hell did it hurt so much? I had Marcus and now Jacob. I didn't need Gideon. But my God damned soul disagreed.

"I should—" I wasn't sure what I should do—

No, I *was*. I needed an excuse to get to Squatters' Row. It was about a twenty-minute walk from Operations, and I had more than enough time to get my contacts fixed right now.

"I should grab something from the cafeteria then lie down. It's been an exhausting couple of nights."

"I'll join you," Marcus said.

Of course he'd offer that, and I ached to say yes.

I grabbed his hands and met his piercing green gaze. I could see his wolf in his eyes, but it didn't darken his expression. It was content.

"If you join me, I'm not going to get the sleep I really need."

"I can be good."

Kol snorted.

Marcus glared at him. "What? I can."

"Bet you another twenty on that," Kol said. "I'm getting the hell out of here, because I can't keep my shields up to the level needed to protect against you two — you *three* for the next three hours." He shrugged and sauntered from the garage.

"Come on, Marcus," Jacob said, jerking his chin to the

door. "We can keep it together without her for three hours."

"I know, but I don't want to." He tangled his hands in my hair and captured my mouth in a fierce kiss. "But I will because you do need the rest."

He turned me to face Jacob, who cupped my cheeks and kissed me tenderly, steadying me from Marcus's ferocious passion and filling me with warm certainty.

"Call if you need us," he said, and they headed inside.

God, I needed them right now. Always.

But I resisted calling them back as my guilt that I'd lied to them twisted in my gut.

This was for the best. Maybe by the time the second spell on the contacts had worn off, the glow would finally be gone from my eyes.

I doubted it, and eventually the truth would come out. But not now. I wasn't ready. I'd just found them, just realized what it was to have someone who cared about me and to be a part of a... hell, of a family. God, I wouldn't ever be ready to lose everything.

CHAPTER 16

I HURRIED OUT OF THE GARAGE BEFORE I COULD CHANGE MY mind. With luck I could sneak back in, grab something from the cafeteria, and get at least an hour's sleep before the morning's meeting. The sun warmed my skin and by the time I'd reached the edge of Squatters' Row I'd managed to work off most the night's bone-deep chill. In fact I felt better than I had in a long time. I'd thought my life before the archnephilim had been fine, but it had been empty. It had been empty since cancer had taken my mom from me just after my seventeenth birthday and I'd been forced to live my life under the radar alone.

Now it was full and amazing and perilous.

God, if my mom could see me now, she'd be horrified. I was a JP agent. And I *wanted* to be one. I was mated to an angel and lived in angel central. She'd say I was asking for trouble and demand to know how I could have been so foolish.

But it was fate. And as much as I didn't believe in fate, that a person made their own fate with their decisions and actions, I couldn't deny it had nothing to do with my situation. I hadn't chosen to have Gideon's brand, and I'd tried to go back to life-as-normal after the archnephilim, but the world of the supernatural had sucked me back in.

I couldn't fight this even if I wanted to. Which I didn't. I might have to accept it was too dangerous to be a part of the team—and God, just thinking that made my stomach churn with frustration—but I couldn't leave my guys. Something deep inside me knew they needed me as much as I needed them. Even Gideon.

I reached the witch's shop in the heart of Squatters' Row. It sat in the back of an abandoned building that used to have a restaurant on the main floor and apartments on the two stories above. The entrance lay around back, off the alley where the restaurant would have accepted deliveries.

A small Eye of Horus drawn in black marker near the top of the solid metal security door was the only indication I was at the right place. I'd found Mystic Mavis by doing an online search on the dark web. I was supposed to only use my dark web connections in an emergency, to change my identity and relocate if JP agents were closing in on me, but given my situation, there wasn't any way I'd be able to go to a registered witch to hide my glowy eyes —at least not without him or her alerting the authorities.

I opened the door, my buzz blazing, setting my skin on fire, and stepped into the long hall between the storage room and the walk-in fridge and freezer. Incense thickened the air with a purple haze that clung in my nose and the back of my throat. Large black glyphs decorated the walls, and low lighting gave the place a creepy ambiance. I hadn't enjoyed visiting Mavis the first time, and so far this time didn't feel any different.

"Changed your mind about a love charm?" a raspy alto said from the end of the hall.

"No." I gritted my teeth against my twitching muscles and stepped into what had once been the restaurant's kitchen. Most of the stainless steel counters had been taken out, replaced by dark-wood bookcases crammed with books and trinkets and boxes and other strange, twisted things. What remained of the counters lay between the sink and stove along the right-hand wall, cluttered with bowls, vials, and jars. One side of the two-compartment sink was filled with dirty dishes, and a pot of something foul-smelling simmered on the stove—and I could only presume the stove was heated by magic, since the building had neither gas, oil, nor electricity.

"I'm sure you've changed your mind," Mavis said.

She sat in the middle of the kitchen in a high-backed wooden chair, behind an intricately carved table. She was bedecked like a gypsy from an old movie with a billowy blouse cinched tight by a black corset that accentuated her ample breasts, and a skirt made of many layers of gauzy material. A multi-strand chain headpiece barely held back her wild black locks, the decorative glass...? or were they actually diamonds...? inset in the delicate gold chains catching the light of the three dozen candles placed around the room.

"I'm not interested in a love charm. Your contacts are failing."

"My spells don't fail." She leaned forward, making her

dozens of bracelets and three necklaces tinkle together, and her large hoop earrings sway.

"Take a look for yourself," I said, keeping my voice even. I needed to approach Mavis from a position of confidence but not confrontation. The witch might look like a pre-war cliché and sell illegal love charms, but she possessed powerful magic. If I hadn't been able to tell by the way my skin crawled the closer I got to her, I still would have known by the reactions she received on the dark web.

Mavis pointed to the stool across from her, and I forced myself to walk the fifteen feet and sit. My buzz snapped and bit and even the magical channels in my head throbbed. Jeez, I hadn't noticed that pain for a while and had hoped that was on the mend.

The purple haze swirled, thickening around Mavis, and her power slid over me, curling against my skin, seeking entrance.

I gritted my teeth. She hadn't done this before—

No, she had. I just hadn't been able to feel it with such clarity before. Which either meant she was using more power or more of me was changing, becoming more sensitive to magic. I really hoped it was the former and not the latter.

She frowned, pursed her small, blood-red lips, and narrowed eyes almost as dark as Jacob's when he revealed his full vampiric nature. Her power tightened, no longer a caress seeking entrance but a slice, cutting into me, drilling into my core to expose the truth.

I held my breath, trying not to fight her. I needed her

spell. I couldn't afford to accidentally force her out. But God, the invasion made my buzz blaze and my heart race.

Please finish. I didn't know how much longer I could resist the pressure building within me. *And please don't let her decide I'm too dangerous to be a customer and tell the JP I'm a nephilim.* Especially since the JP representatives in town were Gideon and the team and the whole point of the visit was to avoid them knowing the truth for just a little longer.

"You're going to need something stronger than just the contacts," she said.

Which of course would cost me more money. A lot of it, probably. "How long will that last?"

"Not forever, if that's what you're asking."

"That's not an answer."

"Feel free to ask around for a better deal." Mavis flashed me perfect teeth with one gold canine. "Oh right, you can't. None of my colleagues are powerful enough to cast what you need. None of my illegal ones, that is."

"I wasn't asking for a better deal, just better details." My buzz snapped in my thigh, and I ground my knuckle into the muscle. I was trapped, and I hated being trapped. If I wanted to keep my secret a little longer, I had to buy whatever Mavis was selling for whatever price she demanded. The only thing I could hope for now was that her spell would last long enough for me to solidify my bond with my guys so they'd be able to come to terms with what I really was.

Except a tiny voice inside me wondered if they ever would. Would I accept one of them if it came out that they were lying to me and had been from the start?

Mavis leaned back, her power slicing into my skin again. "Let's just say I wouldn't make plans more than a year out."

I bit back my relief. I could handle a year. Cassius would be gone—surely he'd be gone—and I'd have time to show my guys who I really was, prove to them I wasn't the monster they thought all nephilim were. Seeing my actions for a whole year would be enough time for them to know me, my soul, and see beyond what I was.

"How much?"

"Two hundred and fifty grand."

"For one year?" That would put a serious dent in my secret offshore bank account and then I wouldn't have much left if I needed to run—not that I could because of the brand—but I also wouldn't have much left for the next year or the year after that.

Except I wasn't going to have the spell recast... right? I only needed it for a year.

But the panic racing through me screamed I'd want more time, I wanted all the time I could get. No one would understand what I was. God, if Gideon hated me now, he'd despise me when he learned the truth.

"Don't try and barter, the cost is non-negotiable," Mavis said.

"I don't have that kind of money," I lied, testing to see if she would just kick me out or if her greed would make her suggest a different price.

"Then you're going to have to find it." A wicked smile pulled at her red lips. "Unless you'd like to give me some of that glow."

"My glow?" I asked, pretending I didn't know what

she was talking about. Sebastian had said some witches paid a lot of money for angelic light magic, but I hadn't had time to learn more about that. Jacob had said angels didn't sell their magic but hadn't mentioned the reason, and I suspected I wouldn't like the answer. But if it kept my secret...

"Your glow. Your light magic. I can feel it in the core of your power." She flicked her fingers and a glass orb rose from a wooden shelf behind her and floated to the table. Light flickered like weak miniature lightning in the churning clouds captured in the orb. "Fill this every year, and I'll keep casting the spell."

Except what was the actual cost? I didn't know enough about what would happen to give her my light. Would I lose the ability to cast the light strike spell? At the moment that was the one thing keeping me alive on the job. Would Gideon or Jacob notice? That would make them ask questions I was trying to avoid. Giving Mavis my light magic could make my situation worse. I needed more information.

"I need to think about it."

"What's there to think about?" Mavis asked, her tone sickeningly sweet. "I could throw in a love charm."

"I don't need a love charm." She really wanted my light, which only made me more reluctant to give it to her.

"Everyone needs a love charm."

"No. Thank you."

"You need my spell. There won't be any place you can hide." Her tone jumped from sweet to dangerous, and she grabbed my wrist with her magic.

My buzz flared, and I jerked to my feet, ripping free of her power. "I need to think about it."

"I wouldn't think too long. My spell on your contacts will fail within twenty-four hours."

"Then I guess I have twenty-four hours."

"Two hundred and fifty grand or your light, little nephilim," she called as I hurried from the kitchen.

I hit the crash bar and stumbled into the alley, my gut churning. There had to be another way. Even if I paid her now, there was no guarantee she wouldn't turn me in, especially if she thought I wouldn't keep paying.

Someone hiding behind the door seized my wrist and wrenched me off balance.

My fear lurched from Mavis to the new danger. I jerked to face my assailant, the palm of my free hand blazing with divine light without me even thinking of the light strike spell, and I came face to face with Kol.

Shit.

The light exploded from my hand, and I wrenched my aim down, blasting a deep gouge in the asphalt at our feet.

He shoved me against the restaurant's concrete wall without even blinking an eye at my blast, his forearm pressed against my chest. Hellfire blazed from his eyes, but with anger not desire. "What the hell are you doing?"

"What are *you* doing?" I shot back as my pulse skyrocketed. He'd figured it out. Of course he'd figured it out. He was the most magically sensitive of the guys, and he wasn't influenced by any kind of bond. He already knew my essence was more light than dark. Hanging out with me was like being with an angel without me being an angel. And God! He'd been able to sense the Divifend. He'd probably noticed the enspelled contacts.

"I'm following an idiot," he said. "That's what I'm doing. What part of no one goes anywhere alone didn't you understand?"

"Kol—" My thoughts raced. What did I tell him? The truth. I had to tell him the truth and pray he didn't arrest me or—

But panic clenched my jaw and made my pulse race. He, out of everyone in the group, had the most reason to fear and hate nephilim. I had to do this delicately, find the right words. I didn't want him reliving whatever horror he'd experienced during the war.

"And don't tell me you didn't think about not sneaking here alone. You're smarter than that." He shoved away from me and ran his hands through his dark locks, mussing them even more and making me heat with desire.

Tell the truth. Come on, Essie. Just do it. It was the only way to salvage this. Perhaps we had a strong enough connection that he wouldn't freak out. Perhaps if he understood why I was so afraid, he'd forgive my lies. *Please, God, he had to understand. They all did.*

"You don't need sex magic to keep Marcus, Essie. Trust me, you're all he needs."

Really? That again? "That's not why I'm here."

"Stop lying. I know what I feel every time you have sex. I can find the charm on you easily enough."

"I swear. I'm not using sex magic. Kol, I—"

"For fuck's sake." He raked his gaze up my body.

My pulse quickened, and the memory of yesterday's

dream flooded me with need. I ached for his touch, his lips, the full force of his power sliding into me. All of him in me, driving me to—

Jeez, if he didn't pull his magic back, I was going to rip my clothes off and beg him to take me.

"Kol, please," I gasped.

His gaze reached mine, his expression hard, making me think of angry, ferocious sex. With his power, he could make pain pleasurable. I'd never wanted that before, but right now if he asked, I'd say yes.

"How the hell do you not have a love spell on you? The power of your energy with Marcus has to be enhanced."

I shuddered, trying to tamp down my desire and draw breath to answer him.

He leaned closer, almost nose to nose. If I shifted forward, I'd be able to kiss him.

Which, God, I didn't want to do. Because he wasn't mine. This was just his power influencing me. That was all. Really.

"What's on your eyes? The spell is so subtle. You're clearly trying to hide something." His breath feathered across my cheeks.

My buzz snapped, slicing through my desire.

He jerked back with a gasp. "Are your eyes glowing?"

"Yes." This was it. Imprisonment or lab rat. Everything my mother had feared for me. "They never stopped glowing after the archnephilim."

"So you decided to visit the shadiest witch in the Quarter? Jeez, Essie. Why didn't you come to us?"

"Why didn't I go to you?" Didn't he realize the truth? And if he didn't, should I keep lying?

"Essie, you can trust us," he said, his tone soft, his eyes sad, heartbroken at the thought that I didn't trust him.

"No, Kol, that's not—"

"I might be able to understand you visiting Mavis after the archnephilim. You were trying to avoid us, but now? After you and Marcus have clearly worked things out, and now you and Jacob—" Kol frowned and pulled his buzzing, lit-up phone from his pocket. The call display only showed a number, but Kol's expression darkened as he accepted the call. "Yeah?"

"Jacob is back early," Cassius said, only audible because of my enhanced hearing. "Summer's lab in ten."

"I'm twenty minutes out."

"Fine," Cassius snapped, and the line went dead.

"Okay, I take it back." Kol shoved his phone back into his pocket. "I completely get why you snuck back to Mavis to respell your eyes."

Except I hadn't paid for the respell and within twenty-four hours I was either going to have to agree to Mavis's demands or risk everyone seeing me for what I really was.

CHAPTER 17

"WE'LL GET RID OF CASSIUS THEN DEAL WITH YOUR EYES," Kol said as we hurried back to Operations. "It shouldn't surprise anyone that you're developing some magic, not with two angelic mating brands, but you're right. Cassius is a complication that's best avoided."

"Why shouldn't it be a surprise?" I asked.

"Angelic mating brands are powerful. They change both—" He flashed me a wicked grin. "—or rather, *all* of those involved. There weren't a lot of recorded bonds with non-angels and only one with a human, but the non-angels always developed or grew their magic. Sometimes in significant ways."

"When did you become an expert on angelic mating brands?"

"I did some reading after you left us."

"Really?" I raised my eyebrows at him. I didn't know why that surprised me, but it did. "After I left you?"

"Fine," he said, "after I realized I missed your energy. I wanted to know if you'd come back."

"According to what everyone tells me, I won't be able to resist Gideon." And the ache in my soul said that was true. Except Gideon was doing a perfectly good job at resisting me.

"You're soul mates, destined to be together."

"But I'm also soul mates with Jacob and Marcus."

"Who says there's only ever one?" Hellfire flickered in his eyes, making me shudder with desire, then his expression turned strange—worried? sad? I wasn't sure—and he yanked his attention back to the street ahead of us. "You humans can be so weird. If incubi could have soul mates, it would have to be more than one. We wouldn't be able to get enough sexual energy from just one person. We'd either starve to death or end up killing our mate."

I had no idea what to say to that, nor to his strange expression, but my phone rang before I could figure out a response. It was the same number that had flashed on Kol's phone a few minutes ago.

"Shaw," I said.

"Summer's lab in ten," Cassius snapped over the line.

"Copy that."

He hung up. Guess I was getting fired in front of the whole team. But hey, at least I had a reasonable explanation for all my weird magic. Everyone would think it was because of the mating brands and no one ever needed to know what I really was.

We made it to Summer's lab barely within my ten-minute deadline. Cassius stood at Summer's keyboard looking at the big screen on the wall, now showing the satellite image of a different, fully abandoned, mostly leveled section of town, while Gideon stood a few feet away, his arms crossed, his expression hard. He'd changed into a dress shirt and slacks, but now that I'd seen his hard, sculpted chest and abs, I couldn't think of anything else.

I resisted the urge to step close to him and fully mute my buzz. It was at the dimmest level it had been all day, almost post-nicotine levels from before the whole arch-nephilim incident, and I needed to just be happy about that.

Marcus and Jacob stood a few feet from Gideon, and I also felt a call to go to them, but for a different reason. Standing with them would make me feel strong when Cassius fired me. And I wasn't going to resist that. To hell with telling Cassius with our body language that there was something going on between us.

I drew up close to them, Marcus in his T-shirt, jeans, and perpetual sexy scruff, and Jacob in an out-of-character long sleeve shirt, the sleeves drawn down hiding the mating brand. They shifted so they stood behind me, showing their support and making Cassius glare at me.

Kol stopped close enough to look like part of the group but didn't actually stand behind me. Instead, he leaned against the same still-empty table from yesterday and crossed his arms, radiating relaxed sexual confidence. I didn't see Summer, but she could have been in one of the other labs attached to hers, or taking a quick break. I didn't know her well enough to know if she was purposefully avoiding the could-cut-it-with-a-knife tension between Cassius, the guys, and Gideon, but it wouldn't have surprised me.

"Marcus, you had another meeting last night with the wolf pack alpha," Cassius said.

"Another five teenagers dead from zip, and one of the wolves who found them accidentally picked up a pill without gloves and is in the hospital."

"Just by touching a pill?" The words blurted out before I could stop them. That put zip in the same dangerous category for supers as fentanyl was for humans.

"The mortality rate is high," Marcus said. "Four times higher than humans. I don't know why supers are even trying the stuff."

"And who's selling it to the pack?" Jacob asked.

"That's too many deaths in a forty-eight hour period." Light flared from Gideon's eyes. "We have to stop this. We should set up a sting, see if we can nab the dealer."

"No," Cassius said, making Gideon stiffen. "We need to stop this at its source. Summer cracked the lock on the pit fiend's phone. It pings the most from a cell tower in the Quarter and this neighborhood." Cassius pointed to the screen. "The last number the pit fiend called is in this warehouse, right now."

"So we're what? Going to blindly run in there?" Marcus asked. "We don't know what's there, if anything, and we don't know how many are inside. The last time we assaulted one of this operation's locations, Gideon almost died. And we'd *known* roughly what to expect."

"I didn't say anything about blindly running in, Agent Diaz." Cassius glared at Marcus. "I'm here to remind your team to exercise caution and not cause another incident with the humans. This is a recon mission. We check out who and what is in this building and the surrounding area." He swept his gaze over the rest of the team. "And yes, this is a part of your evaluation."

"In the garage in five," Gideon said, his tone void of emotion. "Everyone wears a vest."

Jacob, Marcus, and Kol shared a look then glanced at me. So far Cassius hadn't said anything to or about me. He'd barely looked at me, and his emotions were locked down tight. Actually, everyone's were. The room temperature was normal, if a little warm because of my jacket—which I wasn't taking off because that would reveal Jacob's still-healing bite on my neck and the addition to my angelic mating brand.

"Come, Essie," Jacob said. "I'll meet you in the armory and get you set up."

"No. Agent Shaw, you're with me." Cassius strode toward the door, not looking to see if I followed.

Marcus stepped toward me, but I shook my head, stopping him, and hurried after Cassius. My stomach churned and my buzz grew stronger the farther I got from Gideon. I was going to have to face my firing without my guys. Which, as much as I wanted the support of just being near them, was probably for the best. I couldn't afford to make an enemy of Cassius, not when I was permanently bound to his brother, and I didn't want Marcus to lose his temper and ruin his career.

We got into the elevator, but instead of hitting the main floor button to escort me out the door, Cassius selected the basement.

I bit the inside of my cheek to stop myself from speaking. The best plan was to let him make the first move.

There were any number of reasons to take me down to the basement. Perhaps he wanted to fire me as he got ready. Perhaps there were more cells, in the back, beyond the library stacks, where he was going to lock me up to protect Gideon.

The door slid open, and Cassius headed straight to the armory and pressed his thumb to the fingerprint scanner, unlocking the door.

"Gideon's report on the feral vampire nest in the subway tunnel says you're familiar with an M4 carbine." Cassius headed straight to the M4s, pulled one from the rack, and set it on the narrow table in the center of the room, then he grabbed a box of ammo and a magazine from the ammunition shelves. "Ammunition enspelled with a stun spell. Be mindful of your shots. It's expensive. But also don't forget the op from the bar yesterday. The rounds are too small for a strong stun spell, so most supers require two shots."

Now I was confused as hell. It sounded like I was going on this mission. "So you're not firing me?"

He captured me with his icy pale gaze, so much like Gideon's it made me ache. "It's been made clear to me that I have to have a human working actively on the team, even if she is a liability. We need to move on this intel and shut this zip operation down before more supers die, and I don't have time to wait for your replacement to show up."

Ah. So he wanted to fire me but couldn't. Not yet, at least.

He drew my service weapon from the ammunition cabinet and set it beside the M4. "You do what I say, when

I say it, and always stay with a team member." The temperature rose, revealing how much he hated this plan.

I wasn't sure I disagreed with him. I still had no good answer to how I could be a part of the team while ensuring the guys didn't end up hurt.

"Is that clear, Agent Shaw?"

"Yes, sir."

"Your file indicates you'll have trouble with that."

Jeez. I just couldn't get away from that one rookie mistake.

"You stole a divine light ring and snuck out to face an archnephilim alone, and disobeyed a command from a senior agent and left the team while clearing out that feral vampire nest."

"I was the only one free to back up Jacob."

"That's not the point." Light flared in Cassius's eyes, and the temperature rose a few more degrees. "Every time you do something like that, you endanger Gideon."

Not myself and Gideon. Just Gideon.

My buzz flared, and the muscles between my shoulder blades spasmed. I clenched my jaw, putting up with the pain since there was no way to rub it out without contortions.

"Fill that magazine." He jerked his chin to the M4's magazine before turning to the locker with the bullet-proof vests.

I started filling the magazine.

"Your file also indicates Jacob's claim on you is strong enough to enhance your vision." He didn't sound happy about that, and there was no point in denying it.

"Correct."

"At least you won't mess up the team's night vision." He pulled out two vests, set one on the table, and shrugged into the other one.

I finished filling the M4's magazine, inserted it into the carbine's well, and pulled back the charging handle to chamber a round.

"Amiah also says Jacob's claim has enhanced your healing." He set a waistband holster with my Glock on the table.

"Also correct." I checked my Glock's magazine. It had been reloaded since I'd handed it over to Cassius in Hacksaw's parking lot. I chambered a round in my sidearm and holstered it. "Anything else, sir?"

The muscles in his jaw flexed and the temperature flashed to normal. He was locking his emotions down. Not a good sign.

My buzz snapped again, cramping my thigh. Shit.

"Put on your vest." He grabbed a package of red zip ties, then strode to the door and waited for me to pull on the vest and leave the armory before making sure the door was secure.

We took the elevator back to the first floor and met the rest of the guys in the garage. Gideon had changed into a black T-shirt, bulletproof vest, and fatigues. The other guys had just added vests and weapons.

My buzz eased, but the grating tension grew. This was going to be a problem if we didn't get this solved soon.

Cassius handed Marcus the keys to an SUV and we piled in, with Cassius in the front passenger seat. Gideon got in next and there was an awkward moment between Kol and I about who'd get in with him.

"I'm the smallest, I'll fit better with Jacob," I said, my voice low so Cassius and Gideon couldn't hear us.

"You're not going to be able to avoid him forever," Kol said.

"Just as soon as he stops looking at me like I'm his worst nightmare."

"Whenever you're ready, Agent Shaw," Cassius said, his voice thick with sarcasm.

I headed to the back to join Jacob, forcing Kol to get in beside Gideon.

Marcus pulled out of the garage, and we headed out of the Quarter. The satellite image hadn't been wide enough for me to tell which abandoned part of town we were going to, it could have been any number of areas, but the moment we passed through the park ring, we turned south. Guess we were headed toward the industrial area where I'd fought the archnephilim.

My pulse thrummed the closer we got, and even my buzz crackled stronger, as if just drawing close to the spot where I'd blasted myself with massive amounts of divine light set it off.

I gritted my teeth. I was only a few feet from Gideon. That should have been enough to ease it. But it wasn't, and I liked the idea of me participating on this mission less and less. It was dangerous if I couldn't focus.

Jacob squeezed my knee, leaving his hand there, heavy and comforting. "You've got this," he mouthed.

I offered him a weak smile and pressed my hand on top of his. I wasn't sure I had this at all, but I was glad he had my back.

We turned away from the industrial area where everything had changed for me and drove into the old ware-house district near the now-abandoned rail yards. The pain from my buzz didn't diminish, but if I wanted to prove I could handle this job, I couldn't ask to sit this op out. I had taken out an archnephilim and stopped a hell-fire prince from escaping. I could handle a little recon while surrounded by my guys.

The bright morning sun shone on the destruction around us. The buildings had been packed together, sitting side by side with narrow alleys between them or sharing walls, and had been easy targets for Michael's nephilim. One blast had taken out multiple buildings and destroyed goods and supplies that had been unloaded from the trains.

"Jacob and Kol, you've got the rear," Cassius said, turning in his seat and passing a handful of communication ear pieces to Gideon. "Marcus and I will take the front."

We stopped a block from a cluster of still mostly-standing buildings and got out. Birds chirped and some-thing creaked in the gentle breeze. I slipped the sling of my M4 over my head and pushed my sleeves up to my elbows, hoping Cassius wouldn't notice the little bit of exposed extended mating brand. It was just too warm for the jacket and with the physical exertion and adrenalin of doing recon, it was only going to get warmer.

Gideon glanced at my arm, his back stiff, and turned away from me.

"Com test," Cassius said as he handed out handfuls of the red zip ties.

I slipped the ear piece into my ear as Jacob

responded, pocketed a handful of ties, and drew one of his two Berettas.

"Marcus. Check." He drew his sidearm as well and accepted a handful of ties.

Kol took his ties, and drew one of his long daggers from the sheaths hidden on his back beneath his shirt. "Kol. Check."

"Essie. Check."

The muscles in Cassius's jaw flexed, followed by a flicker of heat, and he held out half a dozen ties to me. "They have a magic containment spell that will last an hour."

I shoved the ties into my pocket, surprised that Cassius would include me. Of course, if we needed the ties, that meant the recon mission had turned into a raid, and everyone having the means to contain a super's powers was probably a good idea.

"Eyes open," he said, his voice coming from my left and yet in my ear at the same time.

I raised my M4 and scanned the surrounding rubble through the scope. No sign of movement, but given that I couldn't use the thermal setting on the scope in the bright sunlight, anyone could have been hiding in the shadows.

We hustled as quietly as we could to the closest still-standing warehouse, a three-story red brick structure with a faded black and white logo painted on the side. There wasn't a single sign of activity, no people, no vehicles, nothing, which didn't surprise me. Lots of areas had been destroyed and abandoned, and there were abandoned places closer to the center of town with actual apartments and houses where it was more convenient to squat. I couldn't decide if that meant this was an ideal place for criminal activity or not because no one was around. No one to notice someone coming or going, but also no one to hide among.

"Second building down," Cassius whispered.

Marcus sniffed. "I've got more than five supers, but their scents are old."

"There has to be a fresh one," Cassius said. "We know someone is in the building."

"Could have come from the other direction." Marcus glanced past the open bay door into the abandoned warehouse, then hurried past to the next building, our main objective.

This one didn't have a big bay door, but it also didn't have a door blocking the front so Marcus could easily peek inside. It stood three stories with tall windows, some with large shards of glass still stuck in the frames. The far corner of the top story had collapsed, taking the weight of the four-story warehouse leaning against it.

"Jacob, Marcus, scout around back. Kol, Shaw, stay here." Cassius glanced at Gideon. "You're with me."

Cassius and Gideon hurried down the street ahead of us, while Marcus and Jacob doubled back and disappeared around the side of the red-brick warehouse.

I rescanned the area. Five warehouses stood on the other side of the wide road that was mostly massive potholes. All were missing their windows, and none of them had been boarded up like buildings in the neighborhoods closer to the center of town. A tattered gray tarp fluttered half out of a third-story window, and every time it went limp I could see streaming sunlight from a hole in the roof. I turned my attention to the building beside it and the darkness beyond the second-story windows. No sign of anyone.

"All clear around back," Marcus said over the coms.

"Clear to the end of the street," Cassius said as he and Gideon hurried back, stopping on the other side of the doorway of our target building.

We waited for the others to return, then resumed our previous search order with Marcus and Cassius slipping inside first. I glanced again at the buildings across the street as Gideon entered, then followed him.

For a terrifying moment, going from sunlight to shadow, I couldn't see anything. But I sucked in a steadying breath, and stepped to the side of the doorway to let Jacob and Kol enter, blinking several times to get my eyes to adjust as quickly as possible.

We stood in a thirty-by-thirty square and the only clear area in the warehouse. Ahead of us stood a mess of towering machinery and a narrow hall with at least five doorways. The musty smell of decay filled the air, and dust and debris covered a floor marked with hundreds of footprints, some that looked recent... or at least recentish.

I thumbed the switch on my scope to thermal and searched the darkness among the machinery as we headed to the hall. Still no sign of anyone. My buzz snapped over my arms, and the magic in Gideon's brand softly crackled in response. I couldn't shake the feeling that we weren't alone despite the fact that all evidence said we were.

Marcus and Cassius cleared the first five doorways.

They all led into small rooms, one with a large desk, three that were completely empty, and the fifth filled with rotting cardboard boxes. Then the hall turned and opened into a long narrow room with a maze of interconnected rooms and halls stretching out on both sides. Footprints were everywhere, and the air grew thicker with dust. A weak band of sunlight cut across the ceiling from a crack in the outside wall, giving me enough illumination to see, but still allowing me to use my scope's thermal setting.

The sense that we weren't alone, and yet completely alone, made the hair on the back of my neck stand up. It had to be my nerves. We were expecting at least someone to be here, and yet this place was completely abandoned.

I slid my scope from one doorway to the other. No heat signatures. Nothing—

No, something had glimmered. Something taller than even a super. I moved my scope back to the wall between the last two doorways, and slowly scanned up. There, just where the wall met the ceiling, was a flicker of red... maybe. Now there wasn't anything on the wall.

"Shaw," Cassius whispered, his tone sharp.

I jerked my attention away from the—

There it was again! Definitely something giving off an intermittent heat signature.

"Shaw!"

Marcus, Cassius, and Gideon were almost ten feet down the hall from me, and Jacob and Kol were standing close, waiting for me to continue forward.

"There's no one here," Cassius said. "Don't get distracted."

"Right." Except while I felt certain—too certain—the building was deserted, I couldn't shake the feeling I was wrong.

"Essie doesn't get distracted," Marcus growled.

I would beg to differ with him on that. My buzz was really starting to drive me crazy, and it was taking everything I had not to take a hand off my M4 and scratch my stinging ribs.

"There's no one and nothing here connected to the zip dealers," Cassius said.

"But you saw something," Marcus said to me. "Didn't you?"

"I don't know." I looked through my scope at the wall again. Nothing—

No, there, a flicker of heat. "There's something small, giving off a heat signature, near the ceiling."

Someone blew out a heavy breath, the sound hissing over the coms, but I didn't glance away from the spot to see who.

"Kol?" Gideon asked.

"I don't—" Kol shifted closer to me, heat radiating from his body making me even warmer. "Shit. That's a concealment spell."

"Can you break it?" Cassius asked.

"If a weak amateur had cast it. But I'm not a witch. I didn't even notice the spell on the building walking in."

I turned my attention back to the doorways, my stomach churning with the conflicting sense that we were alone and not alone. "Any idea what it's concealing?"

"Doesn't matter. Back out," Cassius said. "Now."

I turned to leave the way we'd come as a bulky guy

with the feral intensity of a shifter rounded the corner and stepped into the hall. He jerked to a stop and stared at us, eyes wide with surprise.

Jacob lunged for him with his enhanced vampiric speed, clamped a hand over the shifter's mouth, and tackled him to the ground.

"What the—" someone said just around the corner.

"JP agents!" someone else yelled, and more guys rushed toward us from every opening.

CHAPTER 18

I jerked my attention from Jacob, wrestling with the shifter and his two friends who were blocking our escape, to Marcus and Cassius, at the front of our line. If we couldn't go back, maybe we could go forward. But a massive demon who looked like he was made entirely of stone was barreling toward Marcus, while another, smaller demon—actually about my size—with onyx skin bounded from floor to wall and punched at Cassius's head.

"On the ground. JP agents," Cassius barked, but as expected the guys didn't stop fighting.

Kol yanked one of the guys off Jacob, while a vampire with pale skin and hair lunged at Gideon. I fired and somehow managed to hit her shoulder even with her enhanced speed. Red lightning flashed around her. She stumbled, didn't drop, and I aimed to fire again, but something behind me wrapped around my neck and yanked me off my feet.

My assailant wrenched me through a doorway, and

my butt slammed onto the concrete floor, but whatever had my neck yanked up, choking me. I grabbed it with one hand, trying to keep hold of my M4, and my fingers grasped something hard and scaly—

Shit. A naga's tail.

The naga wrenched me up and rammed me against the wall, lunging in fast and punching me in the gut. What little breath I had left burst from my lungs. He tightened his grip around my throat and seized the barrel of my M4, but that still left one hand free to punch me in the gut again.

Black specks danced across my vision and my body screamed for air. Kol had said this type of demon wasn't particularly dangerous. They didn't have any special magic, couldn't cast any spells. They were just quick and strong, and could grab you with their tail. And if I didn't do something soon, I was going to suffocate.

He sneered at me, flashing wickedly sharp teeth. I wrenched at my M4. If I could just nick him, the stun spell on the ammo might be enough for me to break free. But he held tight, so I grabbed my Glock instead.

With a snarl, he batted the gun out of my hand and slammed me against the wall again.

The specks turned into a veil, growing from the edge of my vision, darkening everything. My buzz blazed, biting my skin. Behind him, one of our assailants tumbled past the doorway, and white light flared with Gideon's divine light. A gunshot exploded—Jacob?—and Marcus roared. The guys gasped and grunted and growled over the coms, their voices a strange mix of being in my ear as well as just across the room.

I didn't know how many guys we were fighting, but it sounded like there were enough, or they were powerful enough, to challenge the team. I couldn't count on any of them noticing me in time. It was up to me to break free before I passed out.

The naga jerked his hand back to punch me in the ribs again, and I wrenched my hand up, ramming my thumb into his throat. It wasn't a strong hit, but it made him loosen his hold on me enough for a ragged breath.

"Bitch," he hissed. His tail yanked tight as I twisted the M4 in his grip and fired.

The bullet skimmed his thigh. A flicker of red lightning crackled around his leg, and a zap of magic sliced into me. My buzz screamed in response and divine light stuttered from my hands.

"What the fuck—?" He jerked away and I fired again, point blank into his gut, the bullet exploding into the stun spell instead of driving into him.

This time the lightning burst around him in full, swept to the end of his tail, and zapped into me as well. All my muscles spasmed as if I'd been hit with a Taser, but so did his.

We crumpled to the floor, my buzz blazing through the muscle-contracting magic enough for me to shove away from him and shoot him again.

His body arched off the floor, lightning encasing him, and he went limp, his eyes closed, still breathing but unconscious.

I didn't bother securing him with a zip tie. He didn't have any magic to suppress, and if I didn't secure him to something, he'd just be able to run away or rejoin the fight.

I reholstered my Glock and rushed back into the hall. Three perps lay unconscious, their hands zip tied together. Jacob fought with a big guy in the room across from me, and Marcus still battled the rock demon at the end of the hall.

"Anyone have eyes on Shaw?" Cassius called over the coms. He sounded like he was deeper into the maze.

"I'm in the hall," I said.

Jacob tossed the big guy into the hall, and I shot him. Red lightning raced around him. It didn't drop him, but it was enough for Jacob to grab his wrists and secure a zip tie.

I turned my attention to the rock demon, fired, and missed. The monster punched at Marcus, who bounded out of the way, grabbed it around the neck, and swung in behind, giving me a clear shot of its chest.

"Marcus, let go." I fired, praying he'd let go before the bullet hit, and he wouldn't get zapped with the stun spell.

He let go just as red lightning swept around the rock demon, and I fired two more times. If most shifters took two shots, then I was going to play it safe and hit this rock thing with three.

It staggered, dropped to one knee, and roared.

"Really? More than three?" I fired two more times, and it crashed to the floor.

Something moved at the edge of my vision, and I jerked to face it. Cassius fought, flames blazing from his fists, with a vampire and a woman who could have been any of a number of supers, while a naga rushed toward them.

I thumbed the switch on my M4 to a three-round burst and shot the snake demon in the chest. It dropped with a flash of red lightning, making the vampire, a muscular man abut Cassius's size and build, jerk toward me.

Shit.

He bolted toward me. I had a split-second to decide if I should fire, but Cassius was in my line of sight and the odds were that I'd hit him instead.

The vampire grabbed the barrel of my M4 and yanked. I heaved forward, attached to the weapon by the sling, and the vampire grabbed my ponytail and wrenched my head back. He flashed his fangs, his vampiric intensity more powerful than Jacob's, indicating he was older.

My divine light rushed to my palms without me even thinking the words to the spell and before I could give that a second thought, I rammed my palm into his gut.

The blast slammed into him with almost as much force as the blast that had sent Floyd flying. The vampire screamed, but didn't let go of my hair. We crashed into a heavy metal shelf leaning against the wall. Dust and debris and plastic bits of something showered us.

Dazed, I wrenched my hair from his grip and scrambled back. The vampire's side was scorched and bleeding. He snarled and dove at me, and I shoved the muzzle of my M4 between us and fired.

Red lightning swept around him, and he collapsed on top of me, unconscious and twitching.

Marcus heaved the vampire off me and secured his hands with a zip tie. "You okay?"

"Yeah—" A woman with the ferocity of a shifter in her eyes leaped at Marcus's back. I yanked up my M4 and dropped her with another burst of gunfire. "Just fine."

"Yeah, you are," he said, pride and desire heating his gaze.

Cassius secured his guy, but two tigers bounded through the doorway, followed by another rock demon.

"I'm getting the impression there's more here than just a guy with a cell phone." I fired at one of the tigers, but it lunged to the side, and only one bullet skimmed its flank. Red lightning flickered around it, but not enough to even make it stumble.

Marcus dove for the tiger I missed, his fingers extending into claws, while Cassius sent a whip of pure fire to the other one. Kol rushed in behind the rock demon, slicing at its thigh as he darted past.

"Trade you," he said to Cassius, slashing at the tiger and making it twist out of the way. "My blades are useless on the rock demon."

The guys had all three assailants in the room, and while Jacob snarled over the coms, it didn't sound as if he was in trouble, so I took a second to catch my breath and check my M4's magazine. Seven rounds left and no spare magazine. Just great.

I thumbed the switch back to single shots. How many more of these thugs were in there? Although we probably needed to count our lucky stars that none of them had firearms.

"Jacob. Gideon. What's your head count?" I asked.

"I've got three shifters," Jacob said.

"I'm free," Gideon responded. "I'll— Cassius, I need backup. Two shifters just ran down a set of stairs."

Cassius twisted his fire whip around the wrist of the rock demon, but it wrenched its arm back, yanking him forward, while Kol and Marcus both wrestled with their tigers.

"Shit, another rock demon," Jacob said.

Semi-automatic rifle fire roared from somewhere.

"And they've got AK-103s," Jacob said.

So much for thinking we'd gotten lucky.

I aimed at Cassius's rock demon, but couldn't get a clear shot.

"Cassius," Gideon said.

"Marcus? Kol?" Cassius glanced at the two of them.

The rock demon roared and punched at Cassius's head. His fire whip vanished and he rolled out of the way. I fired and hit the demon in the shoulder twice, and Cassius's gaze leaped to mine.

"Cassius!" Gideon said.

"Could use a little help," Jacob called.

"Shaw, back up Gideon," Cassius said.

"I should back up Jacob. He's in the most immediate danger," I said.

Cassius glared a me, white light blazing from his eyes. "We don't know that. Anything could be at the bottom of those stairs and I want this building cleared."

I bit my cheek against my immediate response. He was right. All of my training said so.

Another burst of gunfire exploded from somewhere across the hall.

"Do your job, Shaw. Jacob can handle this." Cassius slammed a blast of fire into the rock demon, crashing him through the rotting drywall into the next room. "Back up Gideon. Kol, Marcus, stop playing around."

My buzz flared. I wanted to scream at all the conflicting feelings pulling me in different directions, but this was what it meant to be a member of a team where I was emotionally involved with the guys. And they were trusting me to trust them and stay focused. "Copy that. Gideon, what's your location?" I asked.

"Two rights from the end of the original room."

I rushed back into the original room and scrambled past the still unconscious rock demon I'd helped Marcus take down. Someone grunted in pain over the coms. Jacob screamed, and my heart lurched, everything within me saying I had to go to him. I gritted my teeth against the need, the pressure building in my chest, my buzz blazing as if my skin were about to burst into flames.

"On my way, Jacob," Marcus said.

With just those four words, the pressure vanished. I shouldn't have doubted that my mates would have each other's backs. I didn't have to do it all, and I didn't have to do it alone.

I ran through a cramped room with toppled shelves and rotting cardboard boxes. Gideon's divine light shimmered through the doorway ahead of me. Now my chest ached with what lay between us. I shoved that back as well. I could worry about it later when we were out of this mess.

He stood at the mouth of a dark stairwell, holding his blazing sword of divine light. His pale gaze, hard and icy, met mine, and he gave a tight nod then turned his attention back to the stairs.

I scanned the room, but there was nothing in it except for a well-worn trail of footprints leading down to the basement.

The wooden stairs creaked as we quickly snuck down, and the air turned musty and cool. I couldn't hear anything beyond the gasping, grunting, and yelling of the guys still fighting and the gunfire. I also couldn't see any heat signatures through my scope.

The stairs led to a long, narrow hall with a single door at the far end. Light illuminated it, bright in the hall's pitch darkness.

"You open the door. I'll enter first," Gideon said, his voice low as we hurried to the end of the hall.

"Give me a sec to listen." I wasn't sure how good an angel's hearing was, but I was willing to bet Jacob's claim had made mine better.

With no questions asked or any hesitation, he let me hurry past him. I leaned close to the door, slipped my com from my ear, and listened. No voices. No footsteps. Only a strange, low hum—

No, a hum with a faint rattle. "I don't hear anyone, but there's some kind of machinery or something on the other side." I put my com back in and grabbed the doorknob.

"Have we stumbled onto the new lab?" Kol asked.

"There are only two guys with AK-103s," Marcus said. "You'd think this lab would be as secure as the last one."

"Even with only two, this is pretty secure," Jacob gasped. "There weren't any rock demons at the other lab."

I met Gideon's gaze. The glow in his eyes was muted by the stark light of his sword. For a second, he looked haggard and raw, like how he'd looked when we'd rescued Zella from the archnephilim. Then the muscles in his jaw flexed, and his icy mask reformed over his expression.

He pressed his back against the wall to give him the fastest view into the room when the door opened, and nodded.

I yanked the door open. Gideon rushed in, and I followed and froze. A mass of writhing, dark, man-shaped smoke floated twenty feet away. Every muscle within me clenched, and I forgot to breathe. I forgot to do anything. I didn't know if there was anyone else in the room, had no idea how big it was, or what was in it. All I could think was one horrifying word: wraith.

"He's not dead?" The words came out choked and desperate. He had to be dead. I'd killed him. The guys said he'd turned to ash. His brand had become a silvery scar, but it hadn't gone away. Did that mean he could still possess me?

No way in hell was I going to let him or anyone else make me hurt my guys again.

Gideon bolted toward him as I shot two quick rounds. They tore through the wraith's smoke, drawing a howl of pain, but not a flicker of red lightning.

"It's a wraith. The ammo won't work," Gideon said.

"A wraith?" Marcus barked over the coms. "Fuck. Essie—"

"It's not him," Gideon said back. "It's just a wraith. Shaw is fine."

I wasn't fine, but I wasn't immobilized with fear, either. Sure, I'd had a moment—and a part of me was still in that terrified moment, afraid the archnephilim had returned from the dead to take control of me again—but I was fighting through it.

"There's no such thing as *just* a wraith," a masculine voice hissed. The wraith swept a flurry of tentacles at Gideon.

He slashed his sword through them, and drove his blade into the center of the wraith's mass. "Three weeks ago, I would have agreed with you."

I forced my attention away from Gideon to secure the room, something I should have done the moment I'd entered, since we'd originally followed a pair of shifters down the stairs. Harsh fluorescent lights hung from exposed wires on the ceiling, gleaming on two dozen stainless steel tables set up in rows to my left. Crates and boxes were piled on and underneath the tables, and only two of them had beakers, hot plates, rubber tubing, and gloves. The one on the left also had half a dozen sealed jars filled with bright purple liquid. Zip.

The hum with the rattle came from a generator powering the lights, its exhaust vented out a narrow window on the back wall. Beside it were four more generators with the same exhaust setup. They weren't running, but they added to the evidence that this was the new zip lab and it was in the process of being set up.

The shifters stood beyond the tables, about sixty feet away, at the mouth of a dark hall, with a green-skinned demon and a woman with long, wild bright red hair and a complex, colorful tattoo covering her right arm. She didn't have the intensity of a vampire or the ferocity of a shifter, but I could sense a power radiating from her that was so strong it made my buzz snap and crackle, burning through my skin. Even with the wraith in the room, I knew she was the most dangerous super there.

She met my gaze, and I fired at her. One of the shifters, a small stocky guy, lunged in front of her as she ducked into the stairwell. My bullet hit him. Red lightning crackled around him. He staggered, but didn't go down, and the other shifter—a woman about my size—and the demon—also a woman, but bulkier and taller than me—barreled toward me.

Crap. I fired again at the guy. I only had two shots left with the M4 and I wasn't going to waste them by not dropping at least one of the three, especially since I needed to hit them at least twice.

The second shot dropped the guy with a flash of lightning, and I aimed my last shot at the female shifter, who was closer to me than the demon.

She stumbled, her hip hitting the table, giving me the time to flick the quick release catch on my M4's sling, drop the weapon, and draw my Glock. But she was on me before I could fire, swiping at me with long claws.

I wrenched out of the way and tried to shoot her. It didn't need to be a good shot. It just needed to be enough to slow her down for a second.

I missed and the bullet slammed into the far wall. The shifter swiped again, her claws catching my shoulder with fiery agony and wrenching me off balance. My buzz blazed, stronger. I dropped and rolled away to avoid a swipe at my neck, and fired again.

The bullet skimmed her ribs and didn't even make her pause. She lunged at me and I scrambled back, desperate to put any kind of distance between us.

Behind her, the wraith tossed Gideon into a table piled with boxes. One crashed onto him before tumbling to the floor in a mess of empty mini baggies, broken glass, and white powder.

The wraith surged toward him and seized his sword arm with a thick smoke tentacle. He heaved Gideon up, off his feet, but between one blink and the next, his sword vanished and divine light blazed up his arm, searing through the wraith's smoke. The wraith howled and heaved back. Gideon lunged in, his sword forming as he moved, but the green-skinned demon leaped on him and wrenched his sword arm to the side.

Crap. I aimed to shoot the demon, but the shifter swung at me again, reminding me to keep my eyes on my own damned fight.

Her claws caught in my vest, and she jerked me forward. I aimed to shoot her, but she smashed my Glock from my hand before I could pull the trigger. Divine light blazed from my palms, and my buzz set my skin on fire. Her eyes widened with surprise, and she threw me into the table Gideon had just toppled over.

My divine light stuttered and vanished, making the shifter sneer.

The green demon tumbled beside me, clipping my table and sprawling into a pile of boxes. She leaped to her feet and grabbed a jar of the bright purple zip, her furious gaze locked on Gideon.

My pulse froze as she brought her arm back to throw

it. If any of that hit Gideon, it could kill him. It could kill me, too, but odds were better, even if I was half super, that I'd survive.

I scrambled to my feet and dove for the demon. The green demon jerked toward me, eyes wide, and she smashed the jar against my head as I slammed into her.

CHAPTER 19

An inferno blazed across my skin everywhere the zip touched and my buzz screamed, filling me with agony. We crashed to the floor, the liquid zip spraying her in the face as well.

Shock raced across her expression, and the liquid seeped into her skin, completely absorbed, not even leaving a trace of moisture.

"Time," the shifter barked, and the green demon shoved me off her and bolted to the hall.

What the hell?

The wraith blasted Gideon with a pillar of smoke, shoving him into me, and swept toward the hall as well.

A thunderous boom exploded. Part of the ceiling crashed toward me, and Gideon grabbed my vest's shoulder strap and yanked me away from a tumbling beam.

Another explosion roared around us. Gideon hauled me toward the hall where we'd entered as the rest of the ceiling fell. Something heavy smashed onto me, dropping me to my knees. I jerked to the side, slammed into something else— or did it slam into me? I wasn't sure. My head spun, and I couldn't breathe or see. All light was gone, dust thickened the air, and my ears rang.

The roar of chaos snapped to silence and for a moment there was nothing. No dust, no pain, no noise. Then fire blazed through me, and I gasped in a lungful of dust. My ears still rang, and I could hear the guys yelling, but couldn't understand what they were saying.

Light flickered above me and to my left, and I craned my neck and glanced up at it. Gideon stared at me through narrowed eyes, his divine light the flickering illumination. I lay half on his chest with one of his arms wrapped around me.

"—blew up the building," a gruff voice said over the coms.

Gideon closed his eyes, plunging me back into darkness, and panic seized me. I hadn't gotten a good look at him. I didn't know how hurt he was. But I couldn't make my mind work past that to figure out what to do if he was.

"Everyone check in," the gruff voice said.

Recognition swam to the front of my mind. Cassius. That was Cassius.

"I got out," Kol said. "Barely."

"—is trapped under a pile of concrete."

My thoughts tripped and spun. Who'd just spoken? Who was trapped?

"Gideon? Shaw?" Cassius asked.

Gideon's eyes fluttered open, bathing me in light again, but I wasn't filled with relief. His wings were fully extended above us, and they were tattered with one hanging at an odd angle, and a heavy beam sliced deep into his side, pinning him to the rubble behind him and squeezing him against a pile of massive concrete chunks on his other side.

I choked on dust and coughed to catch my breath, setting my whole body on fire, making it impossible to tell where or how I'd been injured. I tried to shift. Lightning cut through my chest, and I couldn't move my leg.

I dragged my attention to my leg. It was like I was thinking in slow motion. A chunk of concrete pinned me to the floor. If I was strong enough, I'd be able to move it. Maybe I could shift it enough to slide free.

"Gideon? Shaw?" Cassius asked again.

"Come on, Essie," Marcus said, his voice tight with fear. "Check in."

"She's here," Gideon said, his breath shallow, ragged gasps. "Alive."

"Status and location, everyone," Cassius said.

"Mostly scrapes and bruises. East side of the building," Marcus said. "Actually, in the building next door. If I have help, I can get Jacob free."

"If I could get the leverage, I could get myself free," Jacob said.

"Shaw and I... are on the west side... near the back." Gideon fought to draw every breath and his wings twitched. It didn't look like he was holding anything up, but he wasn't absorbing them back into his body to heal them, either.

"Can you get out?" Cassius asked.

"We didn't make it out of the basement," I said, the words coming out on a rush of air.

"You're under all that?" Kol gasped.

"Hang tight," Cassius said. "We'll get you out." There was a rustling noise and my best guess was that Cassius was taking out his com to call in backup.

"Can you see any way out?" Marcus asked.

"No, and Gideon is pinned between a beam and concrete." Again, my words came out too fast. What the hell was wrong with me?

Gideon's wings twitched, and he hissed in pain, drawing my attention to the growing pool of blood at his hip. I couldn't feel a pull of strength from me to him through our brand, but I couldn't feel anything but the fire burning through my body.

Which didn't make any sense. I was on top of Gideon. My buzz should be gone.

Except my buzz *was* gone. The biting, stinging inferno had been replaced with a deeper, fiercer blaze that was creeping into my cells and igniting every part of me. It was terrifying, painful. And exhilarating.

Oh, shit. I'd taken a face full of zip before the building had collapsed. Onset was supposed to be twenty to thirty minutes. But that was for an ingested pill, one cut with flour or baking soda. This had been a whole jar of pure zip, and it had probably absorbed into my skin just like it had on the green demon.

"You have to get us out of here," I said, sudden panic raising my voice. I shoved off Gideon and leaned as far away from him as I could in our cramped quarters, shooting agony through my chest and leg. If onset was accelerated, would the violent paranoid delusions come faster, too? "Gideon has to get out."

"We're working on it, Shaw," Cassius said.

"No. He has to get out. You have to get him out of here." It was all I could think of. I was going to hurt him. I might not have a gun, but I had my light strike and at this distance, already injured, I would kill him.

If the zip didn't kill me first... because I'd taken more than enough to OD an elephant.

"Essie, we're working on it. Stay calm," Marcus said.

"I can't be trapped in here with him." I met his gaze. "I can't. I can't—" I couldn't catch my breath, my pulse raced, and the fire within me blazed hotter.

"Work faster," Gideon gasped. "Shaw's... going to OD on zip."

"She's what?" Marcus barked.

"And you're going to bleed out if I don't get violent and kill you first." I had to get him out of there. *He couldn't die. Please, God, don't let him die. And don't let me kill him.*

"Gideon, how badly are you bleeding?" Cassius asked.

My thoughts jerked to Cassius. Of course he wouldn't ask about me. He didn't care what state I was in so long as I lived.

"The beam is holding most of it back—"

"Not all of it." Every minute trapped was a minute where Gideon bled out, or I could lose control and blast him.

"The beam will hold it back long enough. I'm not drawing strength from Shaw, so I'm good." His eyes tightened, dimming the light. "You'll want to have paramedics or better yet Amiah standing by."

"You have to get him out. Now. Please." I shoved my hands into my armpits, desperate to keep my palms away from him. I could control this. I wasn't going to lose my mind. In fact, I was powerful. I could feel my power blazing inside me. I could move this pile of concrete, I could free my leg, I could—

I gritted my teeth. That was the zip talking. I couldn't let it control me, couldn't let it make me do something stupid like shift the rubble around us. That could make everything worse.

"Just focus on something else," Gideon gasped.

"I'm going to kill you and you want me to focus on something else?" My words rushed out and my pulse pounded faster.

The muscles in Gideon's jaw tightened. "Odds are you'll OD first."

"Not helpful," Marcus growled.

Except, strangely enough, it was helpful. I wasn't going to kill him—

Except I still was. If I died, he died or went insane. That was what having his mating brand meant. We were destined to be together. Soul mates. Although no one had said anything about one soul mate hating the other.

I ached with that, the hurt sharp and sudden and reaching deep into my soul. He didn't want me. Logically I knew I shouldn't care. I had Marcus and Jacob. But whatever magic bound us together defied logic. It just couldn't defy his true feelings for me.

He was staring at me like that now with his icy expression, his eyes narrowed as if it pained him just to look at me. And why wouldn't it? I wasn't the angel he was in love with. I was responsible for her death. I was a weak, powerless human who he didn't know and didn't want to know.

My throat tightened and tears filled my eyes. I couldn't keep doing this. No matter what I wanted or where I belonged, his frozen demeanor was shattering me.

"You win," I said. "I'll leave."

Maybe if I didn't have to see him, didn't keep seeing that look in his eyes, I'd be okay. Marcus and Jacob and I would need to figure something out, but I wasn't going to let any of them throw away their careers for me. I'd have to lose my career, but right now, with grief crushing me, living like I was missing a part of myself was better than knowing that part of myself hated me.

"I know I remind you of what you should have had with her, so I'll leave. It'll be better for everyone." I huffed with bitter mirth, sending agony screaming through my chest. "It'll be great for your brother."

Gideon's wings shuddered, blazed with light, but didn't sink back into his body. Gasping, he leaned his head back. "It's only great for Cassius... because he doesn't understand... the situation."

"Yeah, right," I said, unable to keep the sarcasm from my voice. "You didn't tell him how much you loved Zella? How happy you were when you thought the mating brand was with her?" My tears broke free and slid down my cheeks. He wanted her. Not me. He always had. "I know you told him how much you hate that you're mated with me."

"I didn't tell him I hated being... mated with you."

"But you do, don't you? This is your worst nightmare."

His head jerked up, light flaring from eyes filled with heated desire and agony. "It's my worst nightmare because you're Marcus's mate. All I want when I look at you... is to touch you, hold you... tell you how much the distance between us hurts."

"Then why didn't you?" More tears rolled down my cheeks, but the fire in my cells was burning through the heavy grief, turning it into something darker, fiercer. I was pissed that he made me feel this way, pissed that the brand I didn't want made me feel this way. Just plain pissed. I tugged at the collar of my vest, trying to cool my blazing skin. "Why the hell didn't you?"

"Because you're in love with Marcus," he snapped. "It's been obvious... since before our brand appeared." The pain in Gideon's eyes deepened, but that only made me more angry. "The best thing I could do for you was let you... be happy. If I gave into the brand's compulsion... Marcus and I would have fought... over you, and that wouldn't have turned out good for anyone."

What a load of shit. "I heard you," I said, jabbing a finger at him. "I heard you talking to Amiah. You don't care about me. You don't even want to know me."

"I *can't* know you." His wings blazed and shuddered again, leaving him panting in pain. "I can't. I was... already... falling in love with you. If I let you get closer... I wouldn't be able to ignore our bond."

My pulse stuttered at those words. He was in love with me? He couldn't be in love with me. He hated me. It was clear every time he looked at me.

"You're fearless and self-sacrificing. You'd do... anything to save an innocent. I knew fate had picked...

the right soul mate... for me the moment you came to face the archnephilim alone. I knew... why you'd made that choice. Because you didn't want anyone else to get hurt." He pressed a hand to his ribs, as if that would ease his pain. His breath came too fast and too shallow. "If I got to know you better... I wouldn't be able... to do... the right thing and let you be happy with Marcus."

More tears rolled down my cheeks. "Do you know how much that hurt?" I raised my arm with his brand. "You're always here. I can't get away from you, from our connection. And when you look at me—"

"I know you don't want... a bond with me."

"I don't want to feel like a part of me is broken. You look at me with all that ice in your beautiful eyes and I want to scream."

"You have Marcus."

"And Jacob, and I know I'm supposed to." I knew that with certainty in the core of my being. I didn't know why, and maybe there wasn't a reason, but I was destined to belong with these men and they to me. "I'm also supposed to be with you. I don't understand it, but I can't keep going on like this, feeling like this."

"But Marcus—"

"Marcus is an adult," Marcus said over the coms, "and if you'd bothered to ask him, he'd tell you he fully accepts this unusual situation."

"But your wolf."

"Is fine with it," Marcus growled. "You're the only one with issues."

"I don't have a problem... Werewolves... aren't polyamorous. Not with their... destined mates." Gideon's face tightened. "I'm trying to give Essie... what she wants."

"What you *think* she wants," Marcus said. "I tried that once. Worst decision I ever made."

"You did it twice, actually," I said, ripping open the Velcro straps on my vest, desperate to relieve the heat.

"I'm a slow learner."

The light from Gideon's wings blazed brighter, and with a scream that made my pulse stutter with fear, he pulled them back into his body.

"What was that?" Cassius demanded.

"Couldn't get... my wings... in," Gideon gasped. "Too injured." Sweat slicked his brow, and his breath was even more ragged.

My pulse leaped back into a rapid tattoo. "Gideon doesn't look good." *Please, get-us-out get-us-out get-us-out.* I needed to move, to cool off. It was so damned hot in there.

I yanked off my vest, shooting agony through my chest, tearing the shoulder straps instead of releasing the Velcro or pulling it off over my head. What the hell? I stared at the rip, my mind tripping over it as my hands shook, the bright white letters on the front vibrating.

No, *I* was vibrating.

Every cell in my being thrummed with power and strength. Then a wave of pure bliss and power slammed into me as the zip's high roared through me.

CHAPTER 20

ANOTHER WAVE OF BLISS SWEPT THROUGH ME, STEALING MY breath. I was alight with power, every cell awakened to its full potential and beyond. It was the most amazing feeling in the world. I could do anything, face anyone. I was powerful.

"Essie?" Marcus asked, his voice filled with fear and booming in my ear. It made the darkness shudder around me like a massive stone dropped into a still, black lake.

"Focus on me, Essie," Gideon said.

I dragged my attention to Gideon. Pinprick flashes of light sparkled in the glow radiating from his eyes, fireflies dancing from those beautiful blue orbs.

"What's going on?" Cassius asked, his voice another radiating boom.

I could hear everything. Cassius and Marcus breathing over the coms. Kol talking to someone. I was pretty sure he'd taken his com out and was on the phone, but then how could I hear him?

"Zip is kicking in," Gideon said, the flashes in his eyes dancing across the distance between us.

I reached out and one landed on my finger and sank into my skin. It ignited his brand, making it crackle with exhilarating electricity. The power rushed up my arm into Jacob's brand, and entwined with his deep intensity.

"So that's what you feel like," I gasped. So powerful, so quiet and still and certain. I should have expected that. Jacob might look like a wild brawler with his massive build, broad chest, and bulky muscles, but he was still a vampire. The power that had brought him back to life wrapped him in stillness.

"Come on, Essie, look at me," Gideon said.

I dragged my gaze back to Gideon... again. He panted, his complexion gray, and his head lolled to the side as if it were too heavy to hold up. The blood pool at his hip just kept growing, and while I still couldn't feel the pull of strength from the brand, I couldn't just sit there and watch him fade. I had extra strength. I was brimming with it, over-flowing. It blazed from my hands and heart, my whole body.

"Here," I said, and I imagined that power rushing through our bond.

He gasped and his head jerked up. "Don't do that. Save your power."

"I have lots. I have so much." Hell, I'd ripped a Kevlar vest. Hey! I could free my leg.

I grabbed the edge of the concrete chunk pinning me to the floor and yanked it up with so much force it shattered into pieces. The rubble around us shifted, debris showered us, and metal groaned. I was so strong, I could dig us out of there. No problem. The truth of the thought stunned me. This was the power of zip. It was amazing. I could save Gideon.

"Is this what you feel like?" I asked him. "All the time?" I shoved at the edge of a metal beam near my head, and with a boom that side of our pocket in the rubble collapsed.

Oh, shit.

I jerked out of the way, cramming up against Gideon, before I got pinned again. My euphoria snapped into panic. Even with enhanced strength I was a fuck-up. I would always be a fuck-up.

"No wonder you don't want me." My throat tightened again with tears. "I'm so weak. Nothing compared to a super. How could I have possibly thought I belonged on the team, belonged with you or Marcus or Jacob or Kol or anyone?"

"That's the zip talking," Gideon said, wrapping his free arm around me and pulling me to his chest, even though it had to hurt him.

"If how I feel now is how you feel all the time, I'm useless." I pulled out of his embrace, squishing myself against the rubble, embracing the agony in my body. It was the only thing that was real. Pain. Disappointment. Fear.

The fireflies in Gideon's glow turned to stinging embers, biting my skin. He was an angel. He was going to kill me. Marcus and Jacob wouldn't protect me when they learned the truth. I was a naturally born nephilim. That was supposed to be impossible, and my mother told me over and over again that no one would believe me. No one could ever know the truth.

My pulse beat so fast and hard, it felt as if my heart were trying to pound out of my chest.

And why wouldn't it? It didn't belong in my chest.

I clawed at my fitted jacket. I couldn't keep holding my heart hostage. It was fated to be with powerful beings like Gideon and Marcus. My heart didn't belong in a weak human chest.

My pathetic human fingers couldn't dig through the jacket's fabric, so I yanked it off, tearing the seam at the back and shoving it off my arms.

I had to get my heart out. I was killing it, just like I was killing Gideon and Marcus and Jacob and Kol.

"Essie, stop."

But if I stopped, my heart would die.

I dug my fingers into my chest. Surely with my zip-enhanced strength I could dig through my T-shirt. But I was a powerless nephilim, worse than a human. I was half super, and I still didn't have any powers. And my stupid empathy didn't count. It was useless. I was useless.

"Essie." Gideon tried to grab my hand, but couldn't reach me. "Stop."

Blood oozed around my fingers, staining my T-shirt. At least I could do this. At least my heart could be free.

"No. Essie." Gideon flexed his hand and a blast of divine light slammed me into the rubble. My head snapped back, cracking against the concrete, and the rubble shifted, showering us with debris and dust. The beam cutting into Gideon's side dug deeper, drawing a strangled cry of pain.

"What's happening?" Cassius asked, his voice far away, no longer a boom, barely a whisper.

"Get us out of here," Gideon gasped. "Essie, look at me."

I tried to focus on him through the black specks dancing across my vision. My chest hurt every time I took a breath and that was a lot. Blood covered my fingers and the front of my T-shirt, but I couldn't figure out why.

"Tell me something," Gideon said.

His words muddled in my head. "Tell you what?"

"I don't know. Where did you grow up?"

Everywhere and nowhere.

This had to be a trick question. He was going to get me to slip up, reveal the truth, and then kill me.

"Where did you grow up?" he asked again.

"My mom and I moved around a lot."

"Europe? Asia?"

I rolled my eyes at him. "Don't be ridiculous. America."

"Why is that ridiculous?"

"Because—" This had to be part of the trick. "It just is."

I clawed at my arms. My buzz was back with a vengeance, even with Gideon's foot against my calf. I just couldn't get rid of it. Why the hell wouldn't it just go away?

"Just you and your mom?"

"Yeah." I dug my nails into my skin even though I knew it wouldn't stop the buzz.

"Essie," Gideon snapped.

My gaze jerked up to him. I hadn't realized I'd looked

away. He was so pale. His breath was shallow and slow. Why couldn't I feel my strength pouring into him? He needed my strength. But my God damn buzz wasn't letting me give it to him—

Even though he was trying to trip me up and learn the truth.

"You and your mom?" he pressed.

My thoughts splintered and whirled. He couldn't know the truth. He couldn't die.

"Essie."

"Yes," I gasped. "Me and my mom." My mom, who'd fallen in love with an angel before the war had even started. My mom, who'd given up everything to keep me safe. My mom, who'd died from fucking cancer because she refused to dip into my escape money to save herself.

She would be so mad and ashamed of me. I was in love with an angel... and a werewolf... and a vampire... and an incubus. I was a JP agent.

"Focus on... me, Essie."

"Why? You don't want me."

"I've already said I do."

"You're just saying that. The brand is making you say that." This was how it ended. Trapped with an angel and being stupid enough to think that love could conquer everything. The archnephilim and Ibizual had said my guys wouldn't understand me. That no one but them would. The other monsters wanted me. They were coming for me, and Gideon was going to hand me over, because they were who I belonged with. "No. No no no. I won't go back to him. I won't let him control me."

"Who, Essie?" Gideon asked.

"He'll make me hurt you. *I'll* make me hurt you."
Wasn't that the nature of a nephilim? We didn't serve and
protect. We slaughtered. Billions of people.

"Who the hell is she talking about?" Cassius asked.

"The archnephilim," Marcus growled.

"I won't let you keep me."

"She's not making sense," Cassius said.

"I don't make sense. I shouldn't be here."

"Neither of us should be here." Gideon gasped a
ragged breath, his face pinched with agony.

"No, here here." They were going to learn the truth. I
met Gideon's gaze. He was going to lock me away forever.
Wouldn't that be for the best? I was a monster. My true
nature would come out eventually. It would be better for
all of them if I ended it now.

Divine light rushed to my palms. It didn't matter that
I was naturally born. Everyone knew the heart of a
nephilim was black, tainted by her unnatural existence.

I pressed my palms to my chest and pushed all the
power within me, my God damn buzz, the lightning from
Gideon's brand, and the intensity from Jacob's brand, into
my hands. I would burn the abomination and everyone
would be safe.

"No, Essie." Gideon wrenched against the beam,
trying to grab me. "Stop. You have to stop."

"I won't become like him."

"You're not like him. Please, Essie." Blood rushed
down Gideon's side. Light flickered in his palms, but I
sucked that up through the brand.

"And I'll never be." My T-shirt blackened and curled
away from my hands, and my power seared my skin. I

focused my resolve, concentrating on squeezing everything into a final blast. This was how it had to end. I couldn't run from them and I wasn't going to hurt them. I wasn't going to become a monster.

The guys yelled over the coms, demanding to know what was going on.

"This isn't the answer. It's the zip making you think this," Gideon said.

"It's the only answer."

I released the power. It seared into my skin, then swept out of me with sudden shocking cold. Gideon screamed. Power—my power—erupted from him and blazed across his skin, burning him and blackening the concrete around us.

I screamed. He wasn't supposed to die. I was. I couldn't let him do this. I jerked toward him so fast I overshot the distance and slammed my forehead against the concrete above him. Light snapped across my vision and agony seized me. Every muscle, every nerve, every cell blazed with pain, and darkness devoured me.

But the pain kept burning and burning, threatening to consume me. Wasn't this what I wanted? To free Gideon and Marcus and Jacob from me, the monster?

How can you say that? Marcus growled.

I jerked toward his voice but couldn't see anything in the darkness.

You're my soul mate. His fingers slid into my hair and his breath feathered across my cheeks. *My soul wouldn't choose a monster.*

But I am a monster. The archnephilim was right. Ibizual was right.

His lips brushed mine, a whisper of contact that made me flush with need. *They don't know you.*

They know me better than you do. They know the truth.

The truth is that you're mine. His lips smashed on mine. I gasped, and he devoured my breath, stealing it with his passion. *You'll always be mine.*

And mine, Jacob said, his voice that low rumble that always made my soul vibrate until it attuned with his.

A second set of hands slipped under my shirt and skimmed up my ribs. Just that gentle touch, a whisper like Marcus's first kiss that sent a shiver of pleasure rushing through me. Marcus's kiss deepened, and Jacob's fingers brushed my nipples.

I ached for these men, and while I didn't need them, I wanted them. Desperately. But that didn't change what I was.

Which is also mine, Gideon said. A third set of hands pressed against the inside of my thighs, urging me to open to him, to join with him like I'd joined with Marcus and Jacob. Our bond needed to be solidified. Pieces of my soul were breaking away because I hadn't accepted my destiny.

But I couldn't.

Because of what I was.

Essie, accept me. Gideon's hands brushed close to my core and trailed over my abdomen to the waistband of my jeans. *Let me in. You let my power in. Let my body in as well.*

Yes, Kol whispered, his sensual voice sliding like silk over my skin. *Let me in, too.*

His power oozed, molten seduction through my veins, and my senses spun with Marcus's mouth plundering mine, Jacob teasing my nipples, and Gideon undoing my jeans.

Yes, I gasped. *I want you all. I belong to you all. I—*

Sudden cold swept around me, followed by searing agony.

"No, Essie," Gideon said, his voice ragged.

Light cut across my vision. People yelled. A burned leg with bits of fabric charred into raw oozing skin slid past me.

"Get them on a gurney," someone yelled. Loud. Too loud.

I winced, and blessed darkness rushed around me.

Accept me, Essie, Jacob said, his mouth teasing my nipple.

No, me. The pressure on my nipple grew fierce as Marcus sucked on it, drawing it into a tight bud.

The pressure vanished, replaced with a tongue tracing sensual circles. *Essie,* Gideon said, snaps of his electric power dancing over my skin.

Cold swept over me again, and the fiery pain seized me. I screamed and sobbed. I just wanted to go back to my guys, wanted the pain to end.

"Hold on, Essie." That was one of my guys. I knew it even if I couldn't figure out who. His voice was sharp with fear, not soft and sensual.

Then the darkness swept around me, again.

Let me in, Kol whispered.

More searing agony.

Essie. Kol's face materialized out of the darkness, only a breath separating our lips. *Let me in.*

Yes. You, too. Yes.

Sensual heat flooded me and my thoughts stalled. There was only Kol... which wasn't right. There was Marcus and Jacob and Gideon, too.

But I couldn't keep my thoughts focused on them. I kept drifting back to Kol... back to dark, soft nothing... back to Kol and his magic... back to...

Cold swept around me again, but this time the pain that followed wasn't a blazing agony, but a throbbing that radiated pain through every nerve into the core of my being. I yearned to go back to the warm darkness, the nothingness, but the pain persisted.

God, just take me back to the nothingness.

The pain dimmed and swelled, dipping me deeper into the darkness and back out again. Dimmed and swelled. Dimmed and swelled. Floating, bobbing, surrounded by water.

No, not water. It was thicker, warmer, comforting. I was safe in the not-water. I could stay in the not-water forever.

A boom cracked far off in the distance. A flurry of booms followed. It sounded like gunfire. I dragged my eyes open, and met warm brown eyes flecked with gold— Except his eyes weren't flecked with gold, the angel glow in his eyes was. The flecks danced, little pops of light, only noticeable because he stood so close. Gold. That was important. I just couldn't remember why.

He glanced over his shoulder then turned back to me, his hand pressed against something between us.

Gold flecks...

My mother had said my father had brown eyes with gold flecks.

Gold flecks...

The gold melted from his eyes and the brown shifted to warm summer-sky blue. Gideon's eyes. So beautiful. I could spend a lifetime soaring in those eyes, imagining I had the wings to join him in the sky.

But I didn't have wings. I'd never fly. All I'd have was the sky in his eyes. Eyes that watched me with worry and ice. Eyes in a face with an expression so hard, it hurt to look at him.

My consciousness clawed at the soft darkness around me. He was watching me, arms crossed, head tipped back against a window. A harsh beep sliced through the silence, and the rush of air in vents and the hum of machinery followed.

Fire consumed me, my buzz an inferno trying to burn and bite its way out of me. My heart broke at the look in Gideon's eyes, and my throat tightened as my thoughts tripped over what I was looking at. His hair was too short, his eyes farther apart, and his nose was narrower.

"Where's Gideon," I croaked.

Cassius's expression grew grim, and I bit back a sob. It had to be horrible. *God, please let him be alive.*

CHAPTER 21

My pulse on the heart monitor beeped faster. I tried to remember what had happened, but everything was a blur of pain and fear. We'd been trapped. I'd been burning up— Hell, I was still burning up. Then I'd gathered all my power, every last bit and—

A sob broke free. "Did I kill him?" *Please, no. Oh, please, no.* "Is that why you're here? To arrest me? Please, don't let me hurt anyone else. Please. I—"

"I'm not here to arrest you," Cassius said. "And no, you didn't kill him."

Oh, thank God. Relief flooded me for a second, but my grief rushed back in. A tear leaked from my eye, trickled across my temple, and soaked into the pillow.

"He told me what you did."

Another tear rolled across my temple. "I'm sorry. I'm so sorry."

Cassius frowned. "What do you think he told me?"

"That I hurt him or killed him or—"

"I already said you didn't kill him."

Right. But I couldn't stop the flurry of terrified thoughts and tears. "What's wrong with me?"

"Severe depression and anxiety is one of the side effects of coming down from zip." He rubbed his face, and his expression shifted from grim to exhausted. "You know, that drug you got splashed with so Gideon wouldn't."

"The mortality rate for supers is so high," I sobbed. "I couldn't let her throw it at him."

"Now, about the team—"

"I know. I don't belong." More tears leaked from my eyes. "I'm too weak. I'll never be strong enough to take down a super." Which was ridiculous. I'd already taken down a couple of supers. But I couldn't think past the dark, malignant cloud oozing into my thoughts.

"Given that Gideon is still in surgery and has already drained two of the hospital's three healers to deal with the third-degree burns you gave him, I'd say you're more than powerful enough to take out a super."

"I burned him? I—" More sobs broke free. I couldn't hold them back, and my body shook as my skin blazed with fiery agony, thousands of bees stinging over and over again. I could have killed him. I almost had. Three healers and they were still working on him. God, I was a monster.

"Shaw—"

I turned my face into the pillow and cried. I just wanted to curl into a ball and die. A part of me knew this wasn't me, it was the zip, but I wasn't strong enough to fight the overwhelming sorrow.

"Shaw, you didn't— Come on, Shaw," Cassius said.

"Jeez—" Metal like the legs of a chair on a linoleum floor screeched, and his footsteps hurried to the door. "A little help in here."

Soft footsteps rushed to me, and someone murmured something, but I couldn't drag my thoughts away from my grief or my burning skin to understand them. *Please, just let me die.* It was best for everyone if I just died. But then Gideon and Jacob could die. *Oh, God!* I'd almost killed Gideon.

The warm darkness from before swelled at the edge of my senses, and the beep from the heart monitor slowed. I floated again in the not-water, but I couldn't open my eyes to catch a glimpse of the angel with the gold flecks in his eyes. My father.

I'd never dreamed of my father before. Even after my mother had told me about him, her expression soft with wistful sadness. He'd always just been a reminder that I wasn't normal, that I had to hide who I was from everyone, always be on guard and ready to run at a moment's notice. He was the reason the angels would come for me. Except I wanted the angels to come— or rather, one angel. I wanted Gideon. I belonged with Gideon, just like I belonged with Jacob and Marcus.

I bit back a sigh, my pulse tripping at the thought of my guys. I loved them. It was crazy. We barely knew each other, but I did.

The heart monitor beeped at the edge of my senses, and I dragged my consciousness toward it, praying when I opened my eyes, I'd see one of my guys instead of Cassius.

Pale icy eyes stared at me, framed in a face also so pale his skin seemed translucent.

Sebastian Bane.

Soft white-blue light radiated from every inch of visible skin, giving him an ethereal appearance, and his mouth quirked with the hint of a wicked smile.

I frowned, trying to think past my still-blazing buzz. "What are you doing here?"

"Maybe I like to wander Mercy Memorial's ICU," he said, sitting back in his chair.

"The what?" I'd thought I was in a room in Operations, but beyond the window behind him lay a nurse's station, and now that I was paying attention, I could hear the rumble of many voices and someone being paged over speakers somewhere farther down the hall.

"Yeah, nothing but the best for JP agents. And since they don't want to have to keep an eye on two different floors, you're in the room beside Gideon's... when he isn't in surgery draining yet another healer. Not that you weren't touch and go there for a while. First time on zip?"

Grief swept through me, followed by an intense yearning to have all that power back. If I just kept taking it, I'd be strong, I could stay on the team.

I clenched my jaw and fought those thoughts. If I took zip again, I'd kill someone. I'd almost killed Gideon.

"God, Gideon!" I jerked up, sending agony blazing through me.

"Whoa." Sebastian grabbed my shoulders and urged me to lie back. "Gideon is fine. All your guys are fine."

Thank God. They were fine. Everything was fine. Wait

— "Why are you here?" He still hadn't answered my question, and it was still so damned hard to concentrate.

Movement in the doorway at the end of the room caught my attention, and my heart skipped a beat at the thought that my guys were coming. But it was two shifters in nurse's scrubs peeking into the doorway, watching me.

Sebastian frowned and followed my gaze to the door. "Don't you have something to do?" he snapped at them.

The nurses mumbled apologies and hurried away as an orderly walked past the window, blatantly staring at me as he passed.

Sebastian tugged on the cord by his head and released the horizontal blinds, covering the window. "Apparently as the human half of an angelic mating bond, you're a real curiosity."

"You sure they're not looking at the faekin?" Being half human and half fae had to be just as rare as someone with an angelic mating brand.

"No, Kol warned me I'd have to shoo away your audience." He ran his hands through his spiky white and silver hair, drawing my gaze to his delicately pointed ears. "And before you ask again, I'm here because Kol paid me to top up the spell on your contacts."

"You can do that?" Maybe I didn't have to pay Mavis's exorbitant fee. Of course, I didn't know how much Sebastian charged.

"I can only top them up. I can't respell them, and my top up will only last a few weeks unless you do something stupid like channel all your power and fry your angel again."

My throat tightened at that, but tears didn't form in

my eyes this time. Guess the consuming grief from the zip was fading. Now if only my buzz would fade. I kicked a foot out from under the blanket, trying to cool my inflamed skin, but the fire kept burning. "So my light strike is what's burning through the spell?"

He huffed and leaned back in his chair. "Obviously."

"Not obviously. How was I to know?" Jeez, if I'd known that, I wouldn't have used my light strike.

"It's basic concealment magic one-o-one. Everyone knows more powerful internal magics will affect any spell concealing something on the spell caster."

Except if I'd refused to use my light strike, Ibizual would be free or Floyd would have killed me.

Sebastian rolled his eyes at me. "How do you not know this?"

"I never had powers before I got this." I pushed my arm out from under the cover, revealing the delicate, shimmering angelic mating brand, the skin underneath red from my scratching.

"Hunh. Well, it's going to be expensive to keep hiding whatever you're hiding." He ran his hands through his hair again. "I can't believe I'm saying this, you're guaranteed business, but it'd be better for you if you came clean."

"What makes you think I haven't?"

"Because Kol made sure I did this top-up during his shift to watch you, which tells me he doesn't want the others to know." Sebastian frowned, and his gaze grew intense with that look that always made me feel as if he were seeing deep inside my soul. "But I get the feeling even your incubus doesn't know the whole truth."

I shivered under his scrutiny, afraid he'd discover my secret and use it against me. "He's not my incubus."

"You might not have a soul bond with him, but he paid a lot of money to protect you."

"Doesn't mean he's mine."

"So there's room for me, then?" Sebastian's lips quirked back into his wicked smile. "For when you get tired of your other three."

"Not going to happen. Never—"

The temperature plunged, making me gasp. One second it was normal, the next freezing, and frost rushed over my exposed foot, leg, and arm even though my skin still burned with my buzz. Someone was terrified. So scared that the frost swept over all skin not covered by the blanket.

Sebastian's eyes widened, and I yanked my limbs back under the covers as Cassius—strangely now in hospital scrubs when he hadn't been in them before—stormed into my room.

"Essie," he said, his voice ragged.

My heart lurched. Not Cassius. Gideon. Except his hair was cut close to his scalp.

Desperation tightened his expression, and his gaze locked onto mine, capturing my soul. All the ice in his eyes from before was gone, replaced with a heartbreaking fear that clenched my chest.

"Tell me you're okay," he said.

Sebastian rolled his eyes. "You know she's okay. You can feel it in your brand."

Gideon's attention leaped to Sebastian, light blazing

from his eyes, and the temperature snapped to blistering hot. "Get. Out."

"Sure thing." Sebastian jerked to his feet and rushed out the door, pulling it half closed behind him.

The frost reformed—it had barely had time to start melting—and my soul ached at Gideon's pain and fear.

"Tell me you're okay," he said again.

"I'm okay." I raised my hand, inviting him to come to me, needing him to come to me. I trembled with hope that things were different, and yet feared they were back to the way they were before. I needed him to accept me, all of me, and that included Marcus and Jacob.

He collapsed into the chair Sebastian had just left and took my hand. My heart sang at the contact, and my fiery buzz vanished. I groaned in relief, until I realized that under all that fire, my head still burned with the pain of raw magical channels.

"I know the brand says you're physically fine, but Cassius said you wouldn't stop crying." He pressed the back of my hand to his forehead, reminding me of when he'd sat at Zella's bedside. He looked just as raw and haggard now as he had then.

"I'm okay," I repeated. I wasn't, not completely, but there wasn't anything he could do about it. Him being here, beside me, was more than I could have hoped for a day ago.

"He said it was the zip affecting you, but I had to see for myself."

"Gideon, I'm okay." I'd only ever seen him like this for me when I'd been shot and woken up to hear him talking with Amiah about how he couldn't have a relationship with me and didn't want one. And now I had no idea what else to say to him. I ached for him, for his touch, his kiss, and more. We were still two people, destined to be together, who didn't know anything about each other. Our attraction didn't sizzle like what I had with Marcus, but a part of me wondered if that was because both of us had been trying to keep our distance from each other. What would it be like for both of us to accept our destiny?

I searched his face for signs of desire for me, but all I could see was raw fear in his strong, sculpted features, a reminder that, even though I couldn't see signs of the horrible burns I'd given him, I still almost killed both of us. "I didn't mean to hurt you."

"No, you meant to hurt yourself," he said, his tone darkening. "I thought I could ignore the brand and everything would be okay, but the zip took you straight to suicidal grief. Just like the grief the surviving half of a mating brand would experience."

"You thought you were doing the right thing." I huffed a bitter laugh. "I probably could have endured it if I hadn't gotten a face full of zip." Not that I'd wanted to.

He raised his eyes and captured my soul again, his pupils dilated with a hint of desire.

Please, let him feel how I feel. Except I wasn't sure how I felt. Logically I shouldn't feel anything for him, and yet I yearned for him.

"Don't ever do that again," he said, his voice gruff.

"You sound like Marcus." This was a fierce, protective side to Gideon that I'd had no idea existed.

"Sometimes Marcus is right."

"Probably shouldn't tell him that," Kol said from the doorway. He flashed me a panty-melting smile, and my pulse tripped, embarrassingly obvious with the heart monitor. "The doc says Essie is free to go as long as one of us stays with her for the next twenty-four hours. Do you guys want a moment?"

"No—"

"Yes," Gideon said, cutting me off. His grip on my hand tightened. "Please."

A hint of hellfire flickered in Kol's eyes, and he left, fully closing the door behind him.

Gideon opened his mouth, and my pulse stuttered in anticipation. But then he snapped his mouth shut and pursed his lips. His gaze dipped away from me and an awkwardness sank into the silence between us.

CHAPTER 22

I ACHED FOR GIDEON TO HOLD MORE THAN JUST MY HAND. He'd been part of my dream, had slid his hands against my core and begged to solidify our bond, and I could feel his yearning for me in the rising temperature.

The memory of my desire made my pulse pick up, but Gideon didn't seem to notice the faster beeps from the monitor... or he was pretending he didn't. And if the latter was the case, I had no idea why and didn't have the emotional energy to figure it out. His gaze rose and along with a building heat in his eyes, I could see pain and uncertainty. It had to be that uncertainty making him hesitate, even though he'd asked Kol for a private moment to talk with me. And if one of us didn't say something soon, Kol was going to be standing outside the door for a long time.

I shifted to my side and reached to brush my free hand over his too-short hair, but fear he'd pull away stopped me from making contact. "You look like your brother."

He stared at my free hand, but I still couldn't tell how he felt about me not touching him.

"The healers used all their magic dealing with my trauma and the burns, so it was easier just to buzz what remained of my hair," he said. "They'd never seen a light strike that powerful before. It was stronger than what you channeled when you destroyed Ibizual's key."

"Jacob was added to the mix—" Oh, shit. I snapped my mouth shut. I shouldn't have reminded him of our complicated situation. It was awkward enough with just the two of us, and I held my breath, afraid that pointing out I was also bonded with Jacob would make him put his icy walls back up. But all I saw was relief.

"He's the reason we're alive," he said. "His strength, through your bond, kept us both alive long enough for Amiah to stabilize us."

"Is he okay?" Sebastian had said all my guys were fine, but that didn't mean Jacob wasn't running on fumes. A shiver of desire swept through me at the thought of Jacob's magic.

Gideon's gaze darted to the monitor, noticing my change in pulse this time. "He'll need to feed, but he can wait until you've recovered."

"Yeah, about that—" If we were going to build any kind of relationship, I needed to tell him about the whole situation with Jacob.

"I already figured out he's stuck on you after all four of you showed up in the garage this morning. Victoria wouldn't have needed you if that wasn't the case." Gideon gave me a sad, rueful smile. "Which means you're bite locked, aren't you?"

"Yeah."

Realization suddenly flashed across his expression, and he burst out laughing, the change in emotion so quick it stunned me. "So that's why Kol has been dazed the last few days."

The door flew open and Marcus pushed in a wheelchair.

"I said she's having a moment," Kol said.

"They can have their moment after I get Essie out of here." Marcus shot him a fierce look and Kol raised his hands with a chuckle.

"Sorry, guys." He winked at me. "I know you were trying to build up to it."

"She's in a hospital bed," Gideon said. "Anyone could just walk in, as just demonstrated."

"That's what makes it so exciting." Kol flashed another sexy grin, and the heart monitor gave me away again.

"Stop teasing her," Marcus said.

"Yes," Gideon agreed.

I laughed and Kol joined me. "I'm pretty sure he's teasing you two." I reached out my other hand to Marcus, strangely joyful. Perhaps it was another mood swing from the zip, but in this moment things were okay. I knew everything would go back to being complicated as soon as we got back to Operations, hell, with my luck, probably before we got to the parking lot, but there was hope for whatever lay between Gideon and me, and I was going to take it.

The guys wheeled me out of the hospital to the SUV. It was dark out, which meant I'd been in the hospital for at least twelve hours. I doubted it had been more than twenty-four, since Bane had said JP agents got nothing but the best, but still, I had no idea what day it was.

Which was a problem for tomorrow.

We drove the few blocks back to Operations, where Jacob met us in the garage. My pulse fluttered at the sight of him. He looked exhausted, but okay. Thank God, he was okay.

He lifted me out of the SUV, separating me from Gideon and setting my skin on fire, but I didn't complain and managed not to scratch too much. In that moment, he needed me, just like Marcus and Gideon did. I leaned against his chest, savoring the cool radiating from his body, while ignoring his slow heartbeat indicating he needed to feed, and soon.

Jacob carried me up to my room, the rest of the guys following, and for a second I had a moment of wishing everyone would just pile into my bed with me so I could fall asleep with all of them close.

"The docs said we need to keep an eye on her for the next twenty-four hours," Kol said, pulling back the covers on my bed.

Jacob set me on the mattress. I'd made the transfer in my hospital gown since no one knew where my clothes were, and I didn't want to bother trying to hunt them down, so I didn't have anything to do except pull up the covers and pass out.

"Gideon should take the first shift," Marcus said.

Gideon's eyes widened with shock. "Marcus—"

"Pretty sure we've already discussed this." Marcus crossed his arms, as if daring Gideon to disagree.

"We have. You're right," Gideon said. "Still, it might not be the best idea. I might look fine, but I'm exhausted. I'm going to fall asleep, too."

"Then it's perfect." I held out my hand to Gideon. As much as I ached for Gideon, I didn't have the energy for much of anything, either.

"Not for me," Kol said with an exaggerated pout. "All you're going to do is cuddle."

"Pretty sure you and Jacob won't be running low for long," Gideon said, sagging onto the edge of the bed and absentmindedly placing a hand on my calf.

My buzz vanished. Yeah, he was the one I needed to be with right now.

Jacob brushed a kiss across my forehead and headed to the door. Marcus's piercing green eyes darkened, his wolf coming to the surface. He tipped my head up and captured my lips in a fierce quick kiss then left. Kol followed him out.

"I still don't understand how Marcus just accepts this," Gideon said, his gaze on the closed door.

"Marcus knew before I did what our situation was." I laid down and shifted over so Gideon could join me.

He moved his hand from my calf, and my buzz blazed back to life. I swallowed a gasp as he kicked off his shoes and eased in beside me. But he didn't reinitiate contact, and his uncertainty twisted inside me. At least this time I could feel it.

"I'm confused about all this as well." I pressed my hand over his heart, easing my buzz. His pulse raced, but I couldn't tell if it was fear or desire.

The muscles in his jaw flexed and the glow in his eyes

billowed. The temperature flickered with a whisper of heat, but I had no idea what that meant.

This was a mistake. As much as I wanted him near, and not just to ease my buzz but because our bond couldn't withstand the distance between us any more, this was too much too soon. Our emotions were just too confused. Even though we were destined mates, we were going to need time to figure out how we fit together.

I pulled my hand from his chest, but he captured it and pressed it back over his heart. "Why did you think killing yourself was the answer?"

Because I'm a monster. Whether I want to be or not, and you're all going to find out. "That was the zip."

"But it came from somewhere." The light in his eyes dimmed and his uncertainty melted into a soft sadness, forming a delicate mist around me. "Even without me, you have everything to live for. Your connection with Marcus and Jacob should have helped you with the grief of our almost-broken bond."

My throat tightened with a mix of his sadness and mine. "I kept trying to tell myself that. I don't understand why you keeping your distance hurt so much."

"I'd thought it was only hurting me. That what you had with Marcus was stronger because you had it first, but I guess it wasn't. Our bonds are equal. You don't have three parts making a whole. You have three wholes joined inside you, each as significant and consuming as the other."

"Do you still think the brand is a beautiful thing, even though you're mated with a human with two other mates?" Did he feel— did any of them feel like I wouldn't have the time for them because of the others? Not to mention I didn't know if it was worse that they were all co-workers and friends or not.

The light returned to Gideon's eyes. Breathtaking summer sky that made me feel like I was flying. "It's the most beautiful, amazing thing." He brushed his fingers from my hand pressed over his heart to the delicate gold sigil on my forearm. "Just this little touch, and I know this is where I belong, who I belong with. Marcus and Jacob are a part of who you are, just like being a cop or your need to protect us." His eyes narrowed. "Even if that need makes you do dangerous things."

Stupid would be more like it. I knew exactly what he was talking about. "Cassius said you saw that I tackled the demon with the zip."

"That was foolish." His hand trailed up my arm, tracing the lines of Jacob's brand, and clouds passed over his summer-sky eyes, dimming his light again. "It probably saved my life."

"I couldn't let you die."

He brushed his thumb across my jaw, drawing a shiver of desire, and slid his fingers into my hair. His pupils dilated with desire, a desire I'd been aching to see for days now, and his gaze dipped to my lips.

"I couldn't risk that you'd be one of the supers that poison killed," I said, my voice breathy, my pulse racing.

"And yet you were going to burn yourself up with your power." He leaned closer to me, his gaze still locked on my lips.

"I thought I was going to hurt you." *Please kiss me. I need you to kiss me.* God, even exhausted, I needed him to hold me and fill me. Desire heated me, rushing through my body as if Jacob's bite magic was surging through me, or Marcus's wolf was undressing me with his ferocious gaze.

"Pretty sure killing yourself would have hurt me, too." He raised his eyes, and I was falling into a summer's sky.

"I didn't say it made sense." He was so close. If I just leaned in, our lips would meet. But would that be too soon for us? Would that scare him back into his icy demeanor? "I didn't want to hurt any of you. I make everything complicated with you and the team, and—"

He dipped in and kissed me with a tender, aching softness. It made my pulse flutter, and pricks of lightning teased through his brand. The connection between us swelled in my chest, seeping into my cells with desire and certainty, and a sigh of satisfaction escaped my lips. Yes, this was the way it was supposed to be between us.

With a groan, he deepened the kiss, his tongue teasing the seam between my lips, urging me to open to him. I let him in, and his power grew, turning my skin beneath his brand hypersensitive. The sensation sizzled past my elbow into Jacob's brand and swirled into a pulsing intensity that stole my breath.

I moaned and let the power rush through me. The temperature turned sweltering, and every brush of fabric or whisper of breath or shift of Gideon's fingers in my hair sent me gasping. My breath came fast and the room started spinning.

Darkness shuddered at the edge of my vision. My

chest tightened and I couldn't breathe. Everything lurched in and out of focus. The power turned sharp and threatened to roar out of control. I was going to lose my hold on it and hurt him again. *God, no, please.*

Gideon jerked back, frowning, but his expression snapped to worried when he saw my face. "Essie?"

Tears stung my eyes. "I can't control it."

"Control what?" He brushed a lock of hair from my eyes, his expression so tender it broke my heart.

"The power," I said, my throat tight. "There's so much power. I'm going to hurt you again."

"Hey." He pulled me close, resting my head on his chest and holding me tight. His scent of fresh springtime and sun-warmed skin enveloped me. "It'll be all right."

Except I wasn't sure it would be. I fought to concentrate on the sure, strong beat of his heart, and slowly the power from his brand melted back into my skin.

"We have all the time in the world." He pressed his lips against the top of my head. "We'll figure it out. All of us. You're not alone."

A tear broke free. It had to be the zip still affecting me. His words filled me with such hope, and yet they also reminded me of how alone I'd been and how alone I'd be if they learned the truth.

"Just rest, now. Things will look better in the morning."

I sobbed into his chest and didn't fight my exhaustion when it pulled me into a soft, warm darkness. I floated without thought or dream. There was only love and fear. Pure, radiant, soul-affirming love, fighting the terror that I'd hurt Gideon and my guys.

Gentle knocking pulled me out of the darkness, and I dragged my groggy attention to the door as Marcus entered. Gideon, his arms still wrapped around me, stirred and tensed, as if he was expecting Marcus's wolf to lose his shit on us, but Marcus just sat on the edge of the bed and set a hand on my thigh.

"Cassius is summoning us to your office."

Gideon's grip on me tightened. "Can't it wait?"

"Doesn't sound like it," Marcus said. "Cassius sounded more uptight than usual."

Gideon drew in a sharp breath, and the whisper of emotions that had been teasing the temperature around me vanished.

"Okay. We're coming." He eased out from under me and sat up, but I managed to keep a hand on him. I wasn't ready to deal with my buzz just yet.

"Does Cassius's summoning also include me?" I asked. At the moment, I had mixed feelings about the team. I really wasn't strong enough to do the job safely. As much as I could summon a powerful light strike, I couldn't just fry every super we came across.

"I don't care if Cassius's summons doesn't include you. You're part of the team," Marcus said.

"Agreed." Gideon kissed the top of my head, making my pulse trip with a mix of heart-stopping desire and fear, before he slid out of bed.

My buzz exploded, setting my skin on fire, and I bit back a gasp. I wasn't sure why I was still hiding it. I could now easily say my buzz was because of the zip or the archnephilim or the mating brand, but a part of me feared if I said something the guys would want to fix it, and then people would start asking questions and running tests to find out what was going on.

"I'll go change and meet you in the hall." Gideon shoved his feet into his boots and left me with Marcus.

Marcus leaned over me, his wolf's ferocity radiating in eyes filled with desire. I slid my hands over his sexy scruff, tangled my fingers in his hair, and pulled him to me. We'd been intimate and I hadn't lost control. It was safe to kiss him, and I really needed the reassurance of our connection.

Our lips met, and Marcus groaned. He captured the back of my head and plunged his tongue into my mouth, fueling my desire. God, I didn't think I'd ever get enough of him, of his ferocious passion and his searing desire for me. It stole my breath and left me dizzy—and thankfully not in the terrifying I'm-going-to-lose-control-and-burn-you-up kind of dizzy.

With another groan, he pulled away and pressed his forehead to mine, his breath fast. "I really want to stay. God, do I want to stay. But Cassius has been surprisingly subdued about the team since we pulled you and Gideon out of the warehouse, and it would be best if we kept it that way."

"Pretty sure me showing up to a meeting will change all that."

"Not sure." Marcus eased back, leaving me aching at even that small distance between us. "You risked everything to save his brother—" He glared at me. "Stupid move, by the way. Zip can kill humans, too."

"I know." I rolled my eyes at him, only half meaning

my exasperation. "I shouldn't ever do that again. Gideon has already told me."

"Maybe you'll listen to him, since you're not listening to me."

I gave him my driest look.

"Yeah, didn't think that would work. At least you have one hell of a light strike. Cassius lost his shit when he saw Gideon."

"So you all know?"

"That the zip made you try to kill yourself? Yeah." Marcus's fear and sadness swept a cold mist around me. "Jacob felt you pulling power from him, said it was the strangest feeling because he didn't know he had that kind of power, and Gideon was yelling at you to fade it away, don't blast it."

"He said that?" I didn't remember any of that.

"You weren't in your right mind." He pressed his hand against my thigh. "Now, come on. Hurry up and get changed. I'll meet you in the hall."

"You can stay. It's not like you haven't seen me with my clothes off."

"If I stay, your clothes will stay off and we won't leave your bed."

He left and I sat up, trying to figure out what if anything hurt beyond my raw magical channels and my burning skin. I couldn't tell and that worried me. I was pretty sure the healers at Mercy Memorial would have mended any broken bones, but even if I had slightly enhanced healing from Jacob's vampiric claim, I was still also human—or at least they thought I was human—

which meant they couldn't heal me as fast as they could a super.

I shrugged out of the hospital gown, not surprised that I didn't have anything else on underneath, only surprised I'd been too exhausted to notice, and grabbed a change of clothes from my duffle bag. An old pair of runners waited by the door, and I could only assume one of the guys had gone to my apartment and brought me back a pair of shoes. I didn't have another light workout jacket and my skin was too hot for me to even think about covering up the angelic mating brands curled around my right arm, so I was just going to have to accept whatever looks Cassius gave me. Not to mention the looks I'd get from my guys, since it was clear I'd been scratching my arms to the point of bleeding.

After splashing some water on my face—a face that was back to being too pale with shock—I hurried into the hall. Gideon, now dressed in slacks and a dress shirt, waited for me with Marcus without a hint of tension between them, as if that moment when Marcus had first walked in and not reacted badly had been enough to reassure Gideon.

And God, did they look good. Marcus with his piercing green eyes, making my insides sizzle by just standing near him, and Gideon, all ice gone from his expression and the stiffness gone from his posture. He was back to the confident, strong angel I'd first met.

They noticed my scratch marks but thankfully didn't say anything. Although it was clear in their looks that we were going to have a conversation as soon as the meeting with Cassius was over.

We hurried to Gideon's office, where Cassius sat behind Gideon's desk, Jacob perched stiffly on the edge of the couch, radiating vampiric intensity, and Kol leaned against the wall near the door, his arms crossed, looking anything but relaxed. The guys were worried and ready for a fight. This wasn't good.

CHAPTER 23

Cassius studied me as I entered, but with my buzz blazing, I couldn't sense any change in temperature, and his expression remained hard so I had no idea what he was thinking.

Marcus ushered me to the chair—it was slightly farther from Cassius than the couch—and I grabbed Gideon's hand, making my buzz vanish and leaving me cold. I wouldn't be able to concentrate on anything Cassius said with my buzz blazing, and I wanted a clear head, to face whatever was coming.

Gideon's eyes widened in surprise, as if he hadn't expected me to fully embrace our bond right away and in front of everyone, but he stepped up beside me and tightened his grip on my fingers.

Surprise also flashed across Cassius's expression, and he jerked his attention to the open file folder on the desk.

"So?" Marcus growled, drawing up beside Gideon and resting a hand on my shoulder.

"We're being summoned to the mayor's office," Cassis

said. "He wanted to call you in yesterday to discuss the events at the cemetery, but, well, yesterday happened." The muscles in his jaw tightened.

"Screw the political crap," Marcus said. "We all need a day to get our shit together, and if we should be doing anything, it should be hunting down whoever blew up that warehouse and shut down whoever's distributing zip."

"We're a day behind them, and Summer didn't find anything in the rubble that would give us a lead," Jacob said. "And you didn't pick up any scents to follow."

"So we're back to the beginning," Kol said. "The sooner we get back to digging, the sooner we can shut these guys down."

"I agree," Cassius said, "but you can't put off meeting with the mayor. Even if you're all running on fumes and have better things to do, we need to go to City Hall and smooth this over."

"How can we smooth over what happened?" Kol asked. "It's not like we can go back and do things differently."

"Pretty sure the mayor just wants to yell at us and feel like he's in control," Jacob said with a warm glance at me. His still intensity pulsed from his brand, slow and sure, and helped to settle more of my unease about my place on the team and the danger I put my guys in.

"Exactly." Cassius turned a page in the file. "Although it would be better if we didn't have to call in over a hundred citizens for DNA samples to identify the remains of everyone who'd been reanimated."

"There's a lot about the last few days that could have been better," Marcus said.

"But there's nothing we can do about it." Gideon squeezed my hand. "Put on your most diplomatic smiles. We're going to the mayor's office."

"With Essie," Jacob said.

Cassius's eyes narrowed. "Agent Shaw needs more time to recover. The healers couldn't purge all the zip from her system so she's still in the tail end of withdrawal. Not to mention she needs a lot more training."

My thoughts tripped over that. "Are you saying I'm still on the team?" I wasn't sure if that was a good idea or not. Yes, it was what I wanted, but the last two days had proven how unprepared I was for the job.

"If you don't go with us, you won't be on the team," Gideon said. "The mayor will tell the chief of police you didn't show and you'll be reassigned."

"Fired," I corrected.

"So you're going." Marcus glared at Cassius as if daring him to disagree.

"We'll put you on modified duty and start your training when we get back." Gideon released my hand and stepped toward Cassius, adding his glare with Marcus's.

My buzz screamed to life, burning and biting and twitching. I drew in a sharp breath, which didn't help at all.

Jacob said something, I heard his voice rumble, but couldn't make out his words. Kol jerked away from the wall and his mouth moved. I clawed at my arm, unable to stop myself even though I knew it wouldn't help ease my buzz.

Someone else said something, but I couldn't make out the tone well enough to figure out who'd spoken, since neither Jacob's nor Kol's lips moved and I wasn't looking at the others. My hand now dug into my thigh and I noticed I'd changed body parts.

I squeezed my eyes shut and fought to concentrate. The buzz was so much stronger than before. The muscles in my thigh spasmed and I pressed my nails in deeper, desperate to make it stop.

"—of police will have to, except she won't be fully in the field until—"

Cassius's mouth moved in response, but his expression wasn't argumentative, as if he were agreeing with what the guys were saying.

The muscles in my shoulder clenched. I wasn't going to be able to do this.

"I don't think I should go," I said.

They all looked at me. Every one of them, even Cassius, was surprised.

"I'm not— I can't—" God, I had to tell them about my buzz, but I couldn't force the words out. Too many years of hiding in fear held them prisoner. "I'm still shaky from the zip."

"You're coming," Gideon said, his tone clear he wasn't going to argue with me about it. "We'll get you through this. You're a member of this team, and I can't have you fired from the UCPD before the paperwork transferring you to the JP goes through."

"Let's go," Cassius said as he stood.

We headed to the garage, piled into an SUV, where I managed to claim the seat beside Gideon and hold his hand, and we drove into the heart of Union City to City Hall.

It felt so strange, driving with the guys without any tension making the temperature lurch between hot and cold. I got a sense of determination and certainty from everyone, and I was pretty sure that was from real empathy and not my screwy version. I'd been having moments of that for a few days now, and as much as I wanted to pretend it didn't mean I was changing, I couldn't.

When this meeting with the mayor was over, even if Cassius hadn't left town, I was gathering my guys and revealing all my magic. I couldn't keep it a secret any more. I'd have to be careful to frame it in terms of recent events and not make them suspect I'd had magic before being claimed by the archnephilim, but I had to tell them. It didn't matter if they started digging, searching for a solution to my buzz that didn't involve being in constant contact with Gideon—I had to come clean.

Gideon laced his fingers between mine and offered me a soft, reassuring smile, warming my heart. This was the way it was supposed to be between us, not the icy distance.

Marcus turned onto the busy four-lane street that crossed through the heart of Union City's downtown core. The core always struck me as odd, with its strange mix of old and new buildings, and the bustle of people acting as if the new buildings weren't because half of the city's core had been leveled by Michael's nephilim.

We drove past two twisted metal beams—post-war urban art—curled together and standing upright in the middle of a new building's courtyard. A constant reminder of what humanity and supers had survived. Benches and potted trees around it created a welcoming area to sit outside and enjoy the unusually warm early summer day. Over a dozen people in suits were doing just that, even though it was only midmorning.

Marcus parked in a reserved spot on the street in front of the new glass-and-steel sixteen-story City Hall. It wasn't the tallest building in the downtown core, but it was the most impressive, with a large glassed-in rotunda in the front and a wide outside public square with a fountain.

Gideon gave my hand a quick squeeze then let go, and as much as I needed to keep holding his hand, the fewer people right now who knew I was intimate with my coworkers, the better. Marcus flipped the sun visor down to show the JP credentials and got out. Gideon did the same.

I clenched my jaw and fisted my hands at my sides in hopes I wouldn't start clawing at my skin.

People stared, gasped, and pointed at us as we gathered beside the SUV. Only human witches could sense a super's essence, but it was obvious we were supers. There weren't a lot of angels in Union City and they rarely left the Quarter, so the glow in both Gideon's and Cassius's eyes was a dead giveaway as to what they were.

An elderly woman sagged onto a bench and crossed herself, while others gawked with awe. Those who looked away from Gideon and Cassius gave Marcus and me cursory glances—we were the least impressive of the group—and then turned to Jacob.

Jacob had his vampiric intensity pulled back, so most people probably couldn't tell he was a vampire, especially since it was the middle of the day, but he was a big, bulky, dangerous-looking guy.

A moment later, every female eye—and a few male— jumped to Kol, and the awe from the angels turned to lust. He wasn't even radiating his usual sexual grace. In fact, his posture was tense, as if he were trying to hold back like Jacob. But again, like Jacob, even without radiating his magical nature, he would have drawn attention. His small horns poked through his dark hair, making it clear he was a demon, and he was drop-dead gorgeous. Pure sex walking in low-riding jeans and a tight T-shirt.

None of the guys seemed to care they were being stared at, and they headed straight to the building's front doors. I, however, had every alarm in my head screaming at me. Not because people were looking at me, but because they were looking at me and wondering what kind of super I was, and I'd spent my entire life avoiding that. No one was supposed to wonder anything about me. I was a nothing-to-see-here human. And just by getting out of the JP's SUV with my guys, the world looked at me differently.

We marched across the public square with its wide, shallow fountain, and pushed through the revolving doors. The lobby inside was packed with people, and a few hundred foldout chairs had been set up in the rotunda for some kind of event. Janitors and sound technicians talked with two women in crisp navy suits, who pointed at various spots around the rotunda and checked their phones.

Someone gasped. Slowly every eye turned toward us and the roar of voices became silent.

"This is why I hate coming to City Hall," Marcus growled as he glowered at the crowd.

"If you stop looking like you're going to rip someone's head off, maybe they wouldn't look so terrified," Cassius said, his voice low, only audible to our group.

"I don't look like I want to rip someone's head off," Marcus replied, his voice just as low.

"Yeah," Kol said, "You kind of do."

I caught myself scratching my shoulder and jerked my hand back to my side.

Marcus said something else and I strained to focus past the buzz.

A woman a few feet away sighed and sank into a foldout chair, her face flushed.

"At least you don't make people faint just by walking past them," Kol said as we headed toward the hall at the back of the rotunda, where the elevators were.

Marcus snorted. "Don't even try to tell me you don't like it."

"Normally I do. But my shields are still in tatters and all this energy is overwhelming," he said between clenched teeth, hellfire blazing in his eyes. "So can we walk a little faster?"

Two more women and a man had to sit before we reached the back of the rotunda, and I'd never seen Kol so tense before. The tension didn't leave his body when we stepped out of sight, and I had no idea when all those women would stop being excited about him and give him a break.

I shifted closer to him and dug my nails into my ribs, fighting a twitching muscle. "Sorry." It was my fault his shields weren't at full strength.

"Not your fault." He brushed my hand, as if he wanted to hold it, but didn't.

And now all I could think about was the biting agony in my hand. "Kind of is."

"Nah." He flashed me a teasing grin. "It's Marcus's fault."

"Pretty sure it's Jacob's," Marcus said.

Cassius stopped in front of a bank of four elevators, two on either side of the hall. He hit the call button and slid an exasperated look at Gideon.

Gideon shrugged. "We have an incubus on the team. Roll with it or it'll drive you crazy."

"There are rules of conduct for JP agents," Cassius said.

"It's a code, so that's more like guidelines instead of rules, right?" Kol's grin turned mischievous, although I could still see the tension around his eyes and in his shoulders.

"A code *is* a set of rules," Cassius said, as if the idea that the code was merely a suggestion horrified him.

Marcus bit back a laugh, and Kol snickered.

Cassius glared at them, and Kol batted his eyelashes with exaggerated innocence. Jacob snorted, and even Gideon's lips quirked into a smile.

"I should write you up," Cassius said.

"If that deserves a write-up, you're going to spend all

your time filing paperwork." Gideon shook his head at him. "But by all means, go ahead."

Cassius sighed. "This is why I don't work with demons. You're all—" His mouth kept moving, but I couldn't concentrate on his words.

God, when would the buzz end? How the hell was I supposed to do anything?

The guys all turned to face the other way, and I couldn't figure out what they were doing.

"—Essie." Marcus grabbed my hand, jerking my attention to him. "The elevator."

I dragged my gaze to the open elevator behind me. Everyone else was already inside, with Jacob holding the door.

"Right—" I stepped toward them, but a swell of power crackled over me, ratcheting up my buzz.

Marcus's lips moved, and he frowned. He'd told me or asked me something, and I hadn't responded.

"Yeah, sorry." But God, that power. Except it wasn't my buzz. My buzz was responding to it, and it felt familiar. I clawed at my upper arm. *Please, just stop.* I wasn't sure how much more I could take.

Marcus grabbed my hand, blood under my nails, and all the guys had stepped out of the elevator.

Cassius frowned.

"—wrong?" Gideon said. "Are you—"

The power grew stronger, as if it were getting closer, and my whole body was on fire. *I know that power. How the hell do I know that power? And how the hell can I feel it?*

"—back." Worry darkened Jacob's expression.

I gritted my teeth and jerked my attention down the

hall past the elevators. The power was close. It came from over there. And now I knew who it was. The woman from the warehouse.

She rounded the corner thirty feet away and jerked to a stop. Her gaze landed on me and her eyes widened with surprise. Yeah. I was still alive. And buzz or no buzz, I wasn't letting her get away this time.

CHAPTER 24

THE WOMAN JERKED AROUND TO RUN BACK THE WAY SHE'D come, but a group of people in suits came around the corner, blocking her way. With a hiss, she wrenched back to face me and bolted for the door to the stairwell instead of trying to push through the crowd.

I ran after her. Jacob, with his enhanced speed, got there first.

"Marcus. Kol. You're with me in the elevator," Cassius said.

I caught the metal security door before it closed. Somehow the woman had already climbed past the second floor landing, and I could still hear the sound of her feet pounding up the stairs, which meant she hadn't run into the hall. My buzz seared through me, and I gritted my teeth against the pain.

"Past floor two," Gideon said into his phone, coordinating the chase most likely with Cassius in the elevator.

Jacob hit the second floor landing. "Stop. JP agents. There's no place to go."

The woman barked a harsh word I didn't recognize in response, and my buzz exploded into an inferno for a second. Jacob jerked, his body seizing as if hit by a Taser, but I couldn't see any barbs.

"Glyph witch," Gideon said. "With lightning strike. Stay back, Essie." He shouldered past me, the palm of his free hand blazing with divine light.

He passed Jacob, who was still stiff, his expression tight with pain, and glanced up the stairwell, but I could hear the woman running again.

I reached Jacob and waved Gideon on. I'd left my sidearm at Operations. It hadn't even occurred to me to bring my weapon, which only emphasized the point that I wasn't ready to go back to active duty. And while I could cast a light strike, I had no idea how to control it. I was more likely to kill the woman or someone else than I was to stop her. That would make interrogating her impossible. Even if she was in charge, there were still a lot of people in her operation, and we needed to round up as many of them as we could.

Jacob sagged against the railing, his chest heaving with desperate breaths and his complexion gray. "I'm fine. Back up Gideon. I'll catch up when I can."

"I'm unarmed."

Jacob gave me his driest look. " You know you're not, and if Gideon needs you, he'll need your light strike. Go."

God damn, he was right, no matter how much it scared me at the moment to release my power.

"I'm on your six, Gideon," I called up to him as I bolted up the stairs.

"Past the fourth floor," Gideon said.

The woman's footsteps just kept pounding up the stairs. Why wasn't she getting off on a floor and hiding in one of the many offices?

My buzz blazed again, stealing my breath, and Gideon wrenched to the side, pressing his back tight to the cinderblock wall. Lightning burst over the wall at the bottom of the landing ahead of me, and he sent a blast of divine light up at her in response.

The woman barked another strange word that made fiery agony snap over me. Gideon's light exploded against an invisible wall, showering me with stinging sparks. Then the woman was running again before all the sparks had even faded.

She kept running, flight after flight, never getting off at a floor. Fire consumed me, and my legs screamed at the exertion. I fought to breathe, my breath sawing in my lungs.

At the tenth floor landing, she sent another blast of lightning at Gideon. He tried to dodge it again, but it clipped his right shoulder. With a grunt of pain, the lightning shot through his brand into me, leaving him free to keep chasing. My muscles seized, and for a second I thought I'd go down, but cold from Jacob's brand washed through it, bringing a swell of strength from him that consumed the spell.

A part of me wanted to yell at Gideon for using our brand that way. But he was the best person to chase the woman. We both knew that. If he went down, there was no way I'd be able to apprehend her.

She reached the top of the stairwell and ran out onto the roof.

"On the roof," Gideon said and shoved his phone into his pocket.

He slowed, glanced out the door, then ran through.

I reached the top, gasping for air, my body on fire. I glanced out the door as well and couldn't see or hear any fighting. Of course, with my buzz making my thoughts spin, that only meant they weren't fighting just outside the door. A warm wind gusted in my face and the sun beat down on the concrete rooftop. I hurried out and rounded a tall steel HVAC unit near the edge of the building.

Gideon stood with his back to me, facing the woman with long, wild bright-red locks. Power crackled over the tattoo on her arm. Even if I couldn't have seen it, I'd have known it was there from the roar of my buzz. Two other woman, with swarthy skin and dark hair, a stark contrast to the pale-skinned redhead, stood on either side of her. They wore tank tops that exposed the colorful tattoos around their right arms, a match to the redhead's.

"Not smart, taking a fight with an angel to a rooftop," Gideon said.

Hurried footsteps pounded across the roof behind me, and I wrenched around, a flicker of my power blazing in my palms, but I heaved the power back as the rest of my guys and Cassius arrived.

"Make that two angels." With a flash of light, Cassius released his massive white wings.

"Angels are so arrogant," the redhead said.

"They think they're the only ones with wings." The woman to the redhead's left pressed her hand to her biceps and hissed something. Black batwings unfurled from her back, and she shot up into the sky.

Cassius shot up after her as Gideon released his wings. His were also a brilliant white, but unlike Cassius, his glowed with his divine light, as if more than his innate angelic power radiated from them.

He dove for the remaining two women, but jerked out of the way at the last second as the redhead grabbed her wrist and barked the harsh word, releasing her lightning strike.

Marcus grabbed my arm and wrenched my attention away from the fight. "Just stay back, Essie."

On any other day, I'd have argued with him. But I was a mess right now and more likely to get in the way than help.

He didn't wait for a response and dashed across the rooftop to help Gideon. Kol raced after him, drawing his daggers from the sheaths on his back. I didn't know if I should be surprised or not that he'd decided to go to the mayor's office armed.

Jacob drew up beside me, his complexion still too pale.

"How bad is that lightning strike?" I asked. If one hit knocked Jacob out of the fight, this battle could be over as soon as it started.

"The guys can probably take a few hits if they don't get slammed with something else while they're down," Jacob said. "I was low before we went to the warehouse, took a beating during that fight, and just haven't had time to recover."

Because of me. "You should have fed before we left."

"No one expected a fight—" He huffed a bitter laugh. "Well, not this kind of fight."

Marcus lunged at the redhead, slashing at her with his claws, but she pressed a tattoo and he slammed into her invisible wall. The other woman twisted out of the way of Kol's whirling blades, which impressed the hell out of me because he was damned fast, and grabbed her forearm. At this distance, I couldn't tell what image she'd touched, only that it took up as much of her forearm as Gideon's brand did on me and was bright green.

Massive vines shot out of the roof and twisted around Kol. He slashed at one around his leg and jerked out of the way of another about to seize his arm.

A vine shot toward Marcus's back, and I jerked forward, instinct taking over. Jacob bolted past me and grabbed the vine before it grabbed Marcus. Marcus glanced back at Jacob, gave him a tight nod, and lunged at the redhead with his claws again.

Above, the bat woman absorbed Cassius's fire whip into her skin and shot it back at him as a ball of fire. He yanked his wings back, dropped below the blast, and swooped up at her, while Gideon, hovering in the sky, twisted out of the way of another lightning blast from the redhead and shot a light strike of his own down at her.

The power from all three witches roared through me. Every time they activated a glyph hidden in their tattoos, my buzz flared. It made my muscles twitch, threatening my balance, and I staggered to the HVAC unit and leaned against it to keep standing.

The guys lunged and dove, twisted and slashed, but the witches' power didn't fade. Surely, as humans, they'd run out of juice. But I couldn't sense it diminishing. In fact, it felt as if it were still growing, as if they were tapping into a deeper source than just themselves.

My thoughts stuttered and whirled. One minute Cassius was in the sky, the next he slammed into the rooftop with a powerful boom. Marcus still fought the redhead, but Gideon now sliced at the vines holding both of Kol's arms.

I squeezed my eyes shut. My breath still sawed in my chest as if I hadn't had a few minutes to recover from running up sixteen flights of stairs.

Someone yelled. My eyes flew open. Everyone was in a different position again, and I had no idea how much time I'd lost. A vine wrapped around Cassius and slammed him onto the rooftop again. Gideon now flew in the sky, his hand wrapped in the front of bat woman's tank top. Marcus and Kol slashed at vines that just kept growing, and Jacob punched at the redhead's chest.

The world darkened and spun faster. I pressed a hand to the side of the HVAC unit and my pulse stuttered at the divine light blazing from my palm. My skin was already burned and oozing, but with the witches' power, I couldn't feel anything. Not my light or the pain.

Another scream and strength swept from Jacob's brand in my arm into him. My knees gave way, and I sank to the rooftop. Another lightning strike had hit Jacob, and while he was still alive, he was on his knees in front of the redhead, his head bowed, his face filled with agony. Cassius shot a blast of fire at the redhead, and Marcus hauled Jacob back.

I fought to breathe past the agony. My light blazed

around me, and the rooftop under my hands blackened while a part of me screamed that if I didn't get my power under control, I was going to hurt someone.

Gideon yelled, jerking my attention up, as he careened toward the fight on the rooftop with bat woman. He slammed his weight down on her, drawing a strangled scream. Cassius pulled a red zip tie from his pocket, leaped at them, and grabbed her hands.

Bat woman's wings vanished the moment the tie was around her wrists, and the roaring power from the glyph witches contracted as the spell on the zip tie suppressed her magic. The redhead screamed and grabbed the tattoo on her wrist. Cassius wrenched to the side, but he wasn't fast enough, and his body jerked with the full force of her lightning strike, yanking his hand from his pocket and scattering red zip ties on the rooftop.

Marcus tackled the redhead, and Gideon grabbed a tie. A vine seized Marcus's neck and yanked him off the redhead as Gideon seized the woman's arm and secured a tie around one of her wrists.

The witches' power contracted again, but my buzz flared, blazing stronger, spinning my consciousness on the edge of darkness.

Someone yelled and I fought to keep my eyes open. Kol lunged in, his blade severing the vine around Marcus's neck, and he skidded across the rooftop.

"It's over," Gideon said to the remaining swarthy witch, as Cassius wrenched the redhead onto her stomach and secured a second tie, connected to the first around her other wrist, binding her hands behind her back.

"Never," she screamed, and a flurry of vines shot toward the guys. A large one slammed into Cassius, but he'd already finished securing the redhead. Marcus slashed his claws at two threatening to capture his arms and Gideon leaped into the sky, his divine light sword forming in his hands and severing the vine shooting toward him.

Kol sliced through three thin ones, his blades whirling, and rammed his shoulder into the vine witch. All her vines wrenched toward him with a roar of power and darkness rushed across my vision.

One of my guys yelled.

The woman screamed.

My power burned hot within me, blazing bright behind my lids and stealing my breath.

Another scream. This one masculine.

I wrenched my eyes open. Vines crushed Jacob and Marcus against the rooftop, and vine pieces littered the area around Kol. Gideon dove toward the vine witch, a zip tie in his hand, twisting midflight to dodge a shooting vine, and seized her wrist.

She howled and wrenched against his grip. Her vines flailed around her, pounded against Jacob and Marcus, while another grabbed Gideon's neck and choked him.

Kol cut the vine holding Gideon as another thick vine slammed into Kol and sent him flying. He crashed over the rooftop toward me, the vine following and tossing him up and over the edge behind me.

I screamed and lunged for him. He could survive a lot of damage, but I didn't think he'd survive a sixteen-story fall. The vine tripped me as I reached the edge. I caught his wrist, but his weight jerked me forward. Wind rushed around us. Terror filled Kol's eyes, and my buzz snapped into a supernova in my chest, the pressure threatening to tear me apart, even as I felt the last of the witches' power being suppressed with the zip tie.

My power ripped another scream from my throat and exploded with fiery agony, tearing out my back. White flashed behind me. Something jerked me up for a second. My grip on Kol slipped, and I dug my nails into his wrist and seized him with both hands. We plummeted across the street, the wind jerking me up, twisting me to the side. My shoulder clipped the edge of the building across the street from City Hall, and we crashed into an alley.

The impact tore Kol from my grip, and I slammed into a large garbage bin, the world spinning, a trail of white feathers littering the asphalt. Oh, shit. One of the guys had to be hurt.

I twisted to see if Gideon or Cassius were all right and was batted in the face with a wing.

My body spasmed and the wing hit me again.

My wing.

I had wings.

I. Had. Wings.

How the hell did I have wings?

Oh, fuck.

Kol staggered to his feet, his face a mask of pure horror. His body trembled and his breath was ragged, his gaze never leaving my wings.

"You're one of them." His voice broke.

Frost swept over me with his fear, and terror and rage

—*his* terror and rage—exploded within me. God, I'd known the war had scarred him, but he'd put on a good face and hadn't revealed just how deep those scars went.

"Kol, I'm not going to hurt you." I raised my burned and bleeding hands. Just the slight movement sent screaming agony through me and twisted the world around me.

"You're one of them." Fury filled his eyes and the frost vanished, consumed by a searing heat and ferocious fury.

"Kol, I'm not going—"

"I won't go back," he snarled. He wrenched a knife from his boot. "You can't take me back. I won't go back. Ever!"

He dove at me. There was nowhere to go. The world still spun, and I was trapped against a garbage bin.

"Kol. No, please."

He rammed his knife toward my chest as Gideon swooped in and jerked him back. Cassius lunged in, taking Kol's place. He clamped a hand around my throat, seizing both my wrists with whips of fire, and yanked me to my feet.

The world twisted and darkened. White-hot pain swept through me from my buzz and the fall, and the ferocity of everyone's emotions.

He pressed his face close to mine, his eyes filled with a fury darker and more ferocious than Kol's. His hate for me turned the air to fire and blazed through my chest. I was one of the monsters who'd tortured Kol and slaughtered thousands upon thousands of humans and supers. I was an abomination, a monster that wasn't supposed to exist, and I'd made his brother fall in love with me.

Don't miss the next book in the series!

DESTINED STORM
Nephilim's Destiny: Book Four

Time is running out. But what will destroy them first? Secrets? Lies? Or magic?

I'm in trouble. Big trouble. A split-second reflex that saved Kol's life, and all hell busted out. Rather, my secret busted out for all to see. Now the only thing keeping a lid on my wild, unpredictable magic is Cassius's magical handcuffs. Kinky? Yeah, no.

I need to show Gideon, Marcus, Jacob, and Kol that my nephilim blood is the only thing I lied about, even if it means letting my memories be mined for the truth. Except when that soul-scraping spell comes up hard against an unbreakable magical wall, it reveals a secret that's news even to me.

But finding the answers will have to wait. A new danger threatens the city. Three glyph witches so powerful every body-shredding battle leaves my guys barely alive.

We don't know what the witches' end game is, but if we don't figure out how to play—and how to harness my magic—we'll lose. And so will every innocent civilian we've sworn to protect.

Destined Storm is the fourth book in the Nephilim's Destiny series, an action-packed full-length paranormal romance with four irresistible guys and a kick-ass heroine who doesn't have to choose.

OTHER BOOKS BY TESSA COLE

THE NEPHILIM'S DESTINY SERIES

Destined Shadows, prequel story

Destined Darkness, book 1

Destined Blood, book 2

Destined Fire, book 3

Destined Storm, book 4

Destined Radiance, book 5

www.ingramcontent.com/pod-product-compliance
Lightning Source LLC
Chambersburg PA
CBHW020343180626
46812CB00001B/321